Sign up for our newsletter to hear
about new and upcoming releases.

www.ylva-publishing.com

OTHER BOOKS BY EMILY WATERS

Honey in the Marrow

Emily Waters

TWO IS A PATTERN

ACKNOWLEDGEMENTS

Thank you to everyone who helped make this book possible: Charity for being my beta and, so often, my muse. I always want to write something you'll like. Thank you to Astrid for folding me into your cool club of Ylva writers, to Genni for editing with me, and to my partner, Jacob, for loving me unconditionally while so often I'm living in my head. And perhaps most importantly of all, thank you to my dogs, Daniel and Sophie, who sat in my lap or snoozed next to me while I wrote this book. All I ever want to do is go home and hang out with my dogs. This book is for them.

CHAPTER 1

THIRTY-SIX DOWN WAS AN EIGHT-LETTER word for *rueful, remorseful, repentant*. Annie picked up her pen and tapped it against the handle of her ceramic coffee mug.

"I'm not a waitress, Anabelle! You know where the coffeepot is," her mother Patty said, her voice light and airy but her words biting.

Annie looked up from her crossword puzzle, momentarily bewildered, then shook her head.

"Sorry, Mom. No, I was just thinking." Annie was a fidgety person by nature. Always squirming in her seat, drumming her fingers, clicking her pens restlessly until someone made her stop. Her best friend in undergrad—a tall, blonde brainiac named Lori—had once bought her as a gag gift an expensive pen designed for astronauts to take into space. It had been made to look like the American flag—red and blue anodized aluminum with little white stars—and you could write with it anywhere. Upside down or underwater or on practically any flat surface. Lori had said it was the only pen that might actually outlast a stressed-out Annie during finals.

Annie had given it to her father, Ken, who still had it on his desk in his office. It wasn't that she hadn't appreciated the gift or the gesture, but Annie liked her cheap little pens and not having to feel guilty about gnawing up the top of a twenty-four-cent Bic. The pen she held now was resting against her bottom lip, in place to be chewed, but she wasn't thinking about the crossword anymore. She was watching her mother angrily scrub a muffin tin at the sink.

Her parents had been ticked with her for some time now. Ever since she announced her intention to go back to school.

It was Lori's idea, actually. Not another degree, but the idea of going to school out West. They'd both gone to the University of Mississippi and become friends while Annie worked her way through an economics degree and Lori studied prelaw. They had no classes together their first semester, but Lori had lived three doors down from Annie's dorm room. The next semester, they took the same Russian language class. For the next three years, they were nearly inseparable. After graduation, with their matching caps decorated to say *Class of '87*, Annie was recruited to the CIA and went to Georgetown while Lori went to study law at Stanford.

They still kept in touch, though they weren't as tight as when they were twenty. Annie had mentioned in one of her letters last year that she was thinking about pursuing a second master's degree, maybe something more practical than Slavic languages. The government had technically paid for that one, but she'd recently resigned to figure out what she really wanted to do. Law like Lori? Foreign policy? Education? She could teach, maybe.

Lori had written back, expressing support for the idea. She mentioned that there were some great schools out West where she lived and told her not to discount it simply because her parents thought it was all stoned hippies past the Rocky Mountains. Lori probably meant Northern California because she'd settled in Marin County with her husband, Louis, but once Annie started to research, most of the schools she applied to were in the southern part of the state. She'd settled on criminology; it was a career change that would let her utilize her skillset.

Her mom finished scrubbing the muffin tin, banged it into the dish rack, and started on the big cast-iron skillet she'd used to fry bacon for breakfast.

Annie was three days away from moving cross-country, and her parents still were not entirely on board. Her father thought it a waste of time and money, and he was horrified at the amount of the loan Annie had procured. Her mother never tired of pointing out to her only daughter that by the time *she* was twenty-seven, she had a toddler and a baby on the way, and what would Annie have to show for herself except for a pile of degrees and no job?

"Mom, leave that big heavy pan. I'll do it," Annie offered.

"What about next week when you aren't here anymore?" Patty asked. "Who'll do it then, hmm? Me, that's who. So I may as well get used to it."

Annie sighed, picked up her pen, and returned to her puzzle.

Thirty-six down.

Rueful, remorseful, repentant.

Her pen scratched against the newsprint.

Contrite.

Three debate trophies in high school and negotiation training by the United States government and it still took Annie most of the summer to convince her father that she didn't need anyone to drive from Ohio to California with her. At first, both of her parents had insisted on going, and then she'd got it down to just her father.

Two nights before she was due to depart, she got her wish. Her father relented if she promised to stop in Missouri and again in New Mexico to sleep solid nights in hotel beds. He even offered to pay for the hotel rooms, then spent the rest of the evening calling around for the best rates and booking her rooms, reading his credit card numbers over the phone loudly.

Annie hovered in the hallway, fretting.

"He just loves you is all," her mom said, coming up behind her.

"I know. But it's too much money."

"Can't put a price on your safety, honey. It'll make him feel better, so you may as well let him do it."

Annie nodded; the weight of his care heavy enough that it felt difficult to move from the spot.

She'd been feeling guilty about a lot of things lately. Going back to school, moving far away from her parents when she'd just come back to Toledo. Quitting her job with the CIA. Turning down a job offer from the Metropolitan Police Department in Washington DC six months ago even though she had no other prospects. It wasn't the idea of being a police officer she disliked; it was the way Deputy Chief Mason Worth had offered her the job. Worth was a celebrated and decorated officer, but the way he praised her—offering her a better-paying job and an alluring life in a new town—made the hair on the back of her neck stand up. He was so desperate to poach from the intelligence community that he contacted her the day after she left the Company. She had no idea how he knew anything about her, and the nicer he was to her, the more her stomach churned and the worse the fight-or-flight feeling got. So she said no and flew home to regroup.

Anabelle Weaver didn't need another authority figure in her life. She'd already learned that lesson the hard way.

She didn't sleep well the night before she was supposed to leave for California. Part of it was her childhood mattress, narrow and squeaky. But it was also her jangly nerves about her sense of direction. The majority of the trip was driving west on Interstate 40, but first she had to find her way out of the city, then negotiate the freeway system once she reached Los Angeles's outskirts.

Annie had thought seriously about going to UC Berkeley, had even tentatively filled out the form to accept, but at the last minute, she'd mailed the one to UCLA instead. Berkeley had more accolades, but UCLA's program allowed her to earn a master's through the law school without having to become a lawyer. The more temperate climate of Los Angeles was a factor as well, as was the anonymity of a sprawling city like Los Angeles. It was a shame that Lori wouldn't be closer, but, realistically, they'd have little time to spend together anyhow, not like they once had. No movie marathons, no nights at the bar. Lori had a family, and Annie, having one master's degree under her belt already, knew exactly how much work was in store for her.

Too nervous to sleep, she rose an hour before her alarm, well before anyone else in the house stirred. She took a quick hot shower, then carefully braided her hair so it would be manageable during the day. Her natural hair was strawberry blonde—not quite red. She had bleached it for her job in an effort to dim her most memorable feature—not the worst thing she'd ever done for the Company—and right now, she had about three inches of strawberry roots. She was happy to see her true color coming through again.

She studied herself in the mirror. Her braid stretched the skin of her forehead back. Her face was shiny, and she looked tired. For the longest time, she had looked school-age, ambiguously so. If she wore something that pushed her tits up high, she was often mistaken for a coed or a high schooler or the harried grad student she once was. But now time was catching up. She rubbed lotion into the skin around her eyes and onto the dry patch on her forehead.

Walking back to her room, her towel wrapped tightly around her, Annie saw light filtering up the stairs and heard the chug of the coffee maker coming alive. Her parents never bought new things just because they could; they always waited for things to die first. The coffee maker was big, old, and slow, but it still made coffee, so it stayed.

She dressed in jeans, pulled a pair of socks up to her knees. She wore her soft, gray bra, the one that wouldn't dig into her shoulders and poke her in the ribs with the bent, out-of-shape underwire. A long-sleeved white shirt and her sweatshirt over that. She'd be too hot later when the sun came up, but right now she was worried more about comfort. She could always pull over and dig out a T-shirt later.

Her mom was in the kitchen, a pink, quilted robe over her white nightgown. Her hair, mostly white now, stuck up everywhere except at the back of her head, where it had rested all night against her pillow. Her mother greeted her with a smile. It was maybe too early for her to remember that she was sad and hurt and out of sorts.

"Pretty girl," her mother said. "Do you want some coffee?"

She accepted a small cup and sipped it slowly. She wanted to down the whole pot but didn't want to have to stop thirty minutes into her trip to find a bathroom to pee in, or worse.

A little while later, her dad got up. They'd mostly packed the car the night before, filling the trunk and back seat with boxes of clothes, shoes, and books. In the passenger seat was a laundry basket filled with toiletries, towels, and other odds and ends. She'd sold most of the stuff in her apartment when she'd moved back to Ohio, so other than clothes and books, odds and ends were all she had left. And her car, of course, which was by far the nicest thing she owned.

Now her dad loaded the rest, tucking things in wherever there was space. Her mother offered to fix her breakfast, but she waved it away, too nervous to eat.

She didn't want to drag out the goodbyes. She didn't feel ready to leave, but she knew she needed to go and it was time to rip the Band-Aid off, get on the road, and put some miles in before the day got away from her.

There were long hugs and tears, of course. Her dad slipped her two hundred-dollar bills while her mom was busy wiping her eyes. Then her mom slipped her a crisp fifty while her dad was double-checking that the trunk was closed up tight.

Just before she got into the car, her dad handed her the map and handwritten directions he had prepared for her, the addresses and phone numbers of the scheduled motels written in his slanted scrawl. He'd used the astronaut pen. Annie recognized the ink.

Her throat felt thick as she drove away, watching them get smaller in the rearview mirror.

But she didn't cry. Annie was an expert at leaving.

She stopped the first night in Kansas City after driving nearly eleven hours. It was just a Motel 6, but the lobby was clean, and she was weary and rumpled and starving half to death. The man behind the desk barely looked at her, uninterested in a woman traveling alone.

He gave her the key, pointed at the glass door to the lobby, and said, "Go to the left and park over by the fence. You're on the second floor."

She thanked him, returned to her car, and parked where he had indicated.

After checking that the car was locked and nothing valuable showed through the windows, she lugged her suitcase up the stairs and into her room. Then she stepped out to use the pay phone at the end of the walkway.

Her mother picked up after one ring. "Anabelle?" she asked anxiously.

"Yes, it's me," Annie said, equal parts exasperated and grateful. It was quite a burden, all the love her family heaped on her. She didn't always feel like she deserved it, and carrying the weight was sometimes a struggle. "I made it to Kansas City."

They chitchatted briefly as her dad yelled from another room and her mother repeated what Annie had said. She spent another minute and a half trying to extricate herself from the call, promising to rest tonight and drive safely tomorrow, reassuring them that the car hadn't made any funny sounds. Annie had been making good money when she bought the car new a few years back, and she had been out of the country as much as she'd been in it, so the car mostly had sat in her garage. This trip would be the most miles she'd put on it yet.

She hung up and listened as her coin clinked down to the bottom of the pay phone. She froze when she heard footsteps shuffle on the ground below. She moved quietly to the railing and looked down but couldn't see anything. Had someone been listening to her? Not much to hear, really, but it was hard to shake the prickly feeling along the back of her neck.

Then she saw the glow of a cigarette as it arced out and landed on the parking lot blacktop. She heard steps and the sound of a door opening and closing below.

Paranoid, that's what she was. There was no longer any reason to look around corners, to double back to make sure no one was following her, but she found herself doing it all the time. Even here in the States, where she was just another fair-haired and corn-fed American. Nothing special anymore.

That was the way that she wanted it, why she'd left.

She returned to her room and pulled on her hooded sweatshirt. Picked up the canvas shoulder bag that she used for a purse and slung the strap over her head. She had to find dinner, and if her car weren't full of crap and low on gas, she'd drive somewhere. Instead, she walked across the dark parking lot toward the nearest fast-food joint with her hood up and the sleeves of her sweatshirt pulled down to her fingertips.

She bought a sack of greasy fries, a cheeseburger, and a bright blue slushy drink that was so sweet it made her teeth hurt and her blood sing. Sugar could right any manner of wrongs. She walked back to her room with the smell of fries driving her slowly insane, then ate every scrap of food in the bag before falling asleep with the TV on.

She woke up after midnight and stumbled into the bathroom. After she washed her hands and face, she looked in the mirror and saw that the slushy had stained her entire mouth blue.

The next night, Annie spent in Albuquerque, New Mexico, and then it was a straight shot through the Southwest until she picked up Interstate 15 in California.

She honked her horn as she crossed the state line from Arizona, but alone in the car, the gesture made her life seem small. She had listened to the same five cassette tapes on the entire drive, and as she approached civilization, she was happy to switch back to the radio. Even staticky commercials were a refreshing change.

She'd had second thoughts from the moment she left Toledo. Was this the right thing to do? More school and going into debt? No one but her would be paying for this degree, and she wasn't even sure what she wanted to do besides help people in a less shadowy way. Wasn't that what academically inclined people did in times of doubt—fall back on more education to buy time?

She liked to have a plan, to have all the answers before she started something, and this was not that. Still, maybe venturing into the unknown would be good for her. She could go to classes, learn something, figure it out as she went. But it was nerve-racking too. She didn't even have a goal past getting the master's.

She'd overslept that last morning, which meant a delayed start, and she stopped at a gas station somewhere in West Covina to call the residential office to say she'd be arriving later than expected.

She got turned around once she entered the city and had to pull over to study a map. She finally found the campus by dumb luck, then asked someone walking along the sidewalk for directions to the building.

The plan was to live on campus in a tiny graduate student apartment, but when she got to the residential office, an undergrad working the late shift looked up from his book and passed her a voucher with a shrug. She looked at it. At the bottom was a line for when the voucher expired. Someone had written in "8/31/92," which was exactly a week away.

"Stuff fills up fast," the student said. "The university puts up overflow students in a motel for a week while they make other arrangements."

"Other arrangements," she echoed, too exhausted to be mad. "What does that mean exactly?"

"Come back tomorrow," he said. "My boss will be here from eight to five, and he can explain."

"And where is this motel?" she asked, flapping the voucher at him.

"Oh, it's like three blocks from here, I think," he said with another shrug. "Like…north?"

"Write down the address. Written directions, please."

He closed his book with a sigh, pushed back from the desk, and stood up. "Let me ask."

It turned out that the motel was close, though she drove past it the first time. Someone honked at her, maybe because she was going too slow, maybe because she still had Virginia license plates. Maybe Californians liked to honk. She flipped on her turn signal when she saw the motel sign again, parked outside the lobby doors, and shut off the engine. She allowed herself a few moments to collect her thoughts and assess. There was no point in being mad at the situation. The kid at the desk didn't seem to know much at all. She would get everything sorted out in the morning.

Anyway, what was one more night in a motel after two thousand miles?

Annie made the man explain it three times. What it came down to was this: they always overbooked graduate dorms because there were usually a few students who dropped out at the last minute. Financially, it made more sense to overbook than to have empty rooms. But this year, no one had dropped out, and since Annie had waited so long before accepting her slot at UCLA, she was at the bottom of the barrel.

"We give you a week to make other plans," the man said.

"Other plans?" she screeched. "I had plans! You're the one who made them fall through!"

"I understand our system can be complicated—"

"You think it's my failure to comprehend your system?" She made air quotes. "You think that's the problem here?"

"Ma'am—"

"Look, I have been in California for about twenty minutes, and I'm really not equipped to go house hunting on my own. So either you find me the school housing that was promised to me, or you produce a better option."

He pushed his glasses up to rub the bridge of his nose. His plastic name tag said *Paul*.

"I can't help with outside apartment rentals, but I can give you a list," he said finally. "We usually only give it out to postdoctoral and foreign exchange students, but because of this unique circumstance, it might be a good solution for you."

"What list?" she asked.

"It's a list of faculty who are willing to take in students. Rent out rooms in their houses for a quarter or two. It's meant to be short-term, but it should be enough to get you into student housing later."

Annie held out her hand. "Give me the list."

She shoved the list of names into her bag and made her way to the registrar building to sign up for classes. That involved several hours in line. By the time she'd finished, she needed lunch. Then she went to buy books. It wasn't until she got back to the motel and moved the most valuable things out of her car that she even remembered the list.

She called her parents, knowing they'd be out, and left a cheerful but vague message, promising to call again when she was more settled. She'd lie to them if she had to, but she'd rather put off telling them anything for as long as possible. She certainly wasn't going to tell them about this motel, about the overflow situation in student housing, or about how she'd spent all that cash they'd slipped her on textbooks in one fell swoop. And she wasn't going to tell them about feeling totally, helplessly adrift.

She'd made this life, these choices, and she wasn't going to give up in the first week. It couldn't be any harder than moving out of her parents' house the first time or the weeks of endless training at the CIA, no harder than being in a foreign country with a fake name and a list of impossible goals.

While she ran a hot bath, she dug the list out of her bag, smoothing the wrinkles on the narrow desk. There were only about twelve names on it, and she quickly realized that there were only two female names. Something about moving into the house of a male stranger just seemed untenable.

One of the names included a phone number. The other gave only a faculty office number and office hours. That simplified the matter. She'd call the first number in the morning, and if that didn't pan out, she'd stake out the office of this Professor Helen Everton and see what she could find.

CHAPTER 2

The professor who had answered the phone number attached to Annie's Hail-Mary list apologized and said the room was already occupied. So that was that. As Annie made her way onto campus, she read the list of names again and tried to decide which of the men sounded the least threatening.

Michael R. Darby.

As long as he didn't go by Mike.

Neal Halfon.

She crossed that one out with her chewed-up pen. The man could be Santa Claus or Jesus Christ or Patrick Swayze, but she could never have a normal conversation with someone named Neal.

Someone brushed against her, and she looked up. She'd wandered into some sort of new-student orientation fair. Tables were set up displaying banners of different clubs and departments. It seemed to be aimed at undergraduates because there were a fair number of parents escorting their wide-eyed teenage children.

Someone at a table beckoned her to come over and check out something called Bliss and Wisdom International.

She looked down at what she was wearing: jeans, sandals, and a pink T-shirt. Oh God, she looked like an undergrad. She veered away to avoid the girl at the table and looked again at the campus map that she'd stapled to her list.

Everton's office was in the criminal justice building, which meant she taught in that department. Annie paused at the foot of a busy staircase and considered. Did she even want to bother? Would one of her prospective professors even let her rent a room? But Annie didn't remember signing up for a class taught by anyone named Everton, and maybe she was nothing more than an adjunct professor. Tenure-track professors usually didn't need to rent out rooms in their houses.

Beggars couldn't be choosers, and time was ticking down. She had to at least scope this woman out or she might end up living with—she glanced at the list—Aaron L. Panofsky. She'd dated a boy named Aaron once. She crossed that name out too.

Everton might not even be in her office, Annie reminded herself. Classes didn't officially start until next Monday. She'd already shaken a second voucher out of Paul, but she wasn't going to get another one, and she was ready to get out of the motel. Plus, she couldn't avoid calling her parents forever.

She stopped to consult her map and then, leaning against a low wall under the shade of a tree, peered down at the row of buildings. There weren't many people going in and out of Everton's building, though plenty of people were walking by. Since all her classes were going to be in this building, she decided to go in and do a little recon. She could walk around until she found the professor's office.

The dry heat seeped into her like an oven, despite the shade of the tree. She was used to the swampy summers of the Midwest and DC, but the intensity of the California heat was something else entirely. The building beckoned her with the promise of centralized air conditioning.

The first couple of floors were classrooms, and she quickly found the ones where she'd be attending classes. When she climbed the stairs to the third floor, the atmosphere changed. The closed doors were identified with placards. She looked around until she found the room she was looking for at the end of the hall.

H. Everton-323

Compared to the size of the classrooms on the floors below, Everton's office didn't look bigger than a glorified closet, barely big enough to hold a desk, two chairs and maybe a filing cabinet, if she was lucky. The office door had no window, so she couldn't see whether it was light or dark inside, but it sure didn't sound like anyone was in there. She twisted the doorknob gently. It was locked.

It would be hard to stake this spot out inconspicuously, so she went back the way she'd come in. She had passed a room earlier that seemed to be the department office, and when she passed by again, a woman was sitting at the front desk.

Annie plastered a smile on her face. "Hi."

The woman glanced up and smiled in return. She wore a shapeless sweater complemented by a frumpy haircut. "Do you need some help, hon?" she asked.

"I sure do," Annie said in the gushy, saccharine voice she used for church and her mother's crochet circle. "I'm starting classes here on Monday, and I was just wondering if the faculty start their office hours this week or next." She leaned in conspiratorially. "I'm not from around here. I'm just trying to get my bearings."

"Well," said the woman, "not until next week officially, but most of them will pop in at some point this week."

"That's good to hear. I'm Annie, by the way."

"I'm Deb Larson," the woman replied. "I'm sure we'll get to know each other very well over the next few years."

"A pleasure to meet you. This campus is just so beautiful, and the whole city looks like the movies!"

"Where did you move from?" Deb asked.

"Toledo, Ohio, ma'am," she said. "It's not exactly bumpkin country, but it's sure different from here."

"I imagine so!"

"Say, do you all do rosters? The faculty, I mean. I'd like to get a sense of who's who before classes start."

"No," Deb shook her head. "But the library has a set of yearbooks. You'll find faculty photos in any one of them. They republish the same ones every year."

"Good to know." Annie grinned. "Thank you so much for your time today."

"Here to help," she said. "Good luck, honey."

As soon as Annie turned around, the smile disappeared from her face. She pounded down the stairs and headed for the door, nearly colliding with a woman carrying a red-faced baby in a car seat. Annie stood aside to let her pass, then pushed out into the heat and sunshine, intent on the library.

The building was swamped with people being issued new student IDs. Since Annie needed one too, she abandoned her plan to find the yearbooks and instead stood in line to get her photo taken, then stood in another line while someone pasted it onto an ID card and ran it through a laminator. By the time she had her card, she was done for the day.

In her motel room, the piles she'd left everywhere had been straightened up by the maid. She called her parents.

"Anabelle Weaver!" her mother chastised. "You have been purposely calling when we've been gone!"

"No, Mom, that's not true," she lied. "You know it's earlier here. I just forget about the time difference!"

Annie didn't want to admit to her mother that her home life was shaky at the moment, so she told her there was a gas leak in the apartment building where she was supposed to live and that they had her and the other students in a motel until it got fixed. The fib slid out far more easily than any truth.

"What happens if it isn't fixed by Monday?" her mother asked, concerned.

"I don't know. I guess they'll keep us on or make other arrangements," Annie said. "I'll let you know when I'm settled." It was a lie so good, she wished it were true.

After hanging up, Annie warmed up a frozen dinner and watched TV until the sun went down. She didn't think she'd sleep, but even scratchy sheets and the sound of traffic outside didn't keep her awake. She woke once in the night to use the bathroom, banging her elbow into the doorframe, but then she stumbled back to bed and slept until her alarm went off.

The library the next morning was much quieter, and the girl behind the desk wrote down a call number on a slip of paper and directed Annie to an upper floor.

"They're toward the bottom, the newest ones," she said. "I don't think they get used a lot, but there should be one from last year up there." She gestured to the large computer monitor in front of her. "We're still converting everything from cards to a database, so it's been kind of crazy."

The yearbooks were tucked away on the lower part of a tall, dusty shelf. Some of them went back well into the 1950s, taking up one shelf on the bottom. The newer yearbooks were one shelf higher. They were slimmer, cleaner, brighter. Annie crouched down, found the one stamped with *1991* on the spine, and pulled it out.

She ran her finger down the table of contents, found the faculty section, and flipped to the back, leafing through until she hit the names beginning with E. She scanned the pictures: Edison, Engle, Epstein, Ettinger.

But no Everton. Not even an asterisk for the not pictured. Was she new?

She slammed the yearbook shut and slid it back onto the shelf.

She was just going to have to figure this woman out the old-fashioned way. Hunker down outside the building and hope she turned up. Look her up in the phone book, see if her address was listed. Annie was good at finding people; she'd been doing it professionally for years now. She'd find H. Everton.

She went back to Everton's building and sat in the shade on the same low retaining wall where she had sat the day before. She'd checked out a book from the library, and she pulled it out of her bag to use as a prop, opening it to a random page in the center. From this post, she could watch for a while, see what kind of people went in and out.

She should be settling in somewhere, looking for a job, prereading her textbooks, or thinking about her upcoming classes. Buying a binder, maybe, or a pack of pens. Instead, she was doing exactly what she was trying to get away from. God, maybe she'd been wrong to leave. Maybe this really was the only thing she was good at, and she was never going to find anything that suited her better. Maybe she should have learned to live with the things that haunted her: an epic failure, a leering boss who promised her there was nothing in the outside world waiting for her.

A man and a woman went into the building. He held the door open for her. Annie glanced down as if studying her book.

When she looked up again, the man had come out alone. He was of medium height and thin. His black hair was cropped close to his scalp. He wore beige shorts and a powder blue T-shirt. She looked down again, turned the page.

She looked up when someone wearing beige work coveralls steered a squeaky cart along the walkway between her and the building. She watched him until he rounded a bend. The cart squeaked even after he left her field of vision.

Which is why she didn't notice the stroller or the attractive woman steering it until she reached the wall and the shade where Annie was perched. She turned her head to peer into the stroller at the sleeping baby, soon realizing it was the same baby she'd seen yesterday, the one in the car seat. Of course, it was the same woman who'd been carrying it.

The woman pulled the stroller parallel with the wall, then set down her purse and began rummaging through a beat-up brown diaper bag that she was holding against her hip. Her bobbed, dark brown hair reflected auburn in the sunlight and fell forward, obscuring her face except for a pair of wire-framed glasses with large lenses that peeked out between her locks. She wore scruffy clothes.

Annie returned her attention to her book, still watching the woman from the corner of her eye, not looking up until the woman said, "Shit!" The bag had fallen to the ground, its contents spilling everywhere.

The woman sat down on the wall and looked at the mess. Only the stroller separated them; the baby slept tucked under a light blue blanket.

"Here, let me help." Annie set her open book down on the wall, spine up.

"It's okay. It's fine. I'm fine," the woman said, shaking her head. She rubbed her hands on her jeans and half closed her eyes.

"How old is he?" Annie asked, nodding toward the baby as she crouched and started picking things up—a gold tube of lipstick, a tampon, a crumpled receipt.

And an identification badge with the woman's picture attached to a lanyard. The woman hopped off the wall and snatched it away but not before Annie read her name and title.

Helen Everton, Adjunct Professor

Annie handed Helen Everton the items she'd picked up, forcing the woman to stop jamming things back into her bag. When she accepted them and everything was back inside, she gave it a good shake.

"Four months," she finally said, reaching down to pick up her purse. "Almost five now."

"He's beautiful." And it was true. The baby, light-skinned with a tuft of dark hair, was sleeping peacefully.

"Thanks," she said. "He's colicky as hell."

Annie started to laugh and then caught herself. "He your first?"

"Third." She shook her head, her hair swaying with the movement. "No. I mean, I have two of my own, but he's a foster baby. I've only had him for six weeks, and we're still getting used to one another."

"Wow," Annie said. "How old are your other two?"

Everton pushed up her glasses and rubbed at her face. She had no makeup on. She looked tired.

"Eight and ten."

"So you have your hands full," Annie glanced at the entrance to the building.

Everton smiled thinly, then hefted the purse onto her shoulder and picked up the diaper bag.

Sensing that Everton was about to extract herself from Annie's invasive questions, she searched for something to latch onto. Just one small fact about Helen Everton that she could exploit for her own gain.

"I'm Annie, by the way," she said. "Just so I'm not a complete stranger. At least you know my name." She resisted the urge to stick out her hand, thinking Everton wouldn't take it.

"Annie," Everton repeated. "Thanks for your help."

She started pushing the stroller toward the building. As much as Annie wanted to keep talking to her, she didn't want to scare the woman off.

If they went into the building, they'd have to come out again.

They came out much sooner than Annie expected. She'd waited five minutes and then ran into the building to use the first-floor restroom, certain she'd have to sit for a couple hours, waiting for Everton and the baby to emerge once more. But forty-five minutes later, Everton came out, holding the wailing baby and a bottle. The baby's cheeks were bright red in the sunlight.

Annie had moved away from the retaining wall and was sitting on a patch of grass far enough away that the woman wouldn't see her immediately when she came outside again. Sometimes an extra few seconds of observation made the difference between a successful contact and a failed one.

Everton was trying to soothe the child, but the cries were getting louder. Annie closed the book on her lap and squinted. After watching for a few moments, she put the book away, slung her bag onto her shoulder, and approached Everton.

"Hi again!"

Everton looked at her, her expression confused at first and then annoyed.

"Is he okay?" Annie asked.

"As I mentioned." Everton bounced the baby, "colicky."

"I bet he's just overtired," Annie said. "I have, like, a bunch of younger cousins and a baby niece."

Everton nodded distractedly.

"He doesn't want to eat?"

"Oh, I don't know." Everton's voice was tinged with exhaustion. "He never wants anything."

All at once, Annie saw everything she needed to know about Helen Everton. She wore her hair in a sensible shoulder-length bob. Her light-wash jeans showed signs of wear. Her button-down shirt had a small stain at the front hem, like it had accidentally been dragged through someone's dinner plate. Her loafers were scuffed, and her purse strap was fraying.

She was an adjunct professor, so she probably wasn't making a lot of money. And while her clothes were well-made, they were old and worn, suggesting she'd had money at one point but was living leaner these days. She was a mother, but the third baby was much younger and a foster baby. Had she had a change of heart? Was she helping out a family member or friend who had lost custody? Or was she in it for the money that the state paid foster parents?

Annie decided to see if she could get Everton to trust her.

"You look like you could use a break. Want me to hold him for a minute?"

Everton, who'd been spinning in place trying to calm the baby down, looked over at her with suspicion.

"I'm not going to steal him. I'm a really slow runner, I promise. But I am good with babies. Even colicky ones."

Everton studied her a moment longer, then with one more ear-piercing wail in her ear, she decided to trust this complete stranger and shoved the boy into her arms.

Annie couldn't quite believe the woman had agreed, except for the fact that getting people to trust her was something Annie had always been good at. Still, it never ceased to amaze her. It was a game now, in a way, to see how much she could get someone to hand over to her and how quickly. Today it was a harried woman and a foster baby.

The shift was enough to startle the boy into a moment of silence while he reassessed his environment. Annie snatched the bottle before he could begin crying again and put the nipple to his lips, guiding it in and praying that the lie she had spun about being good with children was going to pay off.

She'd had a younger brother, but she'd been only two when Danny was born, so she didn't really remember having a baby in the house. Still, how hard could it be? Feed them, let them sleep. Change a diaper every once in a while.

As luck would have it, the baby started sucking at the bottle greedily, quiet in Annie's arms.

Annie's first out-of-country assignment had been five years ago in St. Petersburg, though it was known as Leningrad back then. She wasn't sure she could ever think of it by any other name. The CIA had been eager to take advantage of *perestroika*, Russian Premier Mikhail Gorbachev's policy reform. Her bosses thought that the restructuring of the political and economic systems would open new leads for informants.

Annie joined the CIA at the height of this disaster. She didn't know that, of course. Most of the turmoil was internal, and they recruited hard that year—visiting universities across the country, promising good pay and a life of excitement.

Annie hadn't seen the recruitment flyers or heard anything about it, though. She'd been studying economics, considering a possible career in finance, or perhaps becoming a high school teacher. Her mother had taught in an elementary school for a few years before she married Annie's father. It never occurred to her that she could work for the government or that they might want her.

She didn't go to the recruitment session, but a recruiter sat in on one of her Russian classes. Annie was almost fluent in German, having taken it in high school, and she was tearing through Russian, listening to language cassettes in her spare time and reading ahead in the textbook. She liked languages; it was like doing puzzles backwards. They were exotic and beautiful, and she liked taking them apart piece by piece.

They had done an exercise that day, performing little conversational skits at the front of the class. Annie was grouped with another woman and a young man. The man was the weak link, fumbling through his lines, sweaty and embarrassed.

Acting was just another language to Annie, and she could spout off simple phrases without effort.

"Dobriy vyecher," she said. *"Meenya zavoot Annie."* The male student was struggling, and she fed him his lines in a stage whisper, causing the rest of the class to laugh through their three-minute performance while the professor scowled and scolded them.

When she went back to her seat, she noticed the man in the dark suit watching them. She noticed him again when she went outside.

"Annie," he said as she passed him. *"Tebe nravitsya puteshestvovat?"*

"Sorry?" She understood the question, but she didn't understand why he was asking it.

He continued in Russian, asking her if she was proud of her country. His pronunciation and accent were perfect, but she could tell he wasn't a native speaker.

"My father's a lieutenant colonel in the army," she answered. "You won't find a more patriotic person than me."

It was a good sales pitch; the recruiters had it down to an art form. She didn't need much convincing. The background checks were inconvenient, but the worst things on her record were a few parking tickets and some detentions in high school for talking too much during class. She said yes when they offered her a job on the day she graduated. Drove out to Virginia with her father; he tried to talk her out of it the whole way. He had spent his career employed by the United States government and knew well the ups and downs, but his jaded warnings could not overcome the high of being wanted by her country.

It wasn't until she was mostly through her training that she realized why the CIA was so desperate for agents; everyone they had in the Soviet Union had disappeared and they didn't yet know why. Would they assign a green twenty-one-year-old to the Soviet–East European division? Surely not!

They did hold her back, for over a year, because she excelled at basic interrogation, and they wanted to beef up those skills. She also took Czech along with more Russian-language classes. In a lot of ways, it was like she'd never left school, only now they were paying her instead of her father writing checks.

Annie landed in Leningrad completely fluent in Russian and German, close to fluent in Czech, and with orders to pose as a university student. She was to look for political students ready to turn on their country and for the wealthy children of known KGB agents. They also told her—informally—that if she could figure out the leak, that'd be great.

Twenty-three, first time out of the country, in over her head.

In the beginning, she was only so-so at actually recruiting potential informants, but she was great at talking to people and found that once she got them warmed up, it was better to hand them off to a more experienced agent for the hard sell. No, what she mostly did in Leningrad was interrogate the CIA's own people. Other agents, support staff, even her superiors. She easily got them talking about nothing, about anything, about everything. Half the story was out before they realized what was happening. Everyone told her over and over that it was a gift, a rare one, and she thrived on the praise. She even had a crack once at a suspicious senior agent named Aldrich Ames, though he was too drunk to really be useful. She had soon discarded him in her mind as too incompetent; on top of being intoxicated, he had been sloppy and arrogant.

She spent nine months in Leningrad before being recalled to the States, not because she hadn't accomplished her goals there but because there was no one left to interrogate, and no one wanted to talk to her anymore.

That became her modus operandi—Berlin for six months, then home for six, working at Langley. Eight months in Ankara and then home just in time for her parent's thirtieth wedding anniversary. Four months in Kyiv before someone broke her cover and she had to tuck tail and leave. She took more language classes here and there, sometimes by mail, and after Ukraine, she asked for a stateside assignment to finish up the coursework and ended up with a master's degree in Slavic languages. After that, she wanted to stay put, tired of the travel, but they sent her to Minsk, where she befriended the wife of a mid-level politician. She tried for nearly three months to get her husband to flip.

One day, she showed up to their meeting place, a small shed at the edge of their property, and discovered the woman and her two-year-old daughter shot in the head. The husband was never found. Two agents assigned to figure out what happened were killed too, and the whole unit was pulled and sent home. All because of Annie.

Annie was unused to failure of any sort, and she arrived back in the United States rattled, immediately resigning. Director Clifton was livid, yelling at her until he was red in the face, telling her she would regret leaving, that no one left his division until he said they could. At the time, she was sure it was a bluff.

She showed up at her parents' door in Ohio, underweight and alone, everything she planned to keep packed into her car.

They let her stay, of course, but she couldn't, and wouldn't, explain herself, and they hadn't been happy about it.

She never did find the mole.

"Please tell me how you did that," Helen Everton said.

On the one hand, Annie knew more about the mysterious professor now than she could have ever gathered from watching the building, but on the other hand, she desperately needed a place to live. There was no easy way to ask for something as personal as a room in someone's house. Maybe this baby was the icebreaker she needed.

"Oh, sometimes babies just want a change of scenery." Annie smiled down at the baby and then back up at Everton. "I mean, you have two older children, so you know what I mean."

"You must have a special touch," she said. "Usually, once he starts fussing, he cries forever. He's nothing like my first two." She looked at her watch.

"Everything okay?"

"I have a lot to do today."

"I'm happy to walk back up with you if you need to get back to work."

"Up?"

"To your office." Annie nodded toward the building. "You said you worked here."

Everton looked at Annie uncertainly. "Did I?"

"Well, you certainly don't look like a student here." Annie tried to steer the conversation away from suspicion.

"Hmm."

Clearly, Everton was not going to be swayed by Annie's charm alone, so she would have to go all in. If she failed, she failed, and she'd figure out a new plan.

"Actually, I know you work here." She held the baby a little tighter. "Helen Everton, I've been looking for you."

Everton was quiet as they entered the building and rode the elevator to the top floor, her mouth a hard line. She kept a tight hold on the stroller and a sharp eye on the woman carrying her baby. Annie let her stew; it was better to explain herself once they got to the privacy of her little office.

Deb was at her desk and smiled when she saw Annie, but her smile froze when she saw Everton. There was some bad blood there, or at least a clash of personalities. Or maybe Deb just didn't like babies. Annie shrugged at the older woman as if to say, *What can you do?* Deb nodded at her gravely. If Everton saw the exchange, she didn't acknowledge it. But then Everton didn't look at Deb at all. She walked past with her nose in the air.

Her office was as small as Annie had imagined. The desk was small too, leaving room for a love seat and just enough space for Everton to walk around to her desk. She parked the stroller in the hallway and left the door open; there was no way the stroller was going to fit.

"Hey, listen—"

Everton plucked the baby out of Annie's arms without a word and laid him down on the love seat. After the bottle, he was drowsy and quiet.

Everton turned to face Annie with a glare. "Who are you?"

"I'm Annie Weaver, ma'am," she said. "You're Professor Helen Everton. I didn't catch his name, though."

"Zachary," Everton said. "Well…Zach, I guess. We call him Zach."

"It's kind of a long story," Annie said. "I was supposed to live in graduate student housing, and when I got here after driving across the country, they didn't have a room for me, so I've been living in a motel. The people from Student Housing gave me a list of professors who rent rooms, but the list was mostly men. There was one other woman and you. The other lady already rented her room out, so I was hoping yours is still available."

"My name is on that list?" Everton asked, holding one hand over Zach as if Annie might try to touch him again.

"Yes, ma'am."

"I asked last year for them to take my number off."

Annie's heart sank. *Shit*. What was she going to do?

"Yours was the only one without a phone number, so I had to hunt you down," Annie said dejectedly. "That's all."

Everton snorted. "I asked them to remove my number, and they literally took the phone number off and left the rest of my information on there." She shook her head. "Idiots."

"So no room, then," Annie said, annoyed that she'd wasted her whole morning on this endeavor. "Well, thanks for your time anyway. It was nice to meet you and Zach."

"I'm sorry," Everton said, and she sounded sincere. "When I put my name on that list, I had a husband and one less kid. We were always going to convert the garage to a spare room, but we didn't get past getting it insulated. The shower doesn't work, and there's no kitchen or hot water."

"I understand," Annie said. "I get it. I do. I don't want to come off as desperate, but if you told me that you had a pole with a blanket draped over it to rent, I would take it."

"There's not much to it," Everton said uncertainly.

"This is my department, so I'm not going to be a stranger," Annie said. "I can pay you in cash every month. I assure you I could pass every background check you can muster."

Everton looked down at Zach, who was completely asleep.

"It would be temporary until student housing became available, which they've assured me is no later than next quarter," Annie said. "And I don't have more than what I could fit in my car, so I don't even have a lot of stuff. Just clothes, mostly, and books."

"Okay, okay. Stop," Everton said. "You are teetering dangerously on the edge of desperate."

Annie laughed nervously, which seemed to break the tension. A tendril of hope sprouted inside of her.

"It's not up to me. I have two other kids, and we're a family, so taking in a tenant is a family decision."

"Okay."

"Come to dinner tomorrow night. You can meet Kevin and Ashley. We'll see how it goes. God knows I could use the money." Everton pulled a business card out of a desk drawer, flipped it over and wrote something on the back, then handed it to Annie. "That's the address."

Annie took the card and stuffed it in her pocket. "Thank you."

"Seven o'clock," Everton said. "Don't be late."

CHAPTER 3

Annie was going to be late.

She had left early—better to sit in her car and wait for time to pass than be late when Helen Everton had specifically told her not to be. But then she got on the freeway going in the wrong direction, and when she finally managed to turn around, she'd gone almost seven miles out of her way.

She'd been distracted when she left. Two cars were always parked in her motel parking lot—a blue Pontiac and a brown Buick—but never at the same time. They always parked in the same space, and she never saw either one arrive or leave. Earlier, she'd walked by the Pontiac and pretended to drop her purse so she could mark the back tire with chalk. When she checked on it later, it hadn't moved.

By the time she'd been ready to leave, the Pontiac was gone and the Buick was in its place.

She knew she was being paranoid, and yet… The cars were both unremarkable, but it was as if they were *trying* to be unremarkable. They were old but not old enough to be interesting. Dirty, but not filthy enough to be noticeable. Annie had learned a lot about blending in during her time undercover, and the way she kept seeing these cars but never the people they belonged to made her suspicious. Maybe they belonged to motel employees. Maybe students were illegally parking in the lot. It could be anything.

She'd thrown her stuff in the car and peeled out of the parking lot, flustered and berating herself for her unshakable paranoia.

She finally found the correct freeway exit, but she was confused by the neighborhood layout, and the sign for Everton's street was obscured by a tree. She made another U-turn and crept slowly along the street while she squinted at the faded numbers stenciled on the curb.

The house was yellow.

Something about that pinged at Annie's heart. It wasn't like the house was familiar to her. It didn't look like her parents' house or any of the dumpy apartments she'd lived in or the halfway decent one in Virginia. But it *was* homey, with a big tree in the front yard and a small porch. Nothing like the wraparound porches from her youth, but large enough to hold a potted plant and a welcome mat.

She parked on the street and turned the engine off.

She slipped her purse onto her shoulder and grabbed the box of chocolates she'd bought. Her first thought had been wine, but that seemed kind of an irresponsible choice with a house full of kids.

And that was the weirdest part. She was so desperate for a permanent address that the idea of moving into a place with three kids seemed like a good idea.

She knocked and waited, waited a few more seconds, then rang the doorbell right as the door opened. Helen Everton looked up at the sound of the bell and then looked back at Annie, scowling a little.

"I…I wasn't sure you heard me knocking," Annie said, embarrassed.

"I did. And the bell."

"Yes," Annie said. "Well, I'm here!" She thrust the box of candy out to Everton, who stared at it uncertainly for a moment, then took it. "Thank you for inviting me, Professor Everton."

"You can call me Helen. Come on in," she said. "We just got home half an hour ago, so excuse the mess, but you should know the truth about how we live, I guess." Helen's glossy, dark hair was up in a ponytail, but several strands had escaped, too short to stay trapped in the scrunchie. She wore a faded plaid shirt over a pair of faded jeans, but the loose shirt couldn't hide her trim figure.

Helen kicked aside a pink canvas bag that had been dropped haphazardly by the entryway. It landed in the hall under a row of hooks piled with an assortment of jackets. She gestured as she led the way. "Living room, den. There's a half bath down here. The kitchen is in the back. All the bedrooms are upstairs."

She stopped at the foot of the stairs. "Ashley! Come down, please!"

A small boy sat at a wooden table in the large kitchen. He was painstakingly printing something with a yellow pencil. Zach was lying in a combination bouncer-rocker toddler seat on the table next to him.

"Kevin, this is Annie," Helen said. "Annie, this is my son, Kevin."

Now, this child looks like his mother, Annie thought. No mistaking this one for a foster child. He had her coloring and the shape of her eyes, though his were dark brown and hers were blue. He looked up at her curiously, then returned to his task, seemingly unimpressed.

"And you know Zach." Helen went to the stove and stirred whatever was in the large pot.

"I do," Annie said. "Hi, Kevin. Hi, Zach."

"Hi," Kevin mumbled. He continued working. Annie glanced down at the large lettering scrawled across the page. His name was printed at the top.

"Homework?" she asked.

He covered the page with his arm and said nothing.

Footsteps on the stairs announced the appearance of Helen's daughter, Ashley. She was less of a copy of Helen but still looked like part of the family set. Her chestnut-brown hair was in two tight braids. She wore a black leotard, pink tights, and a black sweater that wrapped around her and tied at her side.

"I told you to change!" Helen said.

"I had to go to the bathroom," Ashley shrugged.

"You had to take it all off to do that. Why didn't you just change?" Helen asked. Ashley gave her mother the same dead-eyed stare as her brother had. "Go change, Ash. Now."

The girl spun on her heel and went back upstairs.

Helen put her hands on her hips. "That was Ashley."

"Ah," Annie said.

"She's ten going on sixteen."

Annie chuckled nervously. Helen turned back to the stove. Kevin continued scratching out his letters with his pencil.

She was still wearing her light jean jacket, still clutching her bag at her side. Then, realizing that Helen had too much to deal with to make Annie feel at home, she took the matter into her own hands and hung her bag on the back of one of the kitchen chairs. She kept her jacket on, despite the warmth of the kitchen. Her flowered dress was sleeveless and she didn't want to show her bare arms right away. The invitation to dinner was an interview, after all.

Unsure what else to do, Annie touched the baby, resting her hand on his warm stomach. He looked at her when she made contact, gurgled, and smiled. His legs were bare, his thighs chubby rolls. He wore a onesie today, blue stripes with a little train appliqué. The plastic edges of his diaper peeked out at the bottom.

"I hope spaghetti is okay," Helen said. "Ashley has dance on Saturdays until six, so we eat a little later than usual."

"Smells great," Annie said. "Thanks for having me."

"You said that," Helen pointed out with a smirk.

"Sorry," Annie said. "I'm, uh, out of my element."

"Kevin, honey, go set the table."

"It's Ashley's turn."

"She'll do it twice later."

"But I'm watching the baby," Kevin countered.

"I can keep an eye on him," Annie said, slipping her finger into the curl of his little fingers. He hung on tight.

Kevin glowered at her but slid off his chair.

She didn't want to stare at the baby, so she looked out into the backyard instead. Behind the house was a small building that backed up to the fence running along the alley. A gate next to the building provided access to the alley from the yard. The building from the outside looked bigger than her motel room. It might have been a garage at one time, but if so, the fence now blocked where the garage door had been.

"I'll show you after dinner," Helen said.

Annie turned guiltily as if she'd been caught doing something besides looking out the window.

"That'd be fine," Annie said. "Can I help?"

"You can make the garlic bread," Helen said, gesturing with a wet wooden spoon at a loaf of French bread on the counter next to her. Annie hesitated. "There's margarine in the fridge. I find it spreads easier."

Bread and butter; that wasn't too hard. She'd seen her mom make dinner a million times. Helen pulled a serrated knife out of a wooden block and handed it to her.

"Thank you," Annie said.

"Where did you say you were from?"

"Lots of places now," she replied. "But I went to high school in Toledo, and that's where most of my family still lives."

"A good Midwestern girl." Helen's voice sounded slightly mocking, but maybe Annie was feeling defensive, backed into a corner, and desperate to make a bad situation bearable.

"I guess so." Annie pulled open the refrigerator door—covered in drawings and magnets and pictures of the kids—and scanned inside for the margarine. She found a family-sized brown tub, pulled it out, then glanced back at the baby.

Kevin returned and slipped back into his chair.

"Napkins and glasses too?" Helen asked.

Kevin got back up with a heavy sigh.

Annie concentrated on slicing the loaf in half evenly, but when she finished, it looked like it had been sliced by a maniac with a jigsaw. She slathered each half with margarine, hoping no one would notice her botched work.

"Garlic?" she asked.

"There's some garlic powder in the cabinet just there." Helen nodded in the general direction of the cabinets. "I use paprika and parsley usually, but however you like it is fine."

"I'm more of a buy-a-bag-of-rolls kind of cook," Annie admitted.

"There's no such thing as too much garlic," Helen said. "Just a light dusting of the other two."

"I can do that," Annie said, not at all certain that she could. She set the open loaf halves on a cookie sheet and sprinkled everything on. When she was done, Helen looked over her shoulder and nodded.

"Good." She popped the cookie sheet in the oven. "We're almost there."

After everyone had eaten and the adults cleaned up the kitchen, Helen picked up the baby and sat with him on her lap. He reached for her wineglass that was just out of his grasp. Annie had a glass of wine too but was reconsidering the box of chocolates she'd brought that sat forgotten on the counter. If she'd brought wine, she could've kept the entire box for herself.

She picked up her glass and sipped. It was white wine, and Annie preferred red if she drank wine at all, but she was grateful for anything that might help calm her nerves.

The older kids had gone upstairs. They seemed indifferent toward her at best. She'd asked them a few polite questions, gauging their interest in interacting with her. Kevin had been the most responsive. Ashley had given short, clipped answers and glared right back at her mother's stern expression. It wasn't that it went badly; they just didn't take to her right away. Most people didn't.

"You want to see the unit before it gets too dark?" Helen asked finally. Annie hadn't wanted to bring it up, hadn't wanted to pressure her, even though it was the entire reason she'd come this evening. The late summer sun was still setting, and everything was awash in orange-and-gold light.

"Sure."

The backyard was nice, though in need of some attention. Judging by the raised wooden box still full of soil, there had once been a vegetable garden. But now there were only weeds. The whole yard, the whole house even, seemed like it belonged to a woman who once had more time.

Helen, with the baby on one hip, led Annie down the narrow, buckled sidewalk to the side door of the former garage. As Helen reached for the doorknob, she swore.

"I have to go get the key," she said. "Can you take him?"

"Sure." Annie reached out and took Zach. At the exchange, he looked like he might start fussing, but then he melted against her. She propped her arm under his bottom and let him rest his head against her shoulder.

"I'll just be a minute. I'm going to check to make sure my children haven't drowned one another," Helen said as she turned back to the house.

Annie was sure she was kidding. Well, pretty sure.

"Okay, let's peek into this window," Annie said to Zach, though he'd just been fed and was drowsy in her arms. He smelled sweet and clean, and she pushed her nose against his head and breathed him in.

She stepped closer to the window and peered inside, but it was dark and hard to see anything. Mostly, it seemed empty.

"Well," Annie said, "she let *you* stow away on the good ship Everton, so why not me, right?"

Helen came back a few minutes later, keys in hand. "He's asleep!"

"Is he?" Annie asked. She couldn't see his face, mashed up against her shoulder like it was. "We were just chatting."

"You're like a Zach magician." Helen unlocked the door, pushed it open, and flipped on a switch. A single bulb came on, dimly lighting the vacant room. A large area rug covered most of the concrete floor, and she could see a toilet and a narrow shower through the open bathroom door. Her mom and dad's camper had one about the same size.

"Nice," Annie said.

Helen laughed, a low bark. "Well, if you want it, it's yours."

"Really?"

Helen shrugged. "Sure. You don't seem crazy, the kids didn't cry, and the baby likes you. And I could use the money." She cocked her head. "You aren't crazy, right?"

"I mean, I went back to school for a second master's, so I'm not completely sane, but I'm not going to run through the neighborhood naked or anything, no."

"Good," Helen said. "I was thinking three hundred dollars a month."

"Seems fair."

Helen eased the key off her key ring and handed it to Annie.

"I'll pay for my part of the phone bill, of course," Annie promised.

"All right."

Annie took the key with a strong wave of relief. The baby gurgled into her neck.

On the last day before the quarter started, she spent the morning packing up her motel room. She had a voucher for another week, but the place was noisy and small. She just wanted to be settled, even if it was in someone's garage. Obviously, it was not ideal to live on a concrete floor with no kitchen, but she could eat on campus. And how cold did Los Angeles get anyway? Compared to Toledo—hell, compared to Eastern Europe—it might feel like a tropical vacation.

The whole school thing didn't even feel real. The housing situation had eaten up the time she'd buffered in for adjustment, and now here she was, waist-deep and unprepared like always. She still only half believed she'd gone through with this harebrained scheme of applying, then driving across country alone just so she could figure out a way to help people instead of hurting everyone around her.

She'd signed up for three classes this first quarter, all required core classes, including Criminal Law and Legal Research. She hoped that would leave her enough time to get a job. Something part-time. She had some money saved and had gotten a loan, but it'd be nice to have a little extra money coming in. Something for groceries and gas. She wasn't sure what kind of job, though. She was not cut out for retail, was overqualified to wait tables. Maybe something on campus?

Most of the clothes strewn around the room were dirty, so she shoved everything back into her suitcases. She'd forgotten to ask Helen about laundry. Hopefully, there was a washer and dryer in the house. Hopefully, Helen wouldn't mind if she used it.

It took longer to get everything back into her car because her meticulous dad had packed it the first time. Now there were things piled on the passenger's seat, but she just had to go ten miles, so it should all hold for now.

When she pulled up to the house, it looked locked up and empty. The other night, a red Jeep Cherokee that Annie assumed belonged to Helen had been parked in the driveway. Annie pulled around back, easing her car up the alley and parking where the garage door used to be.

Luckily, the gate to the backyard wasn't locked. She used the key that Helen had given her to open the door. It was cool inside and kind of dark, but when she turned on the light, she saw that the area rug had recently been vacuumed. And the bathroom smelled like bleach. Helen had cleaned. That was sweet.

It took an hour for Annie to carry everything in from her car and line it up against one wall. She spent another ten minutes sitting cross-legged on the floor and making a list of what she needed. There was no closet, so she needed someplace to hang or fold her clothes. Also a bed. A table. A hot plate. Everything, basically.

She was just pulling out of Helen's street to head back downtown when she passed the red Jeep going in the opposite direction. Helen didn't glance her way, but then she probably wasn't familiar with Annie's car.

Helen's house was right on the edge of Inglewood, a little closer to the airport than to campus. Annie had looked up a lot of the addresses on the list the residential advisor gave her, and most were within a few miles of campus, some within walking distance even, but Helen was far off the map. It would never work for international students who couldn't drive in a foreign country, so she must have intended it for postdocs or wayward souls like Annie. It was strange; Annie was usually good at reading people, but she couldn't quite get a read on Helen. Who takes in a foster baby as a single mom with a young family and then rents out a room to a stranger?

And would Social Services really entrust Zach to a woman who was suddenly on her own?

Still, Annie had to be careful about asking too many questions in case Helen had questions of her own. Annie had what she needed—a permanent address—so she'd simply steer clear of Helen and her children as much as possible. She wouldn't give them any reason to regret letting her camp out in their yard for a single quarter. At worst, she could live in the former garage until January or until it got cold, if it ever did.

It certainly wasn't cold in the army-navy surplus store, where she bought a cot and a sleeping bag, or at Sears, where she bought plastic bins for her clothes and a hot plate. The place with the best air-conditioning was WalMart, where she bought cans of soup, spiral-bound notebooks, shampoo, and a new backpack.

Nothing made her feel every single year of her age like buying a backpack for a new year of school. She could throw a rock and practically hit thirty. Was she really doing this? Too late for second-guessing now, so she threw the forest-green backpack into the cart and kept moving.

She filled up with gas before she headed home, unloaded her car from the alley, and then drove around to the front of the house and parked on the street.

It felt weird to walk through the house, so she let herself in at the side gate by the trash bins and edged along the side of the building, wishing herself invisible as she crossed the yard and disappeared into the garage. She surveyed the pile of goods she had purchased and the green army cot that was still folded up to fit in her trunk.

She held the pillow she had brought with her to her face; it still smelled like home. Something twinged in her chest, and she thought for a moment that she might cry. Instead, she cleared her throat, swallowed her tears, and figured out how to open the cot. Then she dragged it to the corner away from the window and tossed her sleeping bag and pillow on it.

"Home sweet home," she muttered. It was temporary. Maybe she'd buy a real mattress. Maybe the cot would be fine. Everything was temporary if you thought about it long enough.

Someone knocked and opened the door before Annie could decide whether to let them in. It was Helen's daughter, Ashley, her hair tied up in a high ponytail. She was wearing jeans and a sleeveless shirt with an attached hood—normal kid clothes. Though skinny, Ashley didn't look underfed or scrawny like Annie always had at that age, no matter how much she ate.

"Oh," Annie said, surprised at the sight of her.

"Mom says come in for dinner."

"Oh," Annie said again. "I hadn't—I wasn't going to intrude."

Ashley stared at her blank faced and sighed. "It's enchiladas. Wash your hands first. She can always tell." She turned and walked out the door.

Annie had planned to heat up chicken soup on her hot plate and eat her way through most of a loaf of sourdough bread, but it seemed rude to ignore the invitation, so she dug hand soap out of the WalMart plastic bag and washed her hands in cold water, wiping them dry on her pants.

She crossed the yard slowly, pausing for a moment at the back door just in time to hear Ashley say, "Like a stretcher with legs and a sleeping bag?"

Helen said, "Hmm."

Enchiladas covered with cheese and sour cream were a pleasant surprise, and they were not too spicy for her taste. She ate two while she listened to Kevin complain about having to learn cursive and Ashley talk about some girl named Kerry who had a purple pen even though they were all still supposed to use pencil in class.

"What are you taking?" Helen asked. It took Annie a moment to realize she was being addressed. She looked up and smiled nervously.

"Uh, only three classes. Criminal Law, Legal Research, and something called Crime Control Policy." She shook her head. "I may be in over my head."

"Not taking my class, I see," Helen said dryly.

"Why, what are you teaching?" Annie had followed the university guidelines for first-year grad students when choosing her classes. She didn't have a choice when it came to core classes, so rather than seriously overload her quarter, she'd stuck with the recommended three classes.

"Just two this quarter, on child welfare," she said. "Speaking of which, where's the baby monitor? Kevin?"

"It's right there." Ashley pointed at the counter where a thick antenna was sticking up from behind a bowl of fruit. Helen pushed her chair back and picked it up, holding it to her ear.

"He's fine. We can all hear him when he wakes up without that," Ashley said. "He's the loudest baby ever."

"Thank you for your opinion, Ash," Helen said. "You two clear your plates and go watch TV until it's time to brush your teeth."

"You don't have to feed me," Annie said when the kids were gone. "I mean, thank you. But I don't expect it."

"There's no kitchen out there, no hot water, and it's not furnished. The very least I can do is feed you."

It was a fair point, and it wasn't like Annie was in a position to turn down a free meal, so she thanked Helen again.

"Which reminds me. I called about getting someone to look at the water heater out there, but they can't come out until next week. It'll be inconvenient, but you'll have to come in the house to use the shower."

Annie nodded. That was going to be awkward.

"I'm not going to subject you to the kids' bathroom. It's bigger, but it's always a disaster. Use the one in my room. And you can do your laundry here too, of course. The laundry room is just down the hall. And you know you can always use the kitchen. The key I gave you opens the front and back doors of the house, so you don't have to worry about creeping around. You can just come in whenever you need to."

"I wasn't creeping," Annie said.

"No?"

"I was respecting your space."

"Yeah, okay," Helen said with a small smile. "When is your first class?"

"Ten."

"We'll all be out of here by eight thirty, so you can shower in the morning. Will that work for you?" Helen asked.

"Yes, ma'am," Annie said. "Thank you."

Helen laughed. "You're welcome."

It was still light out, so Annie decided to go for a walk around the block. Her parents always went for a walk after dinner in the summers, and she enjoyed it too. She put on her white sneakers and a light sweater—even though it was still a little warm—and let herself out through the gate into the alley, her purse slung over her shoulder.

No matter where she looked, no matter what direction, she could always see a palm tree. No one had told her that about California.

At the end of the block, she noticed a blue Pontiac with the same license plate as the one that had been camped out at her motel by campus, a good ten miles up the 405.

"You sons of bitches," she muttered, marching up to the car and peering into it. No one was inside, and she saw nothing but a crumpled-up McDonald's bag on the floor of the passenger's side. Still, she was scared and mad and apparently not paranoid enough after all. They'd been watching her all week, maybe longer. She should have trusted her instincts, trusted every time the hair on the back of her neck had gone up since leaving Ohio. Since leaving DC, even. Probably since leaving Minsk.

She looked around but saw no one. She rummaged through her bag and pulled out the Swiss army knife her dad had given her on her thirteenth birthday, flicked open the blade and jammed it into the back tire. Listened with satisfaction as the air hissed out. Dropped the knife back into her bag and pulled out a tube of pink lipstick and wrote STOP in large, bright letters across the back window.

She turned back to the house, threw the lipstick into the trash bin by the side of Helen's house, and locked herself in the garage for the night.

Annie climbed the stairs of the quiet house carrying a little bag of toiletries, a newly purchased towel, and clean clothes. Just like college all over again, walking down the hall to the showers.

Ashley's room was painted pale lavender, Kevin's bright blue. She didn't see a room for the baby, but when she found the main bedroom, there was a crib squeezed against the wall between the bed and dresser. A pile of laundry lay on the floor, diapers were stacked on the dresser, and a white laundry basket held tiny onesies, little socks, and crumpled-up pants.

How did Helen do it? Where did the baby go during the day when Helen was working? And if she was only teaching two classes part-time, what else did she do?

Helen's shower was small but clean and still damp. Annie stood under the hot water spray, enjoying the warmth while popping open bottles of unfamiliar products and sniffing them. The shampoo was what Helen smelled like the most. Her curiosity satisfied, she washed her hair and let the conditioner set while she shaved. The shower was small, requiring some contortion, but she was small too, so it wasn't difficult. It was a good thing about being fair-haired too; when she missed shaving a spot, no one noticed.

She borrowed Helen's blow-dryer, then put on a pair of clean underwear and her bathrobe before returning to her garage room.

She left the house early to give herself plenty of time to find parking. When she got to the end of the street, the Pontiac was gone.

Part of why she'd gone back to Toledo as quickly as she did was because she didn't expect her ex-boss's threats to extend past the Beltway. Frank Clifton was a respected agent of nearly thirty years, and while he was king of his division, he wasn't the head of the whole organization. If he followed through on what he was threatening, his career would be in jeopardy, and Annie wasn't worth all of that, no matter how much Frank had invested in her or what he felt he was owed for his efforts.

So to see now that his reach might be bicoastal sent a shiver up her spine. She hoped he was just rattling her cage, hoping to spook her back into his clutches.

She shook off her concerns and spent the drive thinking about Helen's bedroom. She had a nice bed, a simple, sturdy frame that matched the wooden dresser. The towels in the bathroom were taupe, as were the mats on the floor. She had no pictures, though. Annie's own parents' bedroom was crowded with pictures—of her and her brother, of their granddaughter, not to mention their own wedding portrait hanging on the wall over the bed.

Finding parking on campus took some time. She ended up in the student parking garage. Luckily, she had a parking permit, though it cost her a small fortune; she wouldn't have needed the most expensive one if she'd been living in student housing, though it was a small consolation that they had at least they had reimbursed her for that quarter's payment.

She had two classes today, the same two again on Wednesday, and the third on Tuesdays. Which gave her a four-day weekend every week that she hoped to fill with a job. But with dealing with finding housing and trying to figure out if she was being watched, she worried there'd be no jobs left by the time she got to the work study office.

She'd go between classes today.

In class, she sat at a desk against the back wall. In a briefing or a meeting, she would have sat closer to the front. Today's subject matter was interesting, but her attention wandered.

Everyone in class seemed already familiar with one another. While she'd been hopping around looking for a place to live, they'd been attending orientation and get-to-know-you mixers. Annie felt like a stranger—old too. Everyone in class appeared to be in their early twenties, and she was at the far end of that. There was one older man in a brown V-neck sweater and corduroy pants who did seem even older than Annie, though. This had to be a real career change for him. He might even have a wife and family at home. She took some comfort in that.

When class was over, she gathered up her things. It was almost three hours before her next class started, and she wasn't really excited about searching for a nonexistent job, so she didn't rush out. As she slung her backpack over her shoulder, the man, who had been hovering behind her, spoke.

"Hi. I'm Chris."

"Uh, hi. Annie," she said, glancing around at the room's departing students. Most of them carried totes or messenger bags. She seemed to be the only one with a backpack. It made her look young, but she didn't really care.

"I didn't see you at the mixer on Friday," he said.

"You must be some kind of detective." She wasn't sure why her immediate reaction was sarcasm, except that she was wary of strangers now. "I mean, I wasn't there."

"It wasn't that fun," he said. "Where are you headed?"

"Oh, Work Study Office," she said. "Actually, I should go."

She glanced up front just as the door shut behind the professor. They were alone in the classroom.

Chris' warm smile dropped, and he stood expansively between her and the aisle. Getting around him would be a real challenge if he didn't step aside.

The door opened.

Annie's heart sank.

Before being assigned to his division, Frank Clifton had been one of her trainers. He wasn't someone she would have chosen as a mentor, but he'd taken a shine to her early in training, so she wasn't surprised when she ended up under his supervision. He taught her to be ruthless, and that was a valuable skill, one she'd used many times both professionally and personally, but it made her wary of him as a boss, and it made her even more nervous to see him out of context in her classroom on the first day of what was supposed to be her new life.

"You owe me a tire, Miss Weaver," he said, nodding toward Chris—a name she now knew was a fabrication. "Chris" left them alone in the room.

"No. I left everything nice and square. Plenty of notice. Trained my replacement. Left on good terms. Fulfilled my three-year commitment. Why can't you just let me be gone?"

He chuckled. "Your replacement. You and I both know there's no replacing someone like you. Anyway, do you know how much money we poured into you? Your education and training? I thought we had an understanding. A gentleman's agreement."

"I guess I'm no gentleman," Annie replied.

"That used to be one of the things I liked about you." He looked her up and down.

"I'm not coming back," she said. "So now you're just burning up more money you could use on someone else."

"Everyone has hard assignments, Miss Weaver, and everyone takes breaks. It's fine to take a few months to get your head on straight. But this is throwing away everything we built together."

She shook her head. She didn't have to explain herself to him, especially since she had asked herself the same question not so long ago. To her, Clifton was a boss. To Frank Clifton, Annie Weaver was a possession, a rare gem he did not want to lose. At first it was flattering, but then she grew distrustful of what started to feel like someone blowing smoke. Was she really so special? Was her knack for languages worth all this? Her out-of-line actions had led to the death of two agents, who probably had families.

"Come back to DC, and you'll get a much higher salary step. You won't have to go overseas," he said. "There are plenty of people right here on our own soil who need your special skill set."

"You said all this already, and I turned you down. Mr. Clifton, I have things to do."

"Ah yes, you need a job. You need a bed. You need hot water." He smiled. "Shame about your housing situation."

She sank down into a desk chair. "What else is going to go wrong, I wonder, if I don't come back?"

"What else indeed?" He sat across the aisle from her. "Computers are a miraculous invention. It wasn't hard to hack into the UCLA housing database. Our whole lives are accessible now, Miss Weaver. No matter where you go, I will be there."

She shook her head. "If you force me to return, I'll never be the loyal employee you want. You have to know that."

"You know, the Minsk investigation is still pending. Two dead agents, a missing potential informant with a dead family. A dead *child*. Someone needs to take the fall for that. We both know that person *should* be you."

She felt lightheaded and gripped the edge of the desk to anchor herself.

"Jeffries told you to stay away from the wife, didn't he? It was in the paperwork. But you didn't, did you?"

"No," she whispered.

"Two dead agents," he said again. "Could be a lot of trouble. We could press charges if we wanted. Label you a traitor. Charge you with treason!"

"Stop. I get it. Stop."

"On the other hand, if you come back with me today, that could all go away," he snapped. "Your secrets are my secrets, Annie."

She sat up, feeling her gut instinct rising behind her belly button, above the panic, tossing her a life vest.

"Your secrets are my secrets," she repeated. "Your hands aren't exactly clean." They both knew that Clifton hadn't gotten to where he was playing by the rules. He would order a bottle of scotch and claim it as an expense. He handpicked his favorites and manipulated them like he did to Annie now.

"No," he acknowledged. "Which is why we're offering a compromise." He reached into his suit jacket and pulled out a little black pager. He leaned across the aisle and set it on the edge of her desk, pushing it toward her. "From time to time, different law enforcement agencies need the talents of someone like you."

"Someone like me," she repeated in a low voice, looking down at the dark screen of the pager.

"It's a good deal," he said. "It's good for us to loan out personnel in the spirit of departmental cooperation. It's good for you too. Technically, you'll be paid as a contractor."

"Meaning I can technically disregard the rules about interrogating our own citizens?"

"Don't be crass," he dismissed her. "No one's going to ask you to torture anyone. You'll be asked to talk to people occasionally. That's all."

"I won't take less than $100 an hour." She grasped for a number high enough that he would have to refuse.

But he nodded in agreement. "We'll take care of all that. But on call is on call, and when that pager goes off—whether it's the FBI, the DEA, or any area that LAPD covers—you'll have one hour to answer."

"I don't… I'm not going to miss my classes."

"I'm sure we can work around those."

"I don't really see what's in this for you, though," she said.

"Keeping you active is what's in it for us," he said. "Because one day, that thing is going to buzz, and it's going to be your country needing you to step back up to the plate."

Her laugh was hollow. "Baseball metaphors? Really, Frank?"

She'd never called him by his first name before, and he frowned. "You're a very lucky girl, Miss Weaver. To have thrown away your position and have a way back in. Do this for a few years while you

you work on your degree or come back to us now. Those are your only options."

"Stop having your goons follow me," she said, grabbing the pager and dropping it into the side pocket of her backpack.

He shrugged. "Sure."

She stood up and shouldered her backpack while he watched. "Goodbye for now, Anabelle Weaver. And don't bother calling this in. You won't be able to reach anyone higher than me. I've already told them that you called me and begged for your job back. That you were hysterical. I told them I would take care of it." His eyes glinted in the harsh light of the classroom, and she could feel his gaze on her as she walked out.

CHAPTER 4

Annie made it through the first week of classes without incident. She was tense every minute, though, fully expecting the pager to beep. She tried to distract herself by reading ahead and taking copious notes in her classes. Writing things down sealed information into her brain. It was how she had always worked: copying briefs she received on potential contacts and then burning them once they were committed to memory.

There was no telling how much time Frank would expect her to give up, but reading at a table in the library beat reading in her little shack in Helen's backyard, anyway. By Thursday, she was so far ahead in the reading that she had time to catch up on laundry while the house was empty. She left the door and windows of the garage open to air it out. Even though it was a dry-heat climate, the room could get stuffy without at least running a fan. She went to bed Thursday night after eleven, knowing she could sleep in the next day.

Her eyes opened to an unfamiliar beeping sound. She thought it was her alarm, but it was only 1:24 a.m., and when she hit the snooze button, the beeping continued.

She rolled over, nearly falling out of her cot.

She felt around for the lamp on the floor and switched it on, squinting momentarily in the sudden light. She couldn't place the sound until she got up and stood in the middle of the room.

It was coming from her backpack. Her stomach dropped.

She'd finally managed to put the pager out of her mind. How often could a city the size and scope of Los Angeles possibly need someone like her? Besides, law enforcement agencies were prickly and territorial. They never wanted to call in someone from the outside.

Or did they?

She pulled the pager out of her backpack. The little screen lit up green with a phone number. She pushed the up arrow button and saw they'd called twice. She checked for her keys in case Helen's back door was locked and walked through the backyard in her bare feet, the pager in her hand. The air was cool—Southern California always seemed to cool off a little at night—but the concrete walkway was still warm.

She pushed open the door to the kitchen, surprised to find it unlocked and the light on inside. She heard the baby crying, and a moment later, Helen came in wearing a tattered gray bathrobe, holding him.

Annie froze. She was obviously intruding, and Helen jumped a little when she saw her. They stared at each other for a moment.

"I—" Annie started, but Helen pushed the baby into her arms. "Take him," she said. Annie was too surprised to do anything but receive the squalling child, holding him close as Helen rushed into the half bathroom and closed the door behind her.

The pager beeped again.

"Fine, yeah, okay." She shifted the baby to her hip. He flailed, and she fumbled for a moment, terrified of dropping him, so she tossed the pager onto the counter. It skittered across, then stopped against a porcelain canister containing, if the label were to be believed, flour. She repositioned the baby more securely against her hip while she shushed him and picked up the wall phone's receiver. She pulled the long, twisted, curly cord to where the baby could clutch it. With something to distract him, he quieted down immediately.

She reached for the pager again, holding the phone against her ear with her shoulder, and punched in the number. A man with a tired voice picked up after one ring.

"Identification code?"

"You paged *me*," she said. "At one in the morning, I might add. I don't have an identification code, and you can tell Clifton that he's an asshole."

"Name?" the voice said.

"Annie Weaver."

"From now on, you'll be known as Agent Juno, and your identification code word is Akron."

"Fine," she said.

"Report to 150 North Los Angeles Street in downtown Los Angeles as soon as possible."

"Los Angeles Street in Los Angeles? Seriously?" Annie said. "That sounds fake."

Zach whimpered, then let out a loud wail. Either she didn't hear the man's response or the baby drowned out his voice.

"Okay, I'll get there when I can get there. And for the record, I'm from Toledo, jackass."

She hung up.

So much for sleeping in. Instead, she was cradling someone else's baby in a stranger's kitchen in the middle of the night. She picked up a pacifier that was lying next to a crayon drawing of an airplane on the kitchen table, rinsed it off under the kitchen tap, and put it in Zach's mouth. He took it, sucking noisily.

She had to go, no matter how exhausted she was, but she obviously couldn't bring this baby with her. She walked over to the closed bathroom door and knocked lightly. "Professor?" She heard the sink running. She knocked again. "Helen?"

Helen opened the door. Her eyes and nose were red.

"Annie, I am very sorry," she said. "I didn't mean to do that."

"It's all right. Zach seems calmer now. A little fussy. Aren't we all?"

Helen took him and patted his back lightly. "He never sleeps."

"I'm sorry," Annie said. "I'd stay and help, but I have to go."

"Go? It's the middle of the night. Were you on the phone?"

"I was. I can't explain it to you right now."

Helen stared at her. "That's it?"

"That's it," she said. "Good luck with Zach."

Maybe it was rude, but she didn't owe Helen an explanation. She'd already paid the month's rent in cash, and it wasn't like they were friends.

She dug through the plastic drawers that she was using for her clothes and pulled out a pair of black slacks and a light pink button-down shirt. She'd once had a professional wardrobe, but most of it was still in Ohio because there hadn't been space in the car for everything. Besides which, she thought she wouldn't need it. She buttoned up the wrinkled shirt, put her hair up in a ponytail, and pulled on her jean jacket. She applied lip gloss and mascara, then decided she was too tired to care about makeup and grabbed her coat and her bag. When she went around the side of the house to get to her car, she saw that the kitchen light was now off.

She turned on the dome light and studied the map in her car, but getting downtown wasn't actually difficult, and the building was easy to find because it was large, well lit, and clearly identified as the Parker Center with tall letters on a massive sign. It still had some damage from the Rodney King riots—broken glass on the asphalt, scorch marks on its side—although judging from the fresh paint, some repairs had been made. She had been summoned by the Los Angeles Police Department, currently the least popular agency in the city. It was hard enough to convince her parents that UC Berkeley would be safe; Los Angeles had been a much harder sell. As far as Ken and Patty Weaver were concerned, Los Angeles was still rioting five months after the brutal beating of Rodney King. She could hardly blame them for their fears.

The attack on King—and the riots that had followed—had seriously undermined the LAPD's authority, and it made sense that they'd call in outsiders to help, especially if another agency was footing the bill. Annie had read that the cost to repair the damage to Los Angeles would be over one billion dollars. The city was busted up and broke, and Annie had been recruited to do their dirty work. Not unlike Berlin or Leningrad or… It just seemed as if the America that Annie was living in was not the America she'd been raised to believe in.

In the lobby, Annie showed her Virginia driver's license to the cop at the front desk. She should have gotten an Ohio one when she moved home, but the DMV hadn't been high on her list, and after only a couple of weeks, it still didn't seem that important. Registering for classes, finding shelter, and answering mysterious government pages in the middle of the night really ate up one's time.

The desk sergeant made a show of looking up her name and writing down her information before he finally slid a visitor's pass over to her, telling her at least three times not to remove it.

She clipped the pass to her jacket pocket. "Do you know where I'm supposed to report?"

He sighed and pulled the clipboard back over, the wood screeching along the countertop. "Fourth floor," he said.

He didn't offer to call and let them know she was coming, and she didn't suggest it. Maybe the element of surprise would work in her favor. Give her a chance to scope out the place and the people before they asked her to do something awful.

The elevator opened to cuffed men standing in the hallway and shouting from down a hall where she couldn't see. She stepped out of the elevator and waited, her purse slung across her chest and her hands in her jacket pockets, taking note of burly men with tattoos on their arms, others in leather vests, bored-looking officers in blue uniforms so dark they were practically black, and one man wearing a tired gray suit and a thick red tie. He looked up and spotted her. "Can I help you?" he asked.

"I believe I'm here to help you," she said, projecting her voice without raising it, gave him an easy smile, and gazed at him from under her dark eyelashes. She had no intention of showing how nervous she was. Easy, breezy.

Her heart hammered.

"You're the federal interrogator?" he asked and scoffed.

"Yes, sir," she said and glanced at her wristwatch. "And my time starts now. Let's get to it."

They put her in an interrogation room with nothing but a small table and two chairs. She laughed. "I'm not a wizard. I need the case file. All the information and time to read it." So they put her in a supposedly soundproof empty cubicle with three padded gray walls, but she could hear them talking about her from the other side of the room. Blonde. Teenager. Girl. Fucking joke. Apparently, she'd been called in by the deputy chief, whoever that was, but they didn't really want her there.

Finally, though, they gave her a thick file and a box of evidence. She read everything twice. Pulled a pair of gloves out of her bag to examine the evidence, then decided to take advantage of being ignored.

She slipped out of the cubicle and down the hall to the row of interrogation rooms. The suspects were a brother and sister, twenty-three-year-old twins raised by an abusive stepfather after their mother died of cancer nearly twelve years ago. The stepfather, a member of the sheriff's department, had turned up dead in a ravine not too far from the twins' home. Which was probably why Annie was here. A neutral third party, so to speak.

The boy was in with at least one of the detectives; the girl had been left alone. The rooms didn't have mirrors, which was what she was used to. Instead, officers gathered around the door, listening through an intercom. She could hear the good-cop-bad-cop routine from where she stood.

"Look, Marco, we just wanna help you out of this jam," said one. "We can work with the district attorney if you confess now."

"Maybe you won't have to spend your last days on death row," someone else said.

It sounded like the detective who'd met her at the door. It wasn't a good approach. All good-cop-bad-cop did was confuse the suspect. Gave them whiplash. Especially when used on someone so young.

She pressed against the wall and let herself into the interrogation room with the sister.

"Whew," she said after the door closed behind her. "It's crazy out there! You want a pop or something?"

The girl was suspicious and wary. "No."

"Suit yourself." Annie leaned against the closed door. She sighed loudly and tilted her head. "I'm stuck here too."

"You're not a cop?" the girl asked.

"God, no," Annie said. "Do I look old enough to be a cop?" The girl studied her, and Annie laughed. "Don't answer that!"

"Who are you, then?"

"Oh gosh! I'm so rude! Where are my manners?" Annie sat down across from her. "I'm Annie! I'm an intern here. They asked me to see if you need anything." Annie leaned in a little. "You said no to a pop, but there's a vending machine with snacks, or I could get you some water?"

"I don't want anything," the girl said miserably. "I just want to go home."

"Well, I can't help with that." Annie clicked her tongue. "What's your name anyway?"

"Maria."

"Maria," Annie repeated softly. "You mind if I hide in here a little while with you?"

Maria shook her head.

Annie smiled and reached under the table to activate the intercom and toggle the light on outside the door, indicating that the room was occupied and in use. "Great," she said.

The sun was up by the time Annie dragged herself home, her bones heavy with exhaustion. Maria's brother, Marco, had clammed up and asked for a lawyer after less than an hour. She'd spent nearly five hours with Maria. Getting to know her, getting her to talk. Eliciting confessions took time, and Annie had to first wade through Maria's abusive history with her stepfather before getting to what happened to him.

In the end, Annie got the confession. She usually did. But when she finally emerged from the interrogation room, it seemed like the whole department was waiting in the hallway. The gruff cop was annoyed that Maria hadn't turned on her brother, sticking to the story that she'd killed the stepfather alone.

"You're welcome," Annie said, slinging her bag over her shoulder and heading for the elevator.

She entered the house through the front door, flipping the deadbolt behind her, and walked down the hall, stopping short when she saw Helen sitting alone at the kitchen table, nursing a mug of coffee.

"Oh," Annie said. "You're still here. You okay?"

"Kids are at school, Zach's at daycare, and I called in sick," she said. "Never got any sleep last night."

"I didn't think you taught class on Friday."

"I don't," Helen replied.

They stared at each other, waiting for the other to ask something else. But Annie was tired, especially tired of asking questions, digging for answers, and waiting for the person across from her to slip up.

"Feel better." Annie prepared to slip out the back door.

"Thanks. You want a cup of coffee?"

It might get her through a shower. Annie nodded. "I can get it."

When Annie stayed home sick, which she only did rarely, it was a pajama pity party. She would tuck herself in on the couch, watch stupid movies, and refuse to move all day. But Helen was dressed in jeans, her dark hair clipped back with a silver barrette. She looked pretty. Was she wearing mascara and foundation, or was her skin really that clear, her lashes naturally thick and dark? Hard to say. Some people were just genetically blessed. One of the many unfair things about life.

Annie sat down next to her and set her mug down.

"Your mother called," Helen said.

"What? When? How did she sound?"

Helen lifted her mug in a weak attempt to hide her smirk. It hit the wooden table with a thud on the way back down. "I just told her you were out. She sounded worried."

"I gave her the number, but I told her it was for emergencies only."

"It's fine if your family calls. She seemed very pleasant."

"They're mad I'm out here," Annie confessed. "They're mad I left Toledo."

"It's hard when your kids leave you."

Annie shook her head. "It's not that exactly. I just… I made a big deal of leaving a good job and moving back home, and then I didn't even stay." She looked down at the coffee in her mug, light with cream and sweet with sugar. She ran her thumb across the rim, making the porcelain whimper. "It's hard to know what you want, I guess."

"Where did you work before?"

And there it was. The question. When Annie had first started with the CIA, she backflipped around to avoid answering that question, trying to avoid situations where someone even asked her. It ended up with her sitting alone in her apartment a lot. There were generic answers—she could be vague, say she worked for the government, that she worked for the State Department. Some agents picked a random organization, but that always ran the risk of someone saying, "No, you don't. I work there." And then that became a whole other mess.

Annie simply answered, "Washington, DC."

Helen waited. Annie sipped her coffee.

"Oh," Helen said uncertainly.

"Cost of living there was just terrible. I mean, it isn't great here, is my understanding, but at least it doesn't snow."

"And no humidity."

"Hallelujah."

"So." Helen slowly turned her mug on the table to line the handle up with the edge of a placemat that was buried in coloring supplies. "Part of the reason I stayed in today, other than self-indulgence, is that they're coming to look at your water heater. Someone is supposed to be here between"—she looked past Annie to the clock on the stove—"now and eleven."

There went her dreams of sleep.

"I know you've just moved in and you're only now getting settled," Helen said. "And I know I'm not your mother or anything, but have you thought about…" She paused.

Annie was too tired to follow Helen's prompting.

"What?"

"Furniture? I've sent my children to summer camp with better bedding than what you've got out there."

Annie relaxed a little and laughed awkwardly. "Yeah."

"I wasn't trying to invade your privacy, but I had to go in to read the make and model of that water heater, and—"

"It's your property," Annie said.

"Still, landlords are supposed give notice."

"I have thought about furniture. I just haven't had time."

"I was thinking, since I'm home today"—she took a breath—"we could take the Jeep after the repair guy leaves. There's a really great consignment shop not too far from here. Get you a dresser? A bed?"

"You don't have to go to the trouble."

"It's not any trouble," Helen assured her. "I never get to go shopping, and I never, ever get to go without the kids."

"What about them?" Annie asked. "Won't you have to pick them up from school?"

"It's Sal's weekend." Helen waved her hand.

Annie didn't know who Sal was. She barely knew anything about Helen except that she had blue eyes and thin wrists and wore no jewelry. She had three kids. She lived in this house. She sometimes taught college. End of list.

"The kids' aunt."

"Ah," Annie said.

"Bruce gets one weekend a month, and his sister Sally agreed to supervise his visits because most the time, he doesn't even bother to show up. Instead, he's asleep on top of a secretary somewhere." Helen sounded more tired than upset. As if she'd been worn down all the way to the bone. As if there was no muscle left to fight with.

"I'm sorry," Annie said, lacking anything more helpful to say.

"Me too," she replied. "But I love Sally and the kids get to play with their cousins, and I get a little break. Well, not from Zach, but one after three is still a break."

"I would love to go shopping with you, Helen. I need a shower and a power nap, and then I'm good to go."

"You want to talk about where you were all night?" Helen abruptly changed the subject.

"No. I'm not…ready yet. Is that okay?"

Helen nodded. "Of course it's okay. It's your life."

"Thanks."

"Tell you what. Why don't you shower and nap in my room, and I'll come let you know when they're done in yours."

A hot shower and a nap in a towel for an hour sounded like heaven. "You sure?"

"I had three kids in that bed this morning," Helen said with a chuckle. "At least you won't pee in it. Or leave crumbs."

Annie left to gather her shower caddy, a clean pair of jeans, and a tank top the color of orange sherbet. When she got back to the house, Helen was at the door, talking to a man with a red toolbox, so Annie headed upstairs and closed Helen's bedroom door behind her.

As she showered, she thought about her own mother and all the mornings she and her brother had piled into their parents' bed before they got too old and too cool. She used to have bad dreams and climb into her mom and dad's bed more often than Danny, even though he was younger. She would wake up tucked into her mom's side and find her dad later, snoring loudly in her pink twin bed.

Still wearing a towel, Annie stood at the end of Helen's bed. Light gray sheets clashed with the room's decor, but they were soft. She pulled the comforter up over the sheets, toweled off, then put on her underwear, bra, tank top, and jeans. Then she put her wet towel over one of the pillows, laid on top of the bed, and promptly conked out.

"Annie Weaver!"

Annie sat up like a shot, her heart hammering and her ears ringing. Then she realized she was in Helen's bed and laughed nervously at the thought that she'd almost peed in it after all.

"Sorry." Helen reached out to touch Annie's shoulder. "I didn't mean to scare you. I was just trying to wake you up. I shook you. I said your name. You were dead asleep."

"My dad," Annie said, wiping her mouth with the back of her hand. "He used to use our full names to let us know we were in trouble."

Not exactly true. He was a man with a temper, yes, but her father had been soft with her. He never yelled and rarely even snapped at her. Just turned away with a slow, simmering disappointment. She'd rather he had yelled. Her full name being barked out like that truthfully reminded her of Frank Clifton, but that was something she could not and would not be sharing with Helen.

"Sorry," Helen said, "but not only do you now have hot water, but apparently the only thing wrong with the shower is the showerhead."

"Good news?"

"It is. We can stop by the hardware store while we're out, but we need to get moving. I'm supposed to get Zach by five, and I could use some lunch. Are you hungry?"

"Starved," Annie said.

Helen's Jeep wasn't that old, but it was well used. Annie had to fish a crayon and a toy plastic dinosaur out of the crack of the front seat before she got in. The back was half taken up with a car seat. Helen said they could push the other half of the back seat down to make room for whatever they bought.

"Now, I've been thinking about your budget." Helen pulled out onto the road.

"Mine? Don't worry about that. Even I can afford a used dresser."

"Didn't say you couldn't," Helen said. "But I thought I might at least chip in if we find something we both love. You aren't going to be in school forever. I'll have an easier time renting it out to someone new if it's furnished."

Of course. Annie had promised only a quarter, maybe two if she was lucky. And that was for the best, she told herself again. The more time she spent with Helen, the more she liked her, and that was a complication to her already complicated life that she did not need.

"Let's just see if we can even find anything," Annie said dismissively. "Do you think they'll have batteries for this thing at a hardware store?" She reached into her bag and pulled out the pager that, as if on cue, let out a weak beep.

"What is it?"

"One of those pager thingies," Annie said. "Someone calls the number attached to it, and the number shows up on the screen so I know to call them back." They hadn't given her any replacement batteries. Maybe that was deliberate. If she let the battery die and didn't respond, there would be consequences. If she figured out a way to keep it on, they had her where they wanted her.

"Like doctors use?"

"Right," Annie said.

"What kind of batteries does it take?"

"I'm not sure. I mean, I can't remember what size they are."

She wondered if there would ever be a time in her life when the lies didn't flow out of her so easily.

"Is that where you went last night?" Helen asked. "Heart surgery?"

"I'm a brain surgeon, actually."

Helen laughed. "How about Radio Shack?"

"Yeah," Annie agreed. "Hardware store, Radio Shack, then furniture."

"Don't forget lunch." Helen looked at her over the top of her glasses. "Is Mexican okay? You liked the enchiladas I made, right?"

"Right."

Helen took her to a tiny restaurant in a strip mall that Annie's mom would never set foot in if it were the last place on earth. It was strange for Annie too—the fact she couldn't understand anyone in the kitchen, the loud talking over the sound of sizzling meat and radio music, the brightly colored pop in glass bottles, the tiny television broadcasting a barely visible soccer game mounted up in a corner. It was more foreign to her than many of the foreign countries she'd visited.

Helen ordered for them both, and they sat at a tiny wooden table to wait for their food, a basket of tortilla chips between them. Annie knew she must've looked apprehensive and made an effort to neutralize her expression. "The Mexican food here is more authentic than what we have back home," she said. Her dad thought Taco Bell was exotic. She dipped the corner of a chip into the salsa and took a tentative bite.

"How old are you anyway, Annie Weaver?" Helen asked, biting hungrily into a salsa-laden chip.

"How old are you?" Annie shot back.

Helen laughed. "Thirty-nine."

"Twenty-seven."

"Seriously?" Helen asked. "I was guessing twenty-four at most."

"Hard to be a brain surgeon by twenty-four," Annie pointed out.

"And what exactly brought you to Los Angeles?"

"If we're playing twenty questions, it's my turn," Annie said.

But she didn't get to ask because a woman came with their food. Then, everyone in the dining area close to the small TV cheered, and when things quieted down again, the moment had passed.

They managed to squeeze a wooden chest of drawers into the Jeep, leaving just enough room to pick up Zach on the way home. They compromised on the cost, with Annie buying the chest of drawers and Helen purchasing a twin mattress and a box-spring to be delivered the next day. Helen had suggested full-sized, but Annie said a twin would feel roomy after sleeping on a cot.

They arrived at the day care, and Annie went inside with Helen. The colorful room was loud and bright, and it smelled like formula and diapers and disinfectant. While she liked Zach well enough, didn't even mind Ashley and Kevin, she had no desire for a life with children. The realization washed over her like a wave.

"Here he is!" a woman in a yellow sweatshirt announced brightly. Helen smiled and reached for Zach, who stretched out his arms for her.

"Thank you, Maureen," Helen said.

"Our pleasure," she said, then glanced at Annie.

"This is Annie. She's..."

"One of her students." Annie filled in the gap. "It's a pleasure to meet you, ma'am." Maureen was clearly older than her—older than Helen too—and Annie called anyone older than her *ma'am*.

"Zach just loves her," Helen said when Maureen looked at Annie curiously.

After going out to the car and buckling Zach into his car seat, they headed for home.

"You didn't have to lie to her, you know," Helen said. "To Maureen. About who you are."

"You seemed not to know what to say."

"I was figuring out how to word it, that's all."

"Tenant?" Annie said. "This is my tenant?"

"I was about to settle on *friend*." Helen looked up into the rearview mirror at the baby, who had started to fuss. "It's okay, kiddo. Shh, shh, shh. We're almost home."

Annie thought about it. *Friend*. Well, not like she had a thousand and one of those here. She chatted with people in her classes but made no social plans. She hadn't even talked to Lori yet, the whole reason she'd thought about California in the first place. She'd left her a message that first week in the motel, promising to leave a number when she was settled, but hadn't yet followed up. She'd call her tonight.

Helen pulled the Jeep into the alley and parked.

"I didn't mean to lie." The irony of the statement wasn't lost on her. "Sometimes my mouth fills gaps before my brain thinks about it."

"Let's just get this chest in before the baby loses it completely," Helen said.

It was heavy and awkward, but they finally got it out of the car and into the room. Then Helen took the Jeep back to the house, leaving Annie to move the chest to where she wanted it. She pushed it across the floor, only to have the area rug bunch up beneath it. She was still puzzling out how to fix it when Helen came back with Zach on her hip and the plastic bags containing Annie's showerhead and batteries.

"Annie," Helen said, "I enjoyed going out with you today. Thank you for going with me."

"I had a nice time." Annie pushed her hair out of her sweaty face. She took the bags and set them on the cot.

"I just haven't had a lot of time for friends since Bruce left," Helen confessed.

"You have a lot on your plate." Annie understood how life could spin out of control so fast that friends and morals disappeared into the ether.

"I was thinking that if you wanted to sleep in the house tonight, you could have Ashley's bed or the sofa, even. Just until your mattress comes."

They turned and looked at the army cot at the same time.

"I wouldn't last a night on that thing," Helen said. "You've been on it for a solid week."

"It seemed like a good idea at the time. And I've slept on worse. It's better than the ground."

"Anyway, you're welcome to sleep at the house. That's all."

"Thanks."

After Helen left, Annie changed out the pager batteries. When it lit up green, she watched it to see if she'd missed any calls, but it stayed quiet, and she set it down.

She opened the window to get some air in and stood looking at the house. Helen was standing at the kitchen sink, the phone to her ear. Annie stepped to the side so she could watch from an angle as Helen chatted away.

When Helen looked up, she looked out straight at the garage. Annie froze and held her breath, but it didn't seem like Helen could see her. After a few more moments, Annie turned away.

She was so tired.

She crawled onto the narrow cot, the slippery fabric of her sleeping bag gasping beneath her. She turned onto her side and pressed her face into the pillow. She prayed the pager didn't go off again for a long time.

CHAPTER 5

Annie settled in at one of the pay phones on campus and fished her calling card out of her backpack. It took forever to punch in all the numbers. She was relieved when she got Lori's answering machine again, though it was the very reason she had called in the middle of the day. She left a message apologizing for not calling sooner, gave her Helen's phone number twice, and told her the best times to call. It wasn't that she didn't want to talk to her, but when she pictured explaining her situation to her successful friend, it was embarrassing.

She hung up and started punching in numbers again. Her mother picked up. She started in right away. "I don't like you this far away," she said. "We can never reach you. I hardly know anything about your life. We're worried sick!"

"I'm going to school, Mom. You know that. And I'm living in a house that is so, so much better than a dorm. You talked to Helen. She's nice, don't you think?"

"She seemed very pleasant," Patty conceded.

"I have a lot of work with my classes, but I'm going to be better about calling now that I'm getting settled." Annie made that promise all the time. She always intended to keep it, she did. It was just that life got in the way. Going overseas had been a good excuse for forgetting her promise. Los Angeles, it seemed, was not quite far enough away.

It wasn't that she didn't love her parents. It was just that they had a very simple worldview, one that grated on Annie, one she could do nothing about.

"I'll call again this weekend," Annie said. "I'm between classes, so I gotta run."

"Be sure that you do," Patty said. "Your father has been talking about writing you a letter."

"I'll call!" The last thing she needed was a written scolding. She promised again, her tone softer. "I'll call."

She made it through her next class, which was an hour and a half of discussing and dissecting municipal codes, then headed to the library. So far, the majority of her homework was reading and more reading, but she had to write a few responses to some of the material, and the professor wanted everything typed, not handwritten, and on a computer or a word processor, not a typewriter. "There are plenty available for use in the library," he'd said. "Don't let those expensive machines go to waste."

She wasn't unfamiliar with computers; she'd used them to write reports for her bosses in DC. But she had no idea how they actually worked and no desire to acquire one of her own, no matter how many people told her they were the wave of the future.

The workers at the help desk were busy, and she had to wait in line before she could talk to someone. The woman, obviously a student, wore faded jeans and a T-shirt that said *For People, for a Change* under an image of the governor of Arkansas.

"I need to type something up and print it out. I was told I could do that here?" Annie asked.

"There's a computer room on the third floor," the girl replied. "Check up there."

Ten minutes later, Annie sat in front of a computer monitor. She'd handwritten most of her response on lined paper, so she just had to type it up into the machine. She stared down at the keyboard and sighed. Her brother was great with computers. He had learned to type correctly and everything. Maybe he'd be willing to move out to LA to be her personal typist.

She hunted and pecked her way through the paper and was standing at the printer, waiting for it to chug out her three pages, when she heard beeping.

The pager.

She sighed, tore her pages free along the perforated edge, and went to the desk on the computer floor. She slapped her printed pages down and dug through her backpack while the man at the desk watched her.

"Do you have a phone I could use?" she asked, showing him the pager.

"Is that the Bravo Alpha?" he asked. "Motorola?"

"It's… Yeah," she said. "Yep."

"Cool," he said. "I heard they're designing one with a keyboard attached so devices can communicate with each other without using a telephone as a third party."

"Wouldn't that be something. If I had that, I wouldn't need to use your phone."

"Oh, right." He picked up the phone and setting it on the counter. "One courtesy call."

"Thanks." She dialed the number on the pager. This time, it was a different area code, but when the other side picked up, it sounded like the same man she'd spoken to last time. Like the call was being rerouted.

"Identification?"

"Agent Juno, Akron." She winked at the man at the desk, who was staring at her with his mouth hanging open, then nonchalantly began tearing the edges off the computer paper and separating each page.

"We have an assignment for you," he said. "You're to meet your contact at the following address."

"Hang on." She looked up. "You have a pencil?"

The man closed his mouth and pulled a pencil out of a drawer.

"Okay." She wrote down the address on the back of her paper, pressing lightly so it could be erased later. "What time?"

"One hour."

"I need two," she said, "unless you want me showing up in jeans."

"Two hours," he said and hung up.

Annie sighed. "They never give me enough information," she complained.

"Who…who was that?" the man asked.

"Oh, church social. Thanks for the help."

Annie walked through the empty kitchen, pausing when she noticed a little pile of candy on the table on top of a white envelope addressed to Anabelle Weaver. A tiny Peppermint Pattie, a Hershey's Kiss in gold foil, and a bite-sized chocolate bar.

Helen must have left them there so she wouldn't miss them. Interesting.

She scooped up the candy and dropped it into her bag, then picked up the envelope and tore open the flap. It contained a check for a little over seven hundred dollars.

She felt a little dizzy and sat down at the table. Reaching back into her bag, she pulled out the Peppermint Pattie, looking at the numbers on the check while she peeled back the foil. She popped the candy into her mouth, letting the dark chocolate melt on her tongue, then sank her teeth into the soft, white center. It was hot and cold all at once, and she savored the contrast.

The check gave her a sense of relief. She knew she was being used and coerced because she'd been on the other side plenty of times, using and coercing her way through everything. But she hadn't been sure they'd really pay her, at least not at the rate she asked. It had seemed like an outlandishly high number when she said it, and now she wished she'd asked for more.

You can do this, she told herself. Short bursts of the other life for good money and then back to this one. She was under their thumb, but it was better than being under their entire hand. She would be more careful this time. She wouldn't put herself in a position that put anyone in danger again.

How much damage could she do while sleeping in a garage, listening to the school bus lumber down the street in the mornings? Ashley blasting Paula Abdul and Janet Jackson through her open window. Kevin asking for a computer, the baby crying at night. This was her real life.

She could keep being a part of this life. At least for a bit longer.

And if they kept calling her, maybe she could afford an apartment of her own after a while and wouldn't have to deal with student housing once the quarter ended and her time here with Helen was up.

But they weren't going to pay her at all if she didn't get moving.

She put on a navy skirt and a white blouse, which made her look like a stewardess, but she didn't have a lot of options. She'd ask her mother to send some of the work clothes she'd left behind, or maybe she'd use this money to buy new outfits. She slipped on her black heels, the only pair of work shoes she had here. She clipped her hair back with a barrette and put on some lipstick.

Maybe she ought to be nervous about going to meet a stranger to do God knows what, but she'd done it so many times now in so many places that it seemed silly to be nervous. She opened the map on the hood of her car and tried to write out some directions, but she ended up getting all turned around anyway. She stopped at a gas station to ask for help. The attendant, an old Black man, was watching a portable television. She pushed the paper with the address across the counter in his direction. She was already late.

"That's the church," he said, looking at the address. "Saint Agatha."

"Am I close?" she asked.

"Two blocks that way, honey." He pointed out at the street. "Jesus'll show you the way."

"Thanks," she muttered as she walked out, the sun momentarily blinding her.

It turned out she had driven right past the right place before she got to the gas station but had been expecting to find an office building or a park. Certainly not a church. She pulled into the parking lot.

The church's wooden doors were open. Her eyes took a moment to adjust to the dim lighting. There were only two people inside: an Asian woman kneeling with her head bowed, a rosary clasped in her hands, and a white man in a black suit sitting in a pew, staring up at the crucifix.

Annie wasn't much of a gambler, but she'd bet that was her guy.

She slid in next to him. He glanced at her and then looked away again. He looked younger up close and was not a bad-looking guy, though he carried thirty extra pounds around his middle. Also, he smelled like he was sweating out a bar. Lovely.

"I'm just, uh, waiting for a friend," he said after a few moments of silence. She rolled her eyes.

"You're waiting for me, champ." She could understand people's surprise when she didn't turn out to be what they expected, but she was not okay with flat-out disbelief. "What are you? DEA?"

"FBI," he said. "You're the special agent on loan?"

"That's me. You want to wrap up your business with the Lord so we can get going? I have a life, you know." That life included at least three hours of newly assigned reading for class that she was running out of time to get done. Maybe she could read while she waited for the FBI to pull their heads out of their asses. They always seemed to be standing around.

"Oh," he said. "Yeah, I'm supposed to brief you before I take you to the location."

"You have a car?"

"Yes."

"Can we do it there?" The church wasn't empty, and it wasn't secure.

"I guess, yeah," he said.

She went to pick up her bag.

He stopped her and stuck his hand out. "I'm Agent Sean Katz, by the way."

"Annie Weaver." She pumped his hand once and then letting it go. She slung her bag across her body. "Charmed. Let's go."

It was hard to say which was worse: the two-and-a-half-hour drive to Lompoc with Agent Katz—who apparently found silence uncomfortable because he chatted the whole way there—or the file she was reading that contained two years' worth of investigative material. Reading in the car made her sick to her stomach.

After they arrived at Lompoc, it took a long time to have the prisoner brought out so she could interrogate him. Talking to convicted felons wasn't her specialty. She was great at getting information, even confessions, but the FBI wanted a Hail Mary miracle from a prisoner with no incentive to tell her anything at all.

She stayed with him for three hours. He offered nothing but sexual harassment.

"I don't know what you all expected me to do," Annie said after they took him away.

"You're supposed to be the best," Agent Katz said. "It was worth a try."

"I had nothing to work with! You guys always think I'm going to be some sort of miracle worker, but crappy cases are crappy cases, and I can't squeeze blood out of a stone."

"You did what you could," the agent said. "No one blames you."

"I don't give a shit about blame. I get paid either way." She was exhausted. "Is someone going to drive me back to LA?"

She was hoping for someone other than Agent Katz, but he was her assigned escort for this case.

When they hit Santa Barbara, he said, "What do you say we stop and get some dinner?"

She just wanted this day to be over, but she was starving, jittery, and on edge, so she nodded. "That's fine."

She'd managed to avoid small talk for most of the drive home, choosing to read and be nauseated over listening to him talk about baseball, but it would be too dark to read soon and rude to read during dinner, so she steeled herself. Maybe he'd go through a drive-through somewhere and get greasy hamburgers in a paper sack. He looked like a greasy hamburger kind of guy. But instead he said, "They have great wineries around here."

And that's how she found herself in a nice restaurant with a view of the sun setting over the vineyard. Cloth napkins, white tablecloths, and heavy cutlery.

"You have to try the wine," Agent Katz said when they were seated, but then he ordered a Manhattan for himself. She ordered a glass of Coca-Cola. He ordered a steak. She ordered the chicken.

"So," he said, "tell me about yourself."

She clenched her napkin in her fist and prayed for death.

Helen was sitting in the recliner in the living room with the baby swaddled and falling asleep in her arms.

Annie froze in the hallway, afraid she would make too much noise, but Helen tilted her head to let her know it was okay. She closed the door as softly as she could.

"You look tired," Helen said quietly. Which was kind of Helen to even notice, considering the baby in her arms.

"Long day," she said. "Real…real long."

Helen nodded and looked down at Zach. "I hear ya."

"Could I…" Annie hesitated but then forged on. "Could I hold him for a while?"

"Are you kidding me?" Helen asked. "I'd be so grateful!"

Annie set her bag down and toed off her shoes, leaving them by the front door under the row of coats. She sat on the sofa and put a cushion under her arm for support. Helen stood up and gracefully put the baby into Annie's waiting arms.

He was so warm against her, and he scrunched up his face for a moment but didn't open his eyes. Annie smiled down at the sleeping baby, her throat thick. There was something so simple, so pure, about holding him, and she felt the weight of her day fade away.

"You okay?" Helen asked.

"Yeah."

"You want to talk about it?" Helen pressed, then seemed to change her mind. "I'm going to get some wine. You want some?"

"Maybe just some water," Annie said softly.

She left and came back, setting Annie's water on the end table, holding her glass of wine close to her chest. "Your friend called. Lori."

"Did she?" Annie asked. "She's partly why I came out here. It's been two months, and I haven't even been able to get her on the phone."

"It's not that late. You could call her now."

"She has kids younger than yours," Annie said. "I'll call tomorrow."

Helen sat back down in the recliner, tucking her feet up underneath her. "Okay," she said. "Why don't you tell me about it?"

Annie knew that she shouldn't. She still had to live here at least three more months, maybe four. Things would be easier for everyone if she kept her other life to herself. Her supervisor in Berlin had told her once, "You don't have to lie, but you sure as hell shouldn't tell the truth."

But there was a wide gray area between not the truth and an actual lie. That was where Annie lived.

She snugged the baby a little closer.

"I had to go somewhere for work," she said. "I caught a ride with this guy who wanted it to be, like…a real date, I guess. It was weird and uncomfortable. We both knew I was getting paid to be there."

Helen sipped her wine, holding the liquid in her mouth for a moment before swallowing. "Have you thought about changing jobs?"

"It isn't…" Annie hesitated. "It's not that easy."

"I didn't even know you were working."

Annie said nothing.

"Tell you what. Why don't you go put Zach in his crib and come back down? I made brownies, and there's still half a pan left."

Annie had never put a baby to bed before, not even her niece, and she wasn't sure she had ever carried a baby up a flight of stairs before either. The most time she'd spent with someone else's small child had been in Minsk, and that… She tried not to think of that little girl anymore.

Zach was heavy in her arms, but she made it up the stairs and down the hall. The kids were asleep, their doors open. Kevin had a night-light in his room, but Ashley's room was dark. Helen's room was lit with a lamp on the nightstand, and the baby monitor glowed red next to it.

She was terrified of waking him up when she laid him down in the crib, but he slept through it, the blanket wrapped tightly around him like an all-night hug. Like he was sleeping in someone's arms.

She shut off the light on her way out and went downstairs.

A glass of water and a brownie sat on the coffee table, though Helen was in the recliner, looking as if she hadn't moved at all.

"You did eat dinner, correct?" Helen asked. "With your work companion?"

"Yeah."

"And the baby is okay?"

"He didn't wake up." Annie picked up the fork and cut into a corner of the brownie.

"His social worker is coming in the morning," Helen said. "Are you around?"

"I don't have class until the afternoon," she said, "but I can make myself scarce."

"I meant that I would like for you to meet her. I told her I took on a tenant."

"Oh." She put the bite of brownie into her mouth and let the sweetness spread on her tongue.

"They like to meet the people who are around the baby," Helen said. "So if it's convenient for you…"

"It's no problem."

"I told her you were one of my students," Helen confessed. "I didn't mean it as a lie."

"I'm a student in your department. I don't feel like that was a lie."

"I didn't tell her you worked because I didn't know." Helen sipped her wine again.

"No one has to know," Annie assured her. "Anyway, I'm mostly just a student. Almost all the way just a student."

Helen smiled. "Okay."

"This brownie is really good," Annie said. "Thank you."

"Oh, honey. You are so welcome."

Annie dressed like she was going to class, like she was going undercover to any campus in Leningrad. She dressed like she was trying to look young. She put on a dress her grandma had given her that had a white scoop neck and was patterned with big pink roses. She slipped on her white sneakers. She put her hair up in a ponytail with a pink scrunchie, applied foundation and concealer, and added a hint of pink blush.

The social worker was coming at nine, so at ten after, she went into the kitchen with her backpack on. She heard voices in the living room, then Helen called out, "Annie?"

She pasted a smile on her face and joined the two women.

"Hi, Professor," she said.

The social worker was a friendly looking woman around Helen's age. She had a pad of paper on her lap. Zach was on the floor on a blanket, lying on his tummy and pushing himself up on his arms.

"Annie, this is Miss Oliver," Helen said, "Zach's social worker."

"How do you do, ma'am?"

"It's nice to meet you, Annie."

"Do you have a few minutes to join us?" Helen asked.

"Sure." She let her backpack slip down onto the rug. She took the chair by the window and looked down at the baby, then at Helen, then back to Miss Oliver.

"How long have you lived here now?" Miss Oliver asked.

"Oh, six…seven weeks, maybe? I just started this quarter at UCLA. I'm getting my master's."

"Do you like it here?" Miss Oliver asked.

"I do," Annie said. "It's better than a dorm, and I'm out back, so I'm out of the way." She looked at Helen, who nodded once. "Professor Everton is really nice."

"Where were you before you came out here for school, if you don't mind me asking."

"Ohio," Annie said. "And before that, I was in Georgetown in DC."

"Zach really likes her," Helen said. "Took right to her."

"Well, he seems to be doing really well here," Miss Oliver said. "We'll schedule another visit next month and then talk about the trial."

Helen stood up to see her out. "Thank you for coming."

When she returned, Annie picked up the baby. "What trial?"

"Zach's mother is getting out of rehab," Helen said. "But we'll cross that bridge when we get there, hmm?"

The pager.

She almost didn't hear it. She was on the freeway with the radio turned up, listening to the same ten songs every hour. She turned the volume all the way down and dug around in her bag with one hand, trying to hold the car steady with the other. "Shit! Are they going to call me every damn week?"

It had only been nine days, but still. How incompetent was law enforcement in Los Angeles that they had to keep calling in a semi-retired twentysomething woman? It made her worry for the state of California.

She'd gone to the public library on Manchester Avenue the other day and looked up *Times* articles about the riots and the city's response. The LAPD, the sheriff's department, and the National Guard had all been called up. Apparently, the LAPD had activated most of their reserve officers and were keeping them active while so many of their regular cops were on suspension pending investigation.

She'd read that someone died in Los Angeles County every ten minutes.

If she actually cared about helping, if she cared about anything other than making money and keeping Frank Clifton off her back, she'd tell someone that she'd be a lot more help if they let her go to the crime scenes. If they'd call her before they messed everything up and had no other choice. But being forced into this situation meant she didn't care. About the only thing she could manage was her own survival. Anything left over went to Helen and her kids.

She stopped at the 7-Eleven a few blocks from home and dropped a quarter into the pay phone. She didn't want to make this call standing in the kitchen where everyone could hear and wonder what the hell she was up to.

"You're wanted at Parker Center," the voice told her.

"Now?" Annie sighed. "It's rush hour."

"You were requested by name by the deputy chief of Special Services."

"He asked for Agent Juno, secret company goon for hire?"

"No," the voice said. "But he knew your real name. Most people just ask for our LA interrogator."

It was more than she'd ever gotten out of this man on the other end of the line before, so she decided not to alienate him. "Thanks," she said.

Her name wasn't a secret. She didn't have to live her life undercover anymore. She didn't know what they knew about her or what kind of memo had been circulated that made everyone so willing to call in a stranger to poke holes in their investigations. But she didn't remember meeting any deputy chiefs the last time she was at Parker Center, and the Special Services division handled the cases that were likely to cause a media frenzy. Celebrities and rich people. Successful serial killers.

She went home, letting herself in through the gate instead of going through the house. She opened the door and considered her sparse clothing options.

She settled on a dress with a structured jacket, hoping the shoulder pads made her look more professional. She pushed up the sleeves because the heat during the day was still intense and dry, never mind that it was nearly October.

She threw some snacks into her purse—a little bag of cookies and a packet of trail mix—and locked the door behind her.

Helen was standing in the yard when she turned around, her hands on her hips.

"What did I say about sneaking around?" Helen asked.

"I'm not sneaking. I'm just hurrying."

"I was going to grill tonight since it's still so nice out." Helen shielded her eyes from the late afternoon sun with her hand. "Are you going to join us?"

"Save me some," Annie said.

"Ashley's birthday party is this Saturday," Helen said. "I know she'd like it if you came."

Ashley wouldn't care if Annie fell off a cliff and landed into the open mouths of alligators, but she just nodded. "Okay."

"Be careful out there."

"I always am," Annie assured her. "I'm sorry. I need to go downtown, and the traffic is going to be a nightmare."

"Go on," Helen said. "You know you can always call if you need help."

"Thank you."

As she started the car, she puzzled over the conversation. What did Helen think she was doing that she needed to be careful or might call for help? Maybe she should come up with a lie to cover her tracks better. Working in a doctor's office or temping or something.

She took surface streets, driving by shops with boarded-up windows, the word *OPEN* spray-painted on more than one. A lot of people were starting to get back to normal after the riots, but insurance companies were backed up with claims, and many small business owners couldn't afford repairs before they got their insurance checks.

Two hours after she received the page, which included the hour it took her to get downtown, she arrived on the Special Services floor. She usually came in to the chaos of a case gone wrong, but the elevator doors opened to an empty office. She stepped over the threshold and walked down the hall.

Outside the main room, a man sat at a desk. When the phone rang, he answered with "SSD, this is Woodward."

She stepped in, surveying the cluster of desks. Beyond them was a glassed-in office obscured by long vertical blinds. The door was closed.

The man on the phone held up a finger.

"Okay," he said. "Okay, thanks. Yeah, she's here now." He hung up and looked at her. "The desk sergeant just called to say you were on your way up. Efficient, huh?"

She looked at him, a blank expression on her face.

"You are the translator, right?" he asked. "You speak Russian?"

"I do. That's why you called? You need a translator?"

"You're on the list," he said, holding up a laminated sheet of paper. "Regular one is on vacation, another one is on maternity leave, and the backup is working a case in Topanga. Apparently you're pricey, but the chief got the okay."

"Yeah," she said. "I don't actually work for you guys."

"You do today, sweetheart," he said. "I'll tell the chief you're here. He wants to see you first."

She felt herself relax a little. Translating wasn't that hard of a gig, and maybe she'd be done in time to eat dinner with Helen while it was still warm, before the kids went to bed, before she had to drive home alone in the dark with trembling hands and shuddering breaths, trying to process whatever case she'd just been investigating, before she got to be a normal person again.

She followed Woodward to the closed office door and squinted at the nameplate.

Deputy Chief M. Worth.

A coincidence, she told herself. There was no way it was the same Worth who had tried to lure her from the CIA to the Metro Police Department with a promotion she didn't deserve.

Woodward knocked twice and opened the door without waiting. He stuck his head in. "She's here." He pushed the door all the way open, and Annie walked in.

"Surprise!" Mason Worth waved his hands in the air and chuckled. His cheeks were ruddy, and Annie couldn't tell if it was from excitement or some health issue.

"It certainly is," she said, forcing herself to smile through her shock and trying to scrape together some professionalism. "A real surprise. Truly."

Worth stuck his hand out over the desk, and she reached out to shake it. He held it for a beat longer than he needed to. Behind her, Woodward cleared his throat.

"I've been out here for almost six months," Worth said. "I couldn't pass up such an opportunity. You either, apparently."

"I'm actually going to school," Annie said, still forcing her smile. She glanced back at Woodward, who was looking down at his shoes.

"Fate has brought us together, it seems." Worth grinned, showing teeth yellowed from years of nicotine.

"I, uh, hear you need a translator. Should I be caught up on the case?"

"Oh no, that's not necessary," Worth said. "We just don't know what he's saying."

"Okay. Well, where is he?"

"Interview Two. Woodward will show you. You did such a good job for us last time, by the way. Real nice work."

Annie froze. That had been on a different floor in a different division. Worth was unnerving her. "Yeah. Thanks."

"Good to see you again, Annie."

"Sure," she said. "Uh, you too, sir."

"Didn't realize you were old friends," Woodward said as he shut the door.

"Yeah," she muttered. "Me either."

By the time she got to Helen's house, everyone was already upstairs and getting ready for bed, from the sound of it.

Helen had left a plate for her in the kitchen. It was covered in foil in the center of the table with a napkin on top that had *Annie* written in bright blue marker. She hung her jacket and bag over the back of a chair and sat down. She pulled the plate toward her and peeled back the foil, revealing barbecue chicken, an ear of white corn—it seemed late in the season, but somehow there was always fresh produce in this state—and a little pile of mashed potatoes. She put her finger in the mash and, scooping up a blob, stuck it in her mouth.

She reached back into the pocket of her jacket and pulled out the business card Worth had given her on her way out. On the back, he'd written his home phone number.

She liked law enforcement; she really did. It was a good fit for her, except for this. No matter what the office, no matter what the job, there was always at least one man who made it uncomfortable. Who wanted to take her out for dinner and drinks. Who slipped her his phone number. Who put his hand on the wall next to her head and leaned in. It was never just a job, and she'd never just be a cop or an agent. She would always be a woman first.

She crumpled up the business card and threw it at the garbage. It hit the rim, bounced off the wall, and rolled under the refrigerator.

Close enough. She stuck her finger back in the potatoes and ate half the pile that way, slowly, sullenly, all alone in a house full of people.

CHAPTER 6

It was hot and stuffy in the house, hot and stuffy in the garage. Under Helen's kitchen window, on a patch of grass that was mostly dirt, was the shadiest place in the yard. She was doing her reading for class there. She'd hoped by this point in the quarter that her program would be a little more interesting, but she was starting to realize that most cops were as incompetent as they appeared on TV, and none of her professors were like Columbo or Jessica Fletcher. Solving crimes involved tenacity, intelligence, and sheer dumb luck, and the majority of people in her classes weren't cut out for it, though some would thrive in a lab or do fine with paperwork. But it was starting to haunt her that she couldn't do the good she wanted to do without the weight of the federal government behind her badge. Of all the scenarios she'd spun about herself as a child, she'd never imagined herself in a boring career she couldn't find her way out of.

Still, it was only the first quarter. She was determined to finish. Maybe things would pick up the more she got into the program. Her father had drilled into his children that they should stick things out.

She felt a slight breeze across the back of her neck and closed her eyes to savor it.

It was a rare day for her. She had no classes, and no one was home. She'd planned this day to catch up on schoolwork, and that's what she was doing, heat or no heat. She had a little paper sack of jelly beans—it was too hot for chocolate—and every time she started drooping, she popped a few into her mouth and forged ahead.

She was three pages from the end of a chapter when the window above her slid open. She heard Helen say, "No, I'm home now. I have to get the kids in an hour." Pause. "Yeah, the split shifts aren't ideal."

Annie froze. Her first instinct was to bolt, but that would only call attention to herself. There was no way Helen could see her under the window, even if she looked right out and down. The window was too high up, the ledge out too far, and Annie was in the shadows. She tucked her feet in closer and stayed still and quiet.

"That's going fine, actually," Helen continued. "I was nervous at first, but she seems really smart, and she's quiet. And she pays her rent in cash."

Annie closed her eyes. She was used to listening to other people's conversations but hated listening to people talk about her.

"I'm not—I couldn't say for certain," Helen said and then paused. "Because I don't want to speculate."

She heard the faucet come on, heard the water falling into the sink and moving through the pipes in the wall. Then it shut off again.

"Okay, fine. She has this…one of those little beepers. You know, where you call it and it tells you where to call? And it goes off at the oddest times. Day or night."

Annie opened one eye and looked at her bag of jelly beans. She reached out and stuck her fingers into the opening. The bag crinkled slightly, but Helen didn't seem to hear it. She extracted three jelly beans and carefully pulled them out of the bag.

"I don't think *Pretty Woman* is accurate, no. She is really pretty but too smart for… I think, if anything, it's an expensive escort service, Sal. She's got skin like peaches and cream. I can't stop ogling her sometimes. I feel like an old pervert. She's prettier than Julia Roberts, anyway."

Annie froze in mid chew, the three jelly beans crushed between her molars. Her eyes were wide open now.

Helen thought she was a prostitute. Actually, looking back on the way she'd offered to help Annie, that kind of made sense. And she'd been thinking about a better cover story. She could go on letting Helen think that. What could it hurt?

"Somewhere between Julia Roberts and Michelle Pfeiffer," Helen said.

Annie rested her head against the side of the house. *Jesus.* She didn't want to be hearing this at all. She didn't want to know that Helen thought she was pretty, and she didn't want to know that Helen had noticed her skin. Helen being attractive was something Annie had noticed and intentionally set aside. Helen had an ex-husband and three children and was just a nice woman who happened to let Annie into her life. There was no indication of anything else. But now? The knowledge that Helen thought she was pretty was an elephant in the room of Annie's mind. Or maybe it meant absolutely nothing, and Helen admired her like one admired a finely made piece of furniture or a luxury car, but now the elephant was a permanent, unwelcome resident.

"Right. No one is Michelle Pfeiffer; that's what I'm saying. She's on that spectrum, though. Anyway, she's going to be here Saturday for Ashley's party, so you can meet her then," Helen said and then laughed. "Yeah, I wouldn't…I wouldn't ask her that. No. Please don't."

Annie finished chewing her candy and then closed her notebook. She'd forgotten about the party. She should probably get the kid something.

"Okay, I have to go scrub the bathrooms before the…"

Helen's voice faded away. Annie grabbed her stuff and headed for the garage. She closed the door quietly behind her, then dusted the dirt off her butt, watching it fall on the threshold.

She changed her clothes, put on some lip gloss, and crammed the book she was reading into her backpack. She double-checked that she had her pager and then stepped into her shoes. She had an idea what to get Ashley. She would go put her latest check in the bank, buy Ashley her present, and spend the rest of the day reading at the library.

Helen was standing in the doorway of the half bath when Annie walked through the house. She was holding a stiff brush in her gloved hands. The house reeked of bleach.

"Going out?" Helen asked casually, her voice in a low register that made even innocuous questions sound sensual.

"Yeah," Annie said with a smile. "Duty calls."

Helen raised her brush. "Me too."

"But I'm still planning on Saturday, if you are."

"Yes, of course," Helen said.

"Okay, then. See you later."

Annie could feel Helen watching her leave.

Annie opened the window and sipped at her mug of coffee. She'd bought a coffee maker a few weeks back. Although Helen was happy to share what she made, Annie preferred her coffee to be as dark as mud. She'd picked up three unmatched mugs at the thrift store too. One, dark blue, advertised the mission trip of a local church. Another one was yellow with a pink daisy painted on the side, the handle painted to look like the stem. The one she was drinking out of now was green and large enough to hold a carafe. Plus, it had a picture of a tired-looking Tinkerbell. Annie related to the small, blonde, sassy pixie, even if *Peter Pan* was not her favorite Disney movie.

Ashley was carefully making her way toward the garage, barefoot and still in her pink nightgown. She held something tightly in her arms.

"Morning," Annie called out, surprised to see her, and even more surprised that Ashley was headed her way. She stopped a few steps from the open door.

"Hi," Ashley said shyly. She looked back at the house and then to Annie again. "Do you want to see my party dress?"

"I do," Annie said. "Is that it?"

Ashley unfurled the fabric in her arms and shook it out. The dress had long sleeves and a lacy white collar. The fabric of the body was red velvet, nearly the color of blood.

"Isn't that pretty?" Annie said. "I love it."

"Me too. Are you staying for my party?"

"Yes, ma'am. Is your birthday actually today?"

"Tomorrow," Ashley said. "But Mommy said Saturday is better for a party."

"She's right. Your mom is very smart."

"Mommy said the family is excited to meet you."

Annie raised her eyebrows. "Did she? Who all is coming?"

"My aunt Sal. Uncle Colin, Mommy's brother. My cousins, Stacey and Gina. And Grandpa Peter." She considered for a moment. "And Daddy. Maybe."

"How about your friends from school?"

"My ballet friend Annalisa is coming."

"Ballet friends are good," Annie said gently.

"Mommy said there's waffles. That's why I came out here."

"And to show me your dress."

Annie stepped inside to pull on a sweater, then closed the door behind her to walk with Ashley to the house, coffee still in hand.

"How do you get your hair so curly?" Ashley asked.

"Just how God made me," Annie said. "When I was little like you, all I wanted was straight hair."

"Mine only gets curly if I sleep in braids, but then it's just a little bit, not like yours," Ashley said. "Yours is real. You can put your finger inside the curl."

Annie laughed as she opened the back door. "You could always sleep in curlers. That might work."

"Curlers hurt my head!"

"Beauty and pain go hand in hand. Don't they teach you that in ballet?" Annie teased.

"Morning," Helen said, interrupting their conversation. "Ash, go put that dress in your room. If you get syrup on it, you can't wear it."

Ashley rolled her eyes but headed upstairs. Kevin was already at the table, still in his blue and yellow pajamas. Zach was in his high chair, dry Cheerios scattered across the tray.

The kitchen smelled like sweet batter. The oven was on; the waffle maker on the counter was steaming.

"What can I do to help?" Annie asked.

"Do you think you could feed the baby while I finish up the waffles?" Helen shook a bottle of warm formula and handed it to Annie.

"He'll be happier if you hold him."

Both women turned to look at Kevin.

"He's right," Helen said. "He'd rather be held."

"I can do that. Good tip, Kevin." Annie winked at him.

"My children are very surprising today." Helen opened the waffle iron to reveal a perfectly golden-brown waffle.

Annie pulled the tray off the high chair and set it aside, then unbuckled Zach and picked him up. Cheerios fell from his lap onto the floor. He looked at Annie for a moment with his mouth open, one little tooth peeking through his pink gums. Then he smiled and lunged at her, planting his big open mouth on her cheek.

It was the sloppiest, wettest kiss she had ever received.

No one ever said out loud that getting people to turn on their country involved sex, but even Annie, green and twenty-four-years-old, could read between the lines. Male agents brought informants home all the time, women half their age or the daughters or ex-wives of top government officials. They brought them to America to keep them safe.

Then they married them.

At first, Annie had focused on interrogating the people stationed with her, but Minsk had been different. The agent scheduled for the assignment had gone into the hospital rather suddenly with a burst appendix that was almost fatal, and Annie was tapped as a replacement. All international agents had a cover, so she didn't know who she was replacing, and it really didn't matter. Annie went where she was told.

Annie liked sex well enough. Most of her sexual encounters had been while she was in college, though she'd met a man in a bar a few months back and went home with him. She'd made up a name, a job, a reason for drinking alone that night. Gotten dressed in the darkness and left when the sun was no more than a hint of pink on the horizon. She didn't leave her phone number. She knew going into the encounter that she would never see him again. The sex was fine—parts of it good, even—but lying underneath him, she thought the whole time about what she really wanted instead.

In Minsk, she'd been assigned a midlevel government worker—a lackey for a well-known politician. The intelligence packet on the man contained information about his childhood, his education, his professional career and aspirations, and his family, but she still didn't see a clear way in. She was explicitly directed to stay away from the wife and daughter.

"Do it like in the movies, hon," her supervisor had said with a laugh that sounded like a seal barking when she complained about being stuck. The image of a seal was made more real by the fact that his office always smelled like reheated fish. "Put on a fancy dress and seduce him."

It had been a poor joke, but she had still considered the idea as she lay on scratchy sheets in her twin bed at night. Seduction was just like manipulation with acting on the side, and she was good at both. The problem was her target. She'd been so focused on him that she forgot she could do what most male agents couldn't do without suspicion, and why agents were warned to stay away from families.

She *could* get close to the wife.

Informants simply would not turn on their countries if they found out their handlers had slept with their wives to get close to them, but Annie had other avenues to get close that didn't require sex.

Getting people to turn on their country was a long con but not as hard as one might think, since the countries that American spies infiltrated were often run by harsh governments that used terrorism to keep their people in line. But Dasha wasn't born in Belarus like her husband. She was Russian. It was an interesting time for Annie to be where she was, and it was an interesting dynamic: a husband and wife, Belarusian and Russian, and the Soviet Union dissolving all around them.

Annie didn't hate Minsk, but she preferred Ukraine and Russia if she had to spend any length of time in Eastern Europe. Belarus was unstable; it seemed that the more independent an area became from the Soviet Union, the more that they were just trading one dictatorship for another. Belarus had a corrupt government that favored corporal punishment and communism.

People kept disappearing: agents, government officials, citizens. There was always someone who went missing, never anyone found. Annie kept her gun with her, always on edge, even in her little apartment, even when she was with other agents. She never felt safe, and it was exhausting. She didn't want to get killed, and she didn't want anyone to get killed because of her, and both of those goals seemed less and less likely as the weeks wore on.

But Dasha was a real turning point. Getting close to a family member of a potential target was always a risky route. Annie had managed to avoid it until Minsk because it put the family member in danger and was ethically hard to swallow, even though it was the most obvious way for an agent to pick up information. Family members often had no idea what their loved one was doing. But Annie was out of options, so she made the choice.

Her cover story was that she was born in Canada and had traveled to Eastern Europe on a scholarship but then decided to stay. She introduced herself as Alexa to anyone she met. Her conversational Russian was quite good, her Belarusian limited at best, but no one knew enough about the regions of North America to place her accent anyway.

She met Dasha at a park while the woman pushed her baby in a stroller. It took Annie a few weeks to secure a job watching her daughter, Yeva, three days a week in the afternoons.

"*My budem starat'sya yego,*" Dasha said. *We will try it.*

Dasha didn't work, so Annie wasn't sure why she needed a nanny, aside from the fact that other wives of somewhat important men had them. It didn't take long for Annie to realize that Dasha was lonely and needed someone to talk to who wasn't her husband.

And Annie could talk. Talking was second nature to her. Talking was what kept her in from recess when she was little, what got her spanked after church, and what turned an afternoon of detention into a fairly successful high school debate career. She figured out that she could talk in other languages too and then talked herself right into Langley, sitting in a room full of other wide-eyed recruits in rusty theater seats under a big white dome.

Dasha talked to her for nearly two months before she kissed Annie. It raised the stakes significantly. It put them all in danger, even if the information she got was spectacular. No senior agent would back her up if this came out, and even a whisper of homosexuality would follow her like a specter for the rest of her career. Not to mention, she'd done exactly what she'd been warned against. She'd meant to be a nanny. She'd meant to be a friend, someone Dasha could trust. What had Dasha picked up on? What had Annie done that told Dasha to lean in and capture Annie's mouth practically in midsentence?

It didn't matter ultimately because Annie, lonely and far from home, had enthusiastically kissed her back.

Despite the affair, Annie held her cards close to her chest. She waited another month before she admitted she was American and that she could help get Dasha and Yeva out of Minsk. All Dasha had to do was get as much information out of her husband about his job and the government's plans and then meet Annie at a predetermined location.

The night before they decided to leave Belarus, they were tangled up together under the heavy comforter. "Alexa," Dasha said, *"ya lyublyu tebya."*

No one had ever told Annie that they loved her before, at least not anyone unrelated to her. No boyfriend, no one-night stand, no one. Annie had never felt particularly lovable, and she knew for a fact that she was not easy to love because she was so intense and secretive.

She assured Dasha that everything would be all right, that she would be safe with Yeva in America.

And then the next day, she found Yeva in Dasha's arms, both dead.

She'd called it in, panicked. Her call triggered two agents to look for the husband, and within a day, they were dead too. Everyone involved got sent home. All because of Annie.

Annie stood at the sink in the little bathroom, brushing her teeth. Autumn had finally arrived, and she shivered in the crisp night air despite wearing a pair of socks pulled up to her knees, a pair of sweatpants, and a long-sleeved T-shirt that advertised the Henderson High School debate team of 1983. She leaned over to spit out the toothpaste, then stuck her face under the faucet, slurping up water and spitting it out again. Her face was pressed into her towel when someone pounded on the door. She opened it, towel still in hand, to find Ashley holding the baby and Kevin standing right behind her. They looked terrified.

"What's the matter?" she asked. They'd all had a very good day. She met a whole heap of Helen's family and friends at the birthday party, and Annie gave Ashley three tickets to the Paula Abdul concert at the Forum in December and was rewarded with a hug.

"It's too much," Helen had murmured.

Annie shrugged. "I thought you could take Kevin too, and I can stay in with the baby."

Helen had put her arm around Annie's shoulders and squeezed.

Now Annie leaned over and took the squirming baby from the small girl, whose fear made her seem even smaller.

"Mommy said to come in here and stay with you." Ashley crossed her arms over her chest. It was the same posture Helen took when she felt unsure of herself.

"Why?" Annie asked, shifting Zach's weight to her hip. He was getting bigger. He put his hand in her hair and pulled.

"Because Daddy's here," Kevin said quietly. His demeanor brought out his mother's features in his face.

The elusive Bruce Everton hadn't shown up for his daughter's birthday party. Ashley didn't seem to notice, given she was surrounded by cousins and doting adults.

"Okay." Annie freed her hair from Zach's grasp and laying him down on her bed. "Everyone up here. We'll sit together."

Kevin stepped forward, but Ashley hesitated, looking back over her narrow shoulder toward the house.

"You want to sing a song or something? A few of our favorite things?" Annie offered, patting the mattress. Ashley whipped her head back around and glared at her. So much for that Paula Abdul hug.

"I like that movie," Kevin said. Annie reached out and rubbed the top of his head, keeping her other hand on Zach so he didn't roll off.

"Thanks, kid."

"I think we should go see if she's okay," Ashley said nervously.

"Did they used to fight a lot?" Annie asked. "Before he left?"

"No," Kevin said.

"Yes," Ashley corrected. "You were always asleep because you were little."

"I'm not little. He's little," Kevin said, pointing at Zach.

"Did he ever hurt you?" Annie asked. "Or your mom? Grab you or spank you?"

Ashley thought for a moment and then shook her head. "He just ignored us."

That could feel bad too, Annie knew. Being ignored left a different of bruise, the kind that people didn't see. At least the kids had a mother like Helen. Someone who loved them and worked hard to protect them.

"Okay," Annie said. "Ashley, come sit here with the baby." She got up and dug around in a few drawers until she found what she was looking for: a pair of high-powered binoculars. Ashley watched her from the edge of the bed.

"What are you going to do?" she asked.

Annie rummaged around in another drawer and shook out a black sweatshirt, pulling it on over her T-shirt. Then she put the strap of the binoculars around her neck and tucked them inside her sweatshirt. "I'm going to check on your mom." She leaned over to pull on her sneakers.

Annie hadn't needed to climb up to the roof of the garage, but she had thought about how she would do it. It was second nature to think about entrances, exits, how to get higher, how to go underground, how to make the quickest escape. It was part of her old life that she couldn't shake.

She went around to the alley gate and swung it open to bring it closer to the structure. She pried a paving brick out of the narrow pathway that led to the empty vegetable garden and lodged it firmly against the open gate. She stepped in the vee of the diagonal braces and, climbing to the top of the gate, stepped onto the window ledge. She pulled her upper body onto the flat roof, then shimmied the rest of the way on, breathing heavily for a moment. She had to get back to working out; that climb should have been easier.

Still, she made it up. She crawled across the roof and then got down on her belly. All the lights were on in the house. She brought the binoculars up for a closer look. At first, she saw no one in the kitchen or in the dining room. But then, movement. A shadow. They were in the living room. She adjusted her angle until she could see into a different window.

She recognized Helen but could barely make out a man's arm.

She watched Helen walk into the kitchen, saw the blur of movement, then refocused in time to see Bruce follow her in. He leaned against the doorway, his long curly hair falling into his handsome face. But something wasn't right. He was red-faced and swaying.

He was drunk.

Helen looked tired and angry.

Annie had seen enough.

She rolled back to the edge of the roof, set her foot on the window ledge, and dropped the rest of the way, rolling when she hit the ground. It wasn't the best landing, but it was the fastest way down. She'd be sore in the morning, but no worse than from sleeping on an army cot for two weeks. She stood up with a groan and brushed herself off, then kicked the brick aside and closed the gate.

Ashley and Kevin were still sitting on her bed. Zach was asleep.

Kevin looked up when he heard her come in. "We could hear you up there."

"Did you see anything?" Ashley asked.

"I saw a lot," she said. "You three stay here and lock the door behind me. I'm going to go into the house and make sure everything is okay." She picked up her backpack.

"Why are you bringing all of that?" Ashley asked.

"I'm going to go around to the front door so your father doesn't know I was back here," Annie said, slinging the backpack over her shoulder.

"How do you know how to do all of this?" Kevin asked.

"I used to be a spy. Don't forget to lock the door."

She made a lot of noise coming into the house, dropping her key ring on the porch, scraping the house key against the lock, and jiggling it before opening the door.

She dropped her backpack loudly on the hardwood floor and looked down the hallway. Helen stood in the doorway to the kitchen, her brow creased.

"I'm home!" Annie said loudly.

Helen stepped to the side and crossed her arms the same way Ashley had.

"Who the fuck are you?" Bruce demanded, pushing past Helen.

"I'm Annie Weaver. Who are you?"

"I'm Helen's husband." He looked at Helen. "This the coed?"

"Bruce, please go home."

"Not until I see Ashley."

"Ashley isn't here," Helen said. "I told you: she's at a sleepover."

"Bullshit. Ashley doesn't have any friends," Bruce said. "She's an ice queen, just like you."

"I believe the lady told you to leave," Annie said.

"This is my fucking house."

"You don't live here," Annie said. "You *left*."

"Annie, you don't have to—"

But Annie could tell that Helen wanted him gone, so she was going to make that happen. "You're drunk. I can smell it from here. So why don't you call a cab and go to wherever it is you do live because it sure as hell isn't here."

"Please don't wake up the baby," Helen said, trying to sound calm, though her voice shook. "I will speak to Ashley tomorrow about when she can see you next, and then maybe, just maybe, Bruce, you could show up for the visit. For once in your daughter's life, you could work around her schedule instead of expecting an eleven-year-old child to drop everything for you."

Bruce's expression flickered with hurt that quickly turned to anger, twisting the handsome right out of his features. "I don't want that bitch around my children." He pointed at Annie. Then, with a final snarl at Helen, he headed for the door. Annie stepped aside to let him pass. Once he had stepped outside, Helen hurried to lock the door after him. From behind the door, they watched him stumble to his car parked on the street. Annie realized he shouldn't be driving, but neither she nor Helen moved to stop him.

"Well, I don't know how helpful that was." Helen lifted her glasses to rub at the bridge of her nose.

"Sometimes it just feels nice to tell someone off," Annie said. "Helps you gauge what a person is capable of right away."

"Can easily backfire, though, don't you think?"

"It didn't this time. I poked hard because I wanted to make sure he wasn't going to hurt you. Or your kids."

"That isn't how he hurts us."

Annie stared at her thoughtfully for a moment, then said, "Let's go get them."

Helen hurried out to the garage and bounced impatiently on the balls of her feet while Annie unlocked the door.

All three kids were still on the bed. Ashley held out Annie's pager to her. "This keeps beeping."

Annie got home too late to eat dinner Sunday night. She was behind on homework and in a foul mood. She was not looking forward to her classes next week; they were taught by inexperienced people who had no idea what they were talking about. Full of students who were worried about term papers and group projects, not real life-or-death situations. She was tired and lonely, and she was sick of sunny California. She was sick of men in cheap suits who called for her expertise and then decided they didn't want it when they saw her. Sick of being on call 24-7.

How was she supposed to live like this? With that stupid life dangling over her head?

She walked in on Helen reading a book in the recliner. She looked up when Annie came in, closed the book over her thumb.

"Hi there," Helen said. "Where have you been?"

Annie started to cry.

CHAPTER 7

Helen pressed the cool washcloth to Annie's face until Annie lifted her hands to hold it in place herself. She breathed through the damp fabric, warming it around her lips. It smelled like Helen's bathroom.

She breathed in again shakily. It felt like something inside her gut was coiled up tight. She tried not to think about what the feeling might mean, tried not to think about Helen's kindness: their shopping trip, the little treats Helen left for her, their late-night conversations when she was up late with Zach.

After a moment, Helen stroked a hand against her back. "You're okay," she said softly.

Annie nodded, but Helen's words, meant to comfort and reassure, only brought fresh tears to her eyes. She was thankful that the washcloth hid them.

"Shh, it's all right."

They sat together at the coffee table for a few moments longer, Annie doubled over onto her lap, her face in her hands, and Helen next to her, her hand a steady tether on her spine.

A cry from the baby monitor in the kitchen broke through the quiet.

"That baby has been sleeping like shit." Helen's frustration broke through the soothing tone. "Stay here. I'll be right back."

Where would Annie go? She'd really dug herself into it now. There was being mysterious and self-sufficient, and then there was this—disappearing and coming home in tears. She'd have to tell Helen something. But what?

She wiped her eyes and her snotty nose with the damp cloth, then tipped her head back and let the air dry her face. She heard Zach fussing, heard Helen shush him in the same way she'd soothed Annie—a comforting hiss like a slow leak. She brought him downstairs. His cheeks were wet and rosy. He looked around the bright living room as if it were a foreign planet, so different from the dark bedroom he shared with his foster mother.

It made sense now why Helen had shoved a crib into her own room instead of doubling up the boys. Zach was temporary.

"I'll hold him while you make a bottle," Annie offered.

"All right."

She sat Zach in her lap, his back to her front, and wrapped her arm around his middle. He leaned back against her, looking around. When he started to squirm, she bounced her knees up and down, and he settled down with a giggle.

Helen returned with a wooden tray holding a bottle of formula and two mugs of hot chocolate. "Let's go upstairs," she said.

It felt good to just do as Helen suggested. They crept past the cracked doors of the kids' rooms. Helen set the tray on her nightstand, then closed her door.

Annie put Zach down in the center of the big bed, and Helen handed him a bottle. He could hold it himself now. He slurped at it hungrily until his mouth made a seal around the nipple. As his tummy filled with warm formula, his eyelids drooped.

They sat on the bed between Zach and the nightstand. Helen handed Annie a mug. They sipped quietly for a moment, savoring the warmth of the chocolate.

"You're an adult," Helen said.

"Yes."

"I'm not your mother. I don't think of myself as your mother."

"Definitely not," Annie agreed. "You are not remotely like her."

"But I do feel like I should say something since we're friendly and you are living here with my family."

Annie's stomach bottomed out, but she nodded, curling the fingers of her free hand into the comforter. She would accept whatever Helen decided. She would make it work somehow.

"I don't want you doing something that makes you so unhappy. I don't want you doing something dangerous, Annie." Helen gave her a pained smile. "This job of yours—"

"I'm thinking of dropping out of school!" Annie blurted out.

At Christmastime, when she and her brother were little, her father used to read them the Dr. Seuss book about the mean old monster who lived on top of a mountain, who stole Christmas away in the night. The little kids wake up the next morning, happy anyway, and singing their song. Annie hadn't thought about the Grinch in years, but she remembered that the Grinch was able to come up with a lie quickly because he was so sly.

She remembered it because whenever her daddy read the story, he looked over the rims of his glasses at Annie, his chronic fibber. Annie, who could spin a twisted tale in seconds rather than admit she did something wrong. Annie, who threw her brother under the bus if she saw one coming her way.

The lie spilled out before her brain could process it.

"You are?" Helen asked.

"It may be too much for me." Annie shook her head. "I don't even know why I thought it was a good idea to go back to school. I already have a master's degree."

"I spoke to Greg just last week, and he said your paper was one of the best he's ever seen. He said you speak very eloquently in class."

"You talk about me?"

"All teachers talk about their students," Helen admitted. "The bad ones mostly, yes, though the good ones too."

But the truth was, while there were difficult aspects to her classes, it wasn't hard for her. Most of the subject matter being taught she already knew from experience. In class, she only half listened to lectures, thinking more about how tired she was, about the next time her pager would go off. She stayed on top of the reading, so the lectures were often superfluous. It was as if the whole system was designed for people who weren't going to do their homework.

"I'm glad he thinks so," Annie said uneasily.

"Is that really why you're so upset?" Helen asked, probing gently.

"I'm just…just upset, that's all. Just out of sorts and far from home. Don't you ever feel like you don't know what you're doing?"

"Oh, only eighty or ninety percent of the time," Helen said.

They grinned at one another. Seeing Helen's genuine smile made Annie feel a bit better.

The hot chocolate was delicious, and eventually Zach fell back to sleep. Annie watched drowsily as Helen took his empty bottle, picked him up, and put him back in his crib. Annie moved to get up, but Helen stopped her. "Stay a little longer, would you?"

Annie lay down on the bed and curled up onto her side, her head on her arm.

"I'm going to have to give him back soon," Helen said, peering down into the crib. "His mother will get clean, and the state will return him to her. They always give the mother another chance."

"Maybe you'll get him back again," Annie said sleepily.

"Maybe so. But I'll have to undo the damage all over again, and he's older now." Helen went to the other side of the bed and lay down, her arms resting under her head. "It'll only get harder."

"How'd you get him in the first place?" Annie asked, letting her eyes close. "I mean, as a single parent."

"Bruce and I applied together," Helen said. "At first, I didn't tell them he was gone, and then when the social worker figured it out, she decided he was doing so well that… Anyway, I have a friend in Social Services so I… I don't usually work outside of the system, but he's such a good kid."

"I would've done the same thing," Annie said reassuringly.

But then what wouldn't Annie do if she thought it was in her own best interest?

The next time her pager went off, Annie was in the middle of a midterm. The only sound in the room was the scribbling of pens in blue books, and even though she'd figured out how to keep the device from beeping, it still vibrated loudly enough from inside her backpack that several heads popped up and swiveled around, looking for the source of the sound.

"Sorry," she murmured, digging in her backpack and pulling out the pager. She didn't recognize the number; she never did. She didn't even know the number to the pager to give out if someone asked for it. She pushed buttons until the buzzing stopped. She had one rule, and it was not to be paged during class time.

She dropped the pager into her backpack and picked up her pen.

It went off again two minutes later.

"Problem, Miss Weaver?" her professor asked.

"Nope," she said, silencing it again. This time, she stuck it down her shirt, nestling it against her skin in the soft cup of her bra. At least if it went off again, her body would absorb the sound.

Five minutes later, it buzzed. She ignored it.

She had one more paragraph to write and a conclusion, then she'd be done anyway.

Someone knocked on the classroom door. The professor looked up, perplexed. The door opened, and Deb stuck her head in.

"I'm sorry, Greg, but is… Oh yeah, there she is. Annie? Honey? There's a call for you at the desk."

Everyone turned to stare at her.

"I'm kind of in the middle of something here," she said. "Can you take a message?"

"They said it's an emergency," Deb said with a shrug.

For a moment she panicked, thinking of her parents, her brother, her niece, Helen and Kevin and Ashley and Zach. But then she remembered the buzzing pager. She smiled at Deb. "I'll be just a moment."

She scribbled out a half-assed ending to her essay and tossed her pen into her backpack. Everyone was still watching her as she closed her blue book, kicked her chair in, and tossed her essay onto her professor's desk.

"You sure?" he asked.

"It'll be fine." It was a good essay, even with the rough ending. She knew the material, had used a few intentionally vague real-life examples, and could write well enough. Even if it wasn't her best work, she wouldn't fail the course.

Deb was back at her desk, the receiver next to the phone.

Annie pointed to it. "Me?"

"You," Deb said. "Unpleasant-sounding fellow. Would give me absolutely no details."

"Yeah, he's like that." Annie picked it up and holding the receiver to her ear. "Look, I have, like, one rule in this weird arrangement, and it's don't call during my classes. And you certainly can't call here."

"Identification?" he said.

"Come on. Seriously?"

Silence.

"Juno. Akron. I can't believe you."

"Don't shoot the messenger," he said. "There's been a child abduction. The LAPD is calling in everyone to help."

"I'm not… I don't think I'm a part of everyone."

"It is my understanding that it is the daughter of the Russian ambassador," he said. "They insisted we reach you. Don't take the time to change your clothes. Go straight to Parker Center."

She looked down at her faded jeans that were frayed at one knee, her black boots, her white T-shirt, her flannel jacket.

"Yeah," she said. "All right. I'm on my way."

She reached across the desk and hung up the phone.

Deb stared at her.

"Sick grandma," she said, grabbing her backpack and heading for the door.

Visitor parking at Parker Center was a nightmare, and despite Annie's many assignments over the last few months, she was still considered a visitor. On a day like today, where multiple agencies had been called in, the parking garage was packed. She finally got lucky and found someone pulling out of a spot on the top level, and she swung into it faster than another car coming from the other direction. She didn't feel one bit sorry about it either.

She caught a glimpse of herself in the reflection of a car window as she hurried toward the elevator and groaned. She couldn't look less professional short of showing up in pajamas. She dressed for comfort during test-taking since it involved long periods of sitting, but now she was probably going door-to-door looking more like a Clinton canvasser than someone helping with a kidnapping.

The desk sergeant was unfamiliar with her and busy. When he finally got around to looking at her driver's license, he looked at it for a long time, compared it to his list, then looked at her again before writing something in his logbook and slipping her a visitor's badge.

"You need to go up to Special Services, so take the elevator—"

"I know where I'm going," she muttered, grabbing her backpack and clipping the badge to her flannel.

It took a long time for the elevator to come down, and by the time she got up to the Special Services floor, she realized she was hungry and had to pee. The room was bustling with mostly uniformed officers and men in suits; she recognized a few but didn't know anyone by name.

Chief Worth spotted her the moment she stepped into his bullpen, and he stood up, a look of relief on his face.

He waved her over. So she was going to be the center of this dog-and-pony show, not simply going door-to-door or answering the tip line or processing paperwork or, hell, translating phone calls in Russian or something.

She held up one finger and took a sharp turn into the women's restroom and locked herself in a stall. She peed while rummaging in her backpack for something to eat. She found a Twinkie and ate it in three quick bites, happy there was no one around to judge her for her sins. She disposed of the crinkly wrapper in the menstrual receptacle and flushed the toilet.

She washed her hands and fluffed up her curls before stepping out into the hallway again. Worth was waiting for her.

"The Russian ambassador to the United States is a man named Vladimir Lukin, and he's been the ambassador for nine months," Worth said without preamble. "Lukin is stationed primarily in DC but had business at the consulate in San Francisco and brought his family down to Los Angeles for sightseeing."

"Family?"

"He has a wife and two daughters. The older daughter is twelve and is here with us. The younger daughter, Annika, age seven, has been missing for nearly ten hours."

"Where are the parents?" Annie asked.

"The father has so far refused to leave the embassy. The mother is talking with another translator, and she's hysterical," Worth said. "The sister hasn't said a word, but from what I understand, she was there when Annika disappeared. She may be our only witness."

"What's her name?" Annie asked.

"Tatiana. Annie, we want you to get as much information out of the sister as possible, and quickly."

She would have liked a little more time to prepare, to learn about the family, to learn anything, but missing person cases, especially those involving foreign dignitaries, were different beasts. She hadn't been involved with one before, but by the tone of the room and everyone's anxious, nervous vibe, whatever was happening here was more important than Annie's preference.

"Can I have a piece of candy and a can of Coke?" she asked him.

He looked at her, his brow furrowed. "Uh…"

"For the girl," Annie clarified. "She's probably hungry. And sugar always greases the wheels a little."

"Right," he said. "There are vending machines down the hall."

She stared at him without moving.

Finally, he realized what she was waiting for, pulled a couple of dollar bills out of his wallet, and handed them to her. He made sure his fingers touched her palm in the exchange. Annie ignored the unwanted contact.

"Which room?" she asked.

He pointed to a closed door.

At the vending machines, she chose a chocolate bar and a can of Coke, then returned to the room.

As soon as Annie closed the door to the interrogation room, it got quiet. The girl sat alone at the metal table, shoulders hunched and face wet with tears. She was only twelve and they stuck her in here alone? Where was the mother?

The girl regarded her suspiciously, and Annie returned the stare. She wasn't sure how to start, but she thought she'd do better if she spoke Russian, so she slipped into it.

"Are you Tatiana?" Annie asked.

The girl hesitated and then nodded.

"How long have you been in this room?"

The girl glanced around at the big mirror, the walls, the door. There was no clock. *"A long time."*

"Okay," Annie said. She needed the girl to feel less terrified and abandoned. They really needed her help. "Okay. *Let's go somewhere different. Some place warmer, maybe?"*

The girl started to stand, then sat back down. *"I don't know who you are."*

"Annie," she said. *"I am not a police officer. But I have come to talk to you. Maybe we can go somewhere so you could see your mother."*

The girl nodded and stood, wrapping her skinny arms around herself. Annie knew that she'd been kept separate from the mother to compare stories, to show power, to keep control. But a hysterical mother and a frightened little girl were not hardened criminals.

She opened the door and felt a tug on her sleeve.

"I have to go to the bathroom."

Annie nodded. *"Over here."*

She stood outside the stall while Tatiana used the toilet, then watched her wash her hands. Tatiana looked at the can of Coke and the candy bar that Annie was still holding.

"Are those for me?" she asked in perfect English.

"You speak English!"

Tatiana nodded.

She had an accent, but it wasn't heavy, as if she'd been learning and speaking English for a long time. Given her father and his career, she probably had.

"Let's go sit down, and you can have a snack. I know where we can go."

"Are you going to make me talk about Annika?"

"Yeah," Annie said, her tone regretful. "That's why I'm here."

Tatiana squared her shoulders and nodded. "Very well," she said. "Let us try."

The memory of Dasha popped into Annie's head. *"We will try it."* She did her best to shake it off as she held the bathroom door open for Tatiana.

Annie took her into Worth's glassed-in office because they could see out from there. No one was there to stop them. Most people seemed to be gathered in the hallway outside the conference room while a handful of detectives spoke with the woman—Annika's mother?—inside.

The larger room was swarming with people too, and as Annie closed the office door, she heard someone say, "That bitch from Internal Affairs never checked in."

God, she hated cops. She thought she could be really good at this kind of work. Investigations that didn't end with turning someone against their country or catching a mole. Using her skill and her brain for justice, not to incriminate someone. But it wasn't worth it to be surrounded by sexist assholes who did nothing but ask her to get them coffee. She shouldn't even be in here alone with this little girl. Standard procedure for any sort of interrogation of a minor was to have two people present, especially if the interview wasn't being recorded.

After Tatiana sat down at the table, Annie gave her the candy and the Coke.

"Wait here," Annie said. "I'm going to talk to the chief. But your mom is in that room right over there"—she pointed—"and I can see you through the glass. I'll be back in a couple minutes."

Tatiana nodded.

Worth was facing away from the door when Annie stepped into the bullpen. He turned around, surprised, when she tapped his shoulder.

"You done already?" he asked.

"No. I put her in your office and gave her a snack. And I let her go pee. You can't just leave a minor in there to rot like she's a criminal."

"We were waiting for you," he said. "Wait. My office?"

"She's scared," Annie said. "And I need her not to be. Also, shouldn't there be an officer in there with us? Or someone from Social

Services? If I get anything useful out of her, it may backfire later if procedure was not followed to the letter."

Worth sighed. "Of course. Let me find you a body. Most people are out doing a grid search of where the girl disappeared, but…"

"A woman, preferably."

Worth rolled his eyes. "I'll try." He turned to the cop next to him. "Has the lieutenant from IA shown up yet? Go find her and send her to my office."

She returned to Worth's office and chatted amiably with Tatiana while they waited for the IA officer. Did she like America? How long had they been here? What brought them to Los Angeles?

"We saw the stars on the sidewalk and the letters up on the hill," she said. "And the ocean."

"So you're here on vacation?" Annie asked.

"Papa came for work, and he brought us too."

"When did he tell you you'd be coming out here?" Annie asked.

Tatiana looked at her blankly. She didn't understand. Annie repeated the question in Russian, and Tatiana held up three fingers.

"Three weeks?"

"Mesyatsy," Tatiana corrected.

Three months. That was enough time to plan a political kidnapping.

"Where were you today when you realized your sister wasn't with you anymore?"

"We went to an art museum," she said. "And then after—"

Tatiana looked up when the door opened.

Worth came in, his face red, his voice raised. "Yes, Lieutenant, those are all valid concerns that our translator raised herself, but as you can see, they're perfectly fine!"

Annie pushed herself up from Worth's chair and braced to greet whoever they'd wrangled to be in the room. Annie didn't like working alone, and it wasn't only because she was interviewing a child. She liked having someone else present to maintain a sense of balance in the room. She liked having someone who could pull her back if she started to lose her way.

Worth stepped aside, his hands held up as if in surrender.

It took a moment for Annie to realize whom she was looking at. "Annie?"

The "bitch" from IA wore a crisp, dark blue uniform. Her hair was twisted up and pulled back tightly, and her hat was tucked under her arm above the gun on her hip.

The bitch from IA was Helen Everton.

"You're a cop?" Annie asked, dumbfounded.

"You two know each other?" Worth said. "Good. That'll make it easier."

Annie glanced at him, then looked back at Helen. How had she not figured out that Helen was a cop? She knew she had some other job besides teaching, but how had she missed this?

"Annie, you have half an hour, and then I'd like you to check in with me," Worth said, oblivious to the stunned reactions of the two women. "We have some leads from the mother, but nothing has panned out yet. I want to compare their stories."

It seemed that Worth didn't know the girl could speak English.

Tatiana turned to Annie. *"Why does he think my mother would tell a different story?"* she asked in Russian.

Annie shook her head and replied in the girl's language. *"People remember things differently. We just don't want to miss an important detail."*

"I'll leave you to it," Worth said and shut the door.

Helen stared at Annie with a cold expression. "I'd heard they were using a government contractor to get around some of the new use-of-force policies, but I never dreamed…" Helen shook her head.

"Lieutenant Everton," Annie said. "This is Annika's sister, Tatiana. She was just telling me about what happened to her sister."

Helen straightened up, recognizing Annie's unspoken plea for professionalism, and sat in a chair against the back wall.

Annie continued her questioning where she had left off. She could tell the little girl was holding something back, so she circled around with her questions, tighter and tighter, until Tatiana had nowhere else to go.

"And so you ran," Annie said. "You ran away."

Tatiana nodded miserably.

"Did Annika run with you?"

Tatiana shook her head. "I—" She started to cry, and finally the truth slipped out. "I pushed her. I let them take her instead of me."

Annie leaned back in her chair and picked up the phone.

She couldn't sit in her idling car forever. It was almost midnight, and if the glow of lights in the house were any indication, Helen was still awake, waiting for her to come home. She studied her hands; they were holding onto the steering wheel so tightly that her knuckles were white. She released her grip and felt the tingle of blood returning to her fingertips.

Everything about this situation would be easier if she didn't like Helen. If she hadn't grown fond of her children, her cozy little Inglewood home, the way she smiled at Annie first thing in the morning when all Helen's pretty hair was piled up on her head.

Her last words to Frank Clifton during that last debrief, right before she'd left her letter of resignation in his inbox, echoed in her head. "I got too close," she'd said. "I cared."

She couldn't always turn off the caring, and that particular personality flaw had once more reared its ugly head. She cared about Helen and Zach and Kevin and Ashley. She should sneak around back, put whatever she couldn't live without into her trunk, and drive off into the night.

Running had worked before.

She scoffed. Now she was just lying to herself. If running had worked so well, she wouldn't be tied to an electronic pager like it was a ball and chain. If she were really so cold, she'd have told Clifton to shove it, not caring who he hurt in his pursuit of her. She wished she could be that cold. She wished she'd figured out how to be the kind of agent who was both exceptional at her job and ruthlessly indifferent to the results of her actions, but she'd only ever figured out the first half.

She turned off the engine, and the car went dark. It was cold tonight. She'd told her mother not three days ago that she would come home for Christmas and that she was spending Thanksgiving with Lori in Northern California.

"I won't be alone, Mom," she'd promised.

It wasn't cold enough to see her breath in the air, but she needed more than the thin flannel jacket she had on. She could also use a real coat and a pair of jeans not worn through at the knees. But then, she'd expected to be home hours ago.

Walking up to the front door, she turned the knob. It wasn't locked.

Helen was sitting in the living room, staring at the television. The sound was turned down so low that Annie could barely make out what they were saying, but it looked to be the late news. They probably wouldn't have a story about the Russian ambassador or the body of a little girl on a flight back to Moscow. No, they'd bury that. Americans didn't have sympathy for Russian casualties anymore.

Annie slipped her backpack off and dropped it onto the floor. "Have you got anything besides wine in this house?"

"What do you prefer, Annie?" Helen asked. "Vodka? Is that what you learned to like while you were over there?"

"You can't be mad that I didn't tell you about things I wasn't at liberty to tell you about," Annie said. She'd had the same argument more than once with her father, her brother, and anyone she'd let into her bed more than once.

"I thought you were a prostitute!"

"I know."

"You let me think it!" Helen hissed. "I could have lived without the emotional struggle of thinking a hooker was living in a cop's garage."

"Don't be mad because you drew your own conclusions. I wasn't bringing men home. Besides, it's not like you told me you were a cop." She moved into the kitchen.

Helen followed her in and stood in the doorway. "You never asked. It's not a secret!"

"I thought you were a professor!"

"I am. I thought you were a student!"

"I am!"

Helen's lip twitched just a little.

It *was* rather ridiculous. Annie would laugh if she weren't terrified of being kicked out of the first place she'd thought of as home in a long, long time.

"I'm glad you're not a prostitute, Annie. That really is an enormous load off my mind." Helen dragged a chair over to the refrigerator and climbed up to reach the cupboards over it.

Annie stared at the black leggings that clung to her thighs and calves and the long cream-colored sweater that rode up just a little as she reached up and retrieved a bottle of vodka.

"I do like vodka," Annie said. "More than white wine."

"Zach's asleep, and the kids are at Sal's," Helen said. "So go for it." She handed the bottle to Annie and then pushed the chair back to the table.

But instead of pouring a glass, Annie set the bottle on the counter and crossed her arms with a sigh. Alcohol was rarely the answer for Annie, even when it seemed like a good idea at the time. "You don't really have to liquor me up, Helen."

"I'm not…" She stopped. "It's been a long day."

Annie nodded in agreement.

"I don't like cases involving children, and I especially don't like when they turn out like this one did."

Annie hadn't seen the body or been present for the retrieval. She'd never even left Parker Center. She had been there to gather intelligence, to sort the information, and then snap the pieces together like a puzzle into something recognizable. She didn't usually see the grisly details the cops witnessed. And the one time she had, she hoped would be her last.

"I learned how to make this drink when I was in Leningrad," Annie said. "It had fresh grapes and brown sugar. I'll make us a couple. Then maybe we can start over?"

Helen regarded her for a moment and then opened a cabinet, pulling out a plastic container of brown sugar. From the refrigerator, she pulled out a bag of grapes. Then she dug around in the cupboard next to the pantry and pulled out a cocktail set and two glasses. "Show me how you make it," she said. "I like learning new drinks."

"Okay." If this were an interrogation, Annie would speak softly, reach out, and touch her wrist. Make lots of eye contact. But Annie didn't want to con Helen into liking her, and she didn't want to lull her with lies. She just wanted to get to know her better so that her new life in Los Angeles had a chance of working out.

It was easy to convince herself she was making good choices, living a life of justice when she clipped a government badge to her chest every morning, but here she was, doing the same work for the same people, and she felt like the escort Helen had thought her to be. She felt like trash.

But when she was with Helen, she felt okay. When Helen looked at her, she saw the person Annie wanted to be.

Or at least she had before today.

Annie felt her face grow hot. She swallowed, then said, "First, you muddle the grapes."

Helen dropped four grapes into each glass.

"Now add the sugar and mush it into the grapes." She wiped her face with the back of her hand. "Then add the vodka and ice. I like to stir it up, then add a splash of soda."

"I have Seven-Up," Helen said. "Will that work?"

"Yeah."

Helen finished mixing the drinks and handed one to Annie. She took a drink from her own glass and sputtered. "Stiff," she said.

"Well," Annie said, "Russia is cold."

"You could tell me about what it was like, if you want."

Annie nodded. "Okay."

CHAPTER 8

The social worker came to pick up the baby a week before Thanksgiving. From one perspective, a baby reunited with his birth mother in time for the holidays seemed like a happy ending. But from what Helen had told Annie about Zach's mother, it was only a matter of time before she slipped up again. She lost him the first time after she left him in a mall bathroom soon after he was born while she went to get high. Now, she was sober and recently discharged from a halfway house. It wasn't enough to fix things, according to Helen, but the State of California usually sided with the mother. So until she screwed up again, Zach was going back to her.

Annie was out when the social worker arrived. She'd been spending a lot of time on campus because the end of the quarter was getting close and because Helen was packing up Zach's things. Being in the house—even being near the house—was breaking her heart.

She spent Thursday afternoon standing in line at the registrar's office, signing up for next quarter's classes. She didn't want to spend Friday on campus because more often than not, she got paged on Fridays. Using her was probably cheaper than weekend overtime, and Friday evenings usually bled into Saturday mornings.

She signed up for three classes easily. But her fourth choice was already full. When she asked what other classes were available in that time slot, the woman at the window gave her two options. One of them was Helen's class.

She signed up for it, even though she worried it was a bad idea. But Annie had never let bad ideas stop her before.

When she got back to the house, she was greeted by Sal, Bruce's sister. When Annie had met her at Ashley's birthday party, the woman had been polite, friendly, and chatty, but now her round cheeks were flushed and her short, dirty-blonde hair looked like she had just crawled out of bed.

"Hey, kiddo," Sal said when she spied Annie slipping into the front hall. Sal called everyone *kiddo* regardless of their age.

"Hi," she said.

"Helen called me to come take the kids for the night."

"It's Thursday. Don't they have school tomorrow?"

Sal grimaced. "You haven't seen her since they took Zach away."

"She's taking it rough?"

"I've been here two hours," Sal said. "I wasn't sure if I should leave her alone but…"

"It's okay," Annie said. "I'm in for the night."

"I know it's not your responsibility. It's just that she really likes you."

"Where is she?"

Sal pointed upstairs.

She stopped by Ashley's room. Ashley was sitting on her bed, reading a book, still wearing her dance leotard and tights. Kevin sat on the floor, focused intently on his Game Boy. Their overnight bags were packed and ready to go.

She knocked on the doorframe. "Hey, you guys. How are you doing?"

"Miss Oliver came and took Zach," Ashley said. "Mom is sad."

"Yeah," Annie said. "It's hard to lose someone you love."

"But he wasn't even our real brother," Kevin said. It sounded cruel, but his lower lip quivered like he was about to cry.

"Love doesn't care about stuff like that," Annie said. "Anyway, your aunt is downstairs and ready to go. You guys ready?"

"Can we say goodbye to mom?" Kevin asked.

Who was she to deny these children access to their mother? "Of course." She walked them down the hall, knocked lightly but persistently on Helen's door, then called through the wood. "Kevin and Ashley want to say goodbye."

It was all the warning Helen was going to get. Annie opened the door and ushered the kids inside.

The bedroom was lit only by the lamp on her nightstand. Helen was lying on top of her covers, still fully dressed. But when the children entered, she rolled over and smiled. Annie watched from the hallway. Helen's face was swollen. Her makeup had been rubbed off. She hugged and kissed her children, promising to pick them up from school the next day. She told them that she loved them.

Annie remembered similar scenes from her own childhood—her mother weepy whenever her father was deployed somewhere far away for what seemed like a very long time. But she never let her sadness stand between her and her children, and Helen didn't either.

Helen was a good mother, Annie decided. Better than Annie could ever be.

When the kids came back out into the hallway, Annie asked, "You need help with your bags?"

"We aren't little babies," Ashley said. "It's just one night."

"My mistake," Annie conceded easily. She didn't feel threatened by Ashley. The girl's father had just up and left, a baby had come and gone, and a stranger was living in her garage. The girl had a lot going on, and Annie didn't begrudge her a little hostility.

After the kids had gone, Annie stood in the kitchen, fretting. She didn't know how to be a good friend. Had no idea how to go about comforting someone. Maybe Helen wanted to be left alone. How was Annie even supposed to know?

She picked up the phone to call home but hung up halfway through, deciding her mother's advice wasn't worth the explanation she'd require. Instead, she put on the kettle for tea, then went out to the garage to change into leggings with stirrups and a big sweatshirt.

Returning to the kitchen, she unwrapped several tea bags and poured hot water over them into Helen's pretty white teapot. She was still trying to decide whether or not to carry it upstairs on a tray when she heard Helen come downstairs.

"That for me?"

"I thought we could share it, but if you want it all, I won't fight you for it."

Helen touched the belly of the pot with the pads of her fingers.

"I'm happy to share your tea." They sat together at the kitchen table. The window was open slightly, letting in the first real hint of winter since she had moved to California—but the tea was hot, and they were both dressed warmly. Annie felt downright cozy.

"You want to talk about today?"

"No, thank you."

Annie didn't push. She was the queen of not talking about things.

"You want to watch TV?"

Helen nodded. "Yes."

Annie had never seen this docile side of Helen. Her sadness seemed to linger under a mask of calm. It made Annie nervous—she'd rather see Helen cry or be angry or express something else that she could identify with.

They watched TV until Jay Leno came on. Then Helen stood up. "You can stay, obviously, but I'm going to get some sleep. I have to teach a class tomorrow."

"Oh," Annie said. "I signed up for your class today. I forgot to tell you."

"You did?" Helen rubbed her neck.

"I wasn't planning on it because I thought it might be weird, but I had to fill the slot with something, and I figured…you know…hey."

"Hey. That's most flattering."

"And anyway," Annie continued, "I'll probably be in student housing by then. That was the deal, right?"

"Right," Helen said softly. "When are you planning on moving out?"

"Well, they haven't called yet. But if you're worried about renting the space to someone else, I can go back to the motel or something."

"No, no, nothing like that," Helen said. "Stay as long as you need. The last thing I need is someone else moving out of my house this week."

Annie winced.

"I guess I was trying to ask you if you'd be around for Thanksgiving, that's all," Helen said and shrugged.

"Oh!"

"I know lots of students don't go home for Thanksgiving because they go back for Christmas instead."

"Actually, I'm planning to go up north to see my friend Lori," Annie said. "I figured you'd have some family thing."

"Well, Sal always hosts," Helen said. "The kids play with their cousins, but this year…since Bruce, I just don't think I could stomach it." She smiled, deepening the lines around her eyes, and it was more unsettling than the weird mask of calm.

"Where will you go instead?"

"I never get the house to myself. I'll be fine."

"Or you could come with me," Annie said. "Get out of LA for a while."

Helen raised her eyebrows, her ivory skin shifting into a map of fine lines. And then she became contemplative. And then almost serene. Her cheeks flushed pink. "All right. If you're sure it's okay, I think getting out of town might be nice."

Then Annie flushed too.

It had felt right to invite Helen to visit Lori with her in the Bay Area, and strangely thrilling when she had said yes, but now Annie was faced with the task of calling Lori and making sure it was okay to show up on her doorstep with someone else.

She called in the middle of the day, hoping to get voicemail, hoping to leave a vague, self-deprecating message designed to elicit forgiveness. But Louis answered on the second ring.

"Oh!" she said. "I didn't expect anyone to be home. It's Annie."

"Hey!" he said. "Lindsay stayed home sick from school today, so I called in to stay with her. How are you?"

"Good, thanks. Excited to come see you guys. See the baby and Lindsay."

"Us too. Lori has been talking about it nonstop. She really misses you. She works a lot, so we don't really have time for, you know, friends." He laughed, and she laughed too.

"Hey, speaking of friends," she said.

"Yeah?"

"Would it be terribly rude if I brought someone along with me?" she asked. "I know it's last minute, and if my mother knew I was even asking, she'd lose her mind, but—"

"No! It's fine! The more, the merrier."

"Are you sure?" Annie asked. "We can get a hotel room, if that would be easier."

"Annie Weaver, please. Don't be absurd. Lori would never stand for that. You guys are like sisters, which means you're family, so bring whomever you want."

"Thanks, Lou," she said. "Really."

"You want me to have her call you when she gets home?"

"If she wants," Annie said. "I'm still planning on driving up on Wednesday."

"We'll see you then."

When Annie hung up the phone, something eased in her chest.

The pager woke her up. She hadn't been summoned since Annika went missing, and she'd worried it was because the girl had been found too late. Maybe they thought Annie hadn't done enough. That explained the LAPD not calling, but no one else? She'd started to wonder whether she needed to get a real job instead.

She fumbled for the lamp and reached for the pager. The clock showed 3:44 on Tuesday morning, though she could barely make out the numbers through her bleary eyes. She rolled out of bed and shivered. The concrete floor was cold through the thin area rug. She put on slippers and her big robe. Put her keys and the pager in her pocket and made her way through the backyard.

She unlocked the back door, slipped in, and closed it behind her. She picked up the kitchen wall phone by the door and punched in the numbers by feel, squinting at the green light of the pager.

The phone on the other end rang three times before a familiar voice answered.

"Agent Juno, Akron," she said, then covered the mouthpiece of the phone with her hand while she yawned.

He sounded tired too as he read her the address. FBI again.

"Hey," she said before he could hang up. "What happens if I say no?"

"I'm sorry?"

"It's just that I'm going out of town for a few days, and if I get paged… If I say no, you let them know, right?"

"That is the procedure, yes. What happens from there, well, that's up to your supervisors, I suppose."

"Do people say no?"

He hesitated and then said, "Your case is unique."

She laughed. "Yeah, I bet it is. All right, I'll be there in an hour."

The sun was just starting to lighten the horizon when she pulled into the drab government building's mostly empty parking lot. She'd expected more activity for a middle-of-the-night phone call.

Inside, a receptionist checked her in, went through her bag, and issued her a visitor's pass. Then she waited for someone to come get her.

She recognized the agent that emerged from the elevator and cringed. "Agent Katz."

"We meet again."

She could have gone her whole life without ever seeing him again but forced herself to be cheerful.

"Agent Weaver," he said in greeting.

"Nope. Annie'll do."

He smiled, his cheeks ruddy. "Annie, then. Thanks for coming on such short notice."

"Nothing more thrilling than waking up to a four a.m. summons."

He led her through a maze of hallways into a dark room where another agent was sitting with a cigarette and listening to a tape.

"Even on a good day, people with security clearance who can speak Czech are hard to come by in Los Angeles," he said. "On a holiday week, well, we're glad you're here. There's about four hours of tape, and our assistant director wants it before we all leave for the weekend."

Annie shook her head. "Your tax dollars at work."

Agent Katz looked at her, puzzled. "We're trying to take down a drug ring."

She realized he probably had no idea how much she was paid for this work. "Very noble, I'm sure."

"This is Agent Stevenson," Katz said. "My partner."

Annie nodded at him. They both had dark circles under their eyes and the waxy sheen of people who hadn't had enough sleep and or eaten anything healthy for days. Sweat and grease oozed from their pores.

"You think I could get some coffee?" she asked Agent Katz. He hesitated, looking somewhat offended. He was probably the boy who always got picked last for kickball, and she wondered how smart he was to get here, overweight and barely sober. No slouch, surely.

"Yeah, of course," he said. "Stevenson, get her some coffee."

Agent Stevenson pulled off his earphones. "What?"

Agent Katz scowled. "Never mind. I'll do it."

"Thank you. Thank you so much," Annie said.

She decided then and there to drag out this job as long as possible, to work right up to the last second, fretting over translating words she knew by heart, just to watch these two agents scramble and panic while she got paid for every minute of it. Just because she could.

She nearly rear-ended someone on the way home, and even the adrenaline of the near miss wasn't enough to keep her sharp. She drove past Helen's street and had to make a U-turn at the next block. Once inside the house, she made it only as far as the living room sofa before she collapsed and fell asleep.

She woke up when Helen and the children came home in the afternoon. Kevin ran in first, sneakers pounding on the floor as he shot up the stairs. Ashley was next, her ballet slippers gliding softly. Then Helen closed the door behind them, shifting a bag of groceries on her hip. Annie sat up, rubbed her eyes, and fluffed her hair. Only then did Helen see her, startling at the sight.

"Are you all right? You look awful!"

"Fine, fine. I had an early call and fell asleep as soon as I walked in."

"I didn't hear anything about a case," Helen said.

"Not for you guys. Don't worry."

Helen frowned. "Do you want to go sleep in my bed?"

"What?" Annie said. "No. I mean, thank you, but I'm just going to go take a shower, I think."

"Okay."

Annie got up and started to walk past her, but Helen reached out and pressed the back of her hand against Annie's forehead.

"I'm fine."

"Dinner in an hour," Helen murmured, her hand lingering.

Annie nodded against her fingers.

They decided to take the Jeep. Helen said it had more space, and Annie couldn't disagree, so she just nodded dumbly, still too tired and surprised that Helen was even going with her at all. If Helen didn't mind adding eight hundred miles to her odometer, Annie didn't either. It was a relief to have Helen driving too, because napping too much during the day meant her sleep suffered at night. Plus, Annie had stayed awake most of the night worrying about getting lost. But when she handed Lori's address to Helen, scribbled on the back of a paycheck envelope, Helen studied it for a moment and said, "I'm sure we can find this."

It had put Annie at ease, even if it might only be a confident-sounding lie.

They piled the bags into the cargo area of the Jeep, the kids got in the back, and Annie sat in the front. With a car seat no longer in the back, there was more elbow room, though the kids knew better than to point this out to their mother. They would stop at Sal's, deposit the kids, and then head north on Interstate 5 for the next six hours.

Helen asked Ashley and Kevin three times if they would be okay without her, if staying two nights was too many, until finally Kevin leaned forward, put his hand on the center console—the farthest he could reach toward the front of the car—and said, "Mommy, chill out."

"I'm chill," Helen said as Annie stifled a laugh. "I'm a chill mommy."

"Tell you what," Annie said. "We'll make sure Aunt Sal has the phone number of where we're staying, okay?"

"If you miss me, you can call," Helen added.

"Where are you going again?" Ashley asked.

"Marin County."

"Yeah, but where exactly?"

"We're staying with my friend from college and her husband in a town called San Rafael," Annie said. "She's got two little girls."

"Girls?" Kevin asked. "Only girls?"

"Lindsay and…" She stopped. "Oh shoot, I forget the little one's name. Something with a K, I think."

"Wait. Your friends Lori and Louis had a baby and named her Lindsay, then had another baby and didn't give her an *L* name?" Helen asked.

"I'm, like, seventy percent sure it's a *K*." Annie shrugged. "They didn't consult me. I haven't even met the baby yet."

"Why not?" Ashley asked.

"I was away when she was born."

"Away where?"

"Somewhere too far to come home to meet a baby."

"Yeah, but where?" Ashley asked.

"The Soviet Union."

"Where is that?" Kevin asked.

"It's nowhere anymore," Helen said. "Enough questions. We're almost there, so promise me you'll behave for your Aunt Sal and be nice to your cousins."

It took nearly forty-five minutes to unload the suitcases, settle the children, and chitchat with Sal. The first thing Helen said after they pulled away from the house was, "I didn't know they had such little kids."

"Lindsay is preschool age. Four? The baby is maybe a year now. Kylie? Krystal? God, what is her name? I really hope it's not Krystal."

"Krystal with a *K* sounds like a stripper name," Helen said.

"If it is Krystal, maybe we keep that observation to ourselves," Annie suggested.

Helen hummed agreement, then entered the access lane to get on the freeway.

"I didn't think about the baby. I hope that's okay."

"Of course it's okay," Helen said. "I love babies."

And she's just lost hers.

They drove in silence for a few minutes. Then Annie leaned down, rummaged through her bag and pulled out an old book of unfinished crossword puzzles. It was something she'd picked up back when she spent a lot of time on long flights across oceans. When she found it while packing up for this little trip, she brought it along in case they needed something to pass the time.

"Are you a puzzle person?" Annie asked.

"I think my skills are more in the jigsaw area," Helen said. "But I'm game."

"I like 'em. Keeps me sharp."

"Okay, but how does one driving do a crossword puzzle with another person?"

"We take turns with clues. At least, that's how my dad and I play it. I get the evens; you get the odds. And the first one is easy. One down, the clue is long ago and it's four letters."

When Helen didn't answer, Annie looked at her. "It's *once*."

"Of course. Why don't you fill in what you know, and if you get stuck, maybe I can help." She turned on the radio and tuned past stations, finally settling on a woman belting out a love song.

Annie looked up from the puzzle and listened to see if she recognized the song. When she didn't, she tuned the music out and focused on filling in as many of the short words of the puzzle as she could.

"Okay, okay, gimme a clue." Helen turned off the radio when the song ended.

"Six letters, pick up the phone," Annie said.

Helen squinted at the road ahead. "I don't think I can do this without seeing it."

"It's got a 'W' in it," Annie hinted.

"Answer."

"Yeah."

Helen glanced at her. "You aren't writing anything. I didn't mean give me a clue you'd already filled in!"

Annie closed the crossword book, leaving her pen to mark the page, and shoved the book back into her bag. "We can do something else."

"Do you think I'm dumb?" Helen asked and laughed. "Oh God, I'm the dumb one."

"I do not at all think you're dumb."

"You're like a CIA protégé, and I'm a cop who can barely hang on to her teaching job. This is tough. I'm used to being the smart one."

"Why did you become a cop?" It was something Annie had been wondering about for a while, but they rarely had a quiet moment alone long enough to have a normal conversation. Usually one of them was crying or it was the middle of the night or the kids needed something or Annie's pager went off.

"It certainly wasn't the plan," Helen said. "The plan was to teach so I could get a discounted rate for the law school. But once the kids were born, with Bruce still in graduate school, it wasn't enough to make ends meet. So I joined the reserves."

"Oh," Annie said. "You're a reserve corps officer?"

"Yeah. Or I was. After the riots, so many officers either quit or were put on probation that a lot of the reserves got called up and were offered permanent full-time or part-time positions. Once I was made permanent, the pay and benefits were better than teaching, so after Bruce left, I figured I might as well stick with it."

"But you're still teaching. I signed up for your class."

"Yeah. I keep thinking if I keep at least one class, if I keep my foot in the door, I can still go to law school. But come on, I'm in my late thirties, and I have little kids. I should probably just be realistic."

"I think it's never too late to go back," Annie said. "Obviously."

"Anyway. I transferred to Internal Affairs a few months ago because the LAPD needed serious overhaul after the bad press we got after Rodney King, and I think it's probably the only way I'll get promoted anytime soon."

"Makes sense."

"Being in IA does not, however, make me popular."

Annie recalled hearing the detectives call Helen "the bitch from Internal Affairs" not too long ago.

"You are not dumb," Annie repeated. "You might not be popular now, but my guess is you're smarter than most of the guys on the force, and eventually things will come out in your favor."

"That'd be nice," Helen said. "A hopeful view of things."

They drove in silence for several miles until Helen asked, "What about you? You told me how you joined the CIA and that you left, but you never told me why or what the deal really is with that pager."

"I'm just a contractor now," Annie said carefully. She worked to keep her expression neutral. She shouldn't be talking about it at all. "Technically, CIA officers aren't supposed to do interrogations on American soil, but if they keep me on as a contractor, they don't have to rely on FBI or locals to do their dirty work for them."

"That's…"

"Awful, I know," Annie said.

"So you don't like it?"

"I like it better than going overseas, I guess."

"Is that why you left in the first place? The travel?"

Annie pictured the blood, the chalky faces, how tiny the little girl looked. She swallowed. "Yeah. The travel."

"You could always quit."

"It's not that simple," Annie said. "Anyway, it beats waiting tables or working retail. I make okay money, and since I have a lot of school left, I can't complain."

Annie fiddled with the hem of her sweater. She could lie through her teeth with barely a second thought, but honesty made her fidget.

"Have you ever thought about being a police officer?" Helen asked.

Annie sighed. "Deputy Chief Worth—Mason Worth—actually tried to get me to join his previous department out in DC. I think that's half the reason the LAPD calls me so much."

Helen snorted. "No wonder you said no."

"Yeah, he's certainly not subtle."

"Please tell me if he harasses you in any way going forward," Helen said. "I'm serious."

"I will," Annie promised.

"Annie, thank you again for letting me tag along. I already feel, um, lighter somehow."

"I'm so happy. You'll like Lori and Louis. They're good people. Funny and down-to-earth. Lori put up with me for years, so you know she's made of sterner stuff than most."

"Putting up with you doesn't seem like a chore, for the record."

"Wait and ask her that," Annie said with a laugh, "before you make your conclusion."

Helen glanced at her. "I will."

Annie shifted in her seat. Rolled down the window a bit to let some fresh air in; it was cool against her face. Took a deep breath and another, and then, when she became a little lightheaded, she rolled the window back up.

Helen turned the radio back on and hummed along with the music.

CHAPTER 9

Helen's sense of direction was much better than her own. Annie squinted at the map on her legs, looked up to peer out the window at passing street signs. But Helen seemed to need only her intuition and turned confidently onto Lori's street.

"I think… What number was it?"

"It's 108," Annie said and pointed. "There."

Helen turned the Jeep around in an empty driveway and parked in front of the house. It was built up against the side of a hill, giving it a feeling of seclusion. Two cars were parked on the steeply sloped driveway—a small sedan like Annie's and a pickup truck. Wooden stairs led up to a wide porch and the front door. Lori was a high-end lawyer while Louis worked in construction, which—by the size of their midcentury dream home and the expensive-looking neighborhood—was booming.

"Jesus." Annie peered up at the house. "This really puts a garage-slash-apartment into perspective."

"Stop it," Helen said, killing the engine and unbuckling her seatbelt. "There's nothing wrong with a more compact life."

Annie burst out laughing. "Keep it up. Lori loves funny women."

It was much cooler than in LA, breezier too, and Annie zipped up her sweatshirt before shouldering her bag and walking up the driveway to the porch. White, fluffy clouds moved through a clear blue sky.

"Are you nervous?" Annie asked before she rang the bell.

"No," Helen said. "My friends' parents always love me."

Annie snorted, then pushed the button, causing a cacophony on the other side of the door, though they couldn't see anything through the frosted glass panels. A dog was barking. Someone was yelling.

Then there was a loud bang. Finally, she heard footsteps, and the door flew open to reveal a small girl with shiny blonde hair.

"It's Annie and her friend! They're here!" she shrieked.

"Lindsay, you're supposed to wait for a grown-up!" The voice was Lori's younger sister, Kelly. "Sorry. Come in! Come in! Annie and… Annie's friend!"

"This is Helen," Annie said. She walked in and hugged Kelly, touched the top of Lindsay's head, and looked around the foyer of the beautiful house. Helen stepped in after her and shook Kelly's hand.

Louis descended down the ornate wooden staircase wearing jeans and a cable-knit sweater. He looked like he had walked off the page of a catalog. He embraced Annie, shook Helen's hand, and then picked up Lindsay. "Lori's upstairs giving the baby a bath. We had a diaper malfunction."

"She pooped everywhere!" Lindsay said.

Louis chuckled. "She did indeed. Thank you, sweetie."

"Daddy," Lindsay said, "Annie didn't bring a boy."

Kelly snickered.

Ignoring Lindsay's comment, Louis turned to Helen. "Welcome to our home! Do you have bags? Can I help you?"

"Kelly can get them," Lori called from the top of the stairs. They all looked up just as she paused on the landing next to a stained-glass window. The golden light illuminated her and the baby in her arms like some sort of tall, thin Madonna figure. Her blonde hair was cut into a sleek bob. Annie fought the urge to touch her own frizzy mop.

Annie hurried up the stairs two at a time, impatient to hug her friend. She wrapped her arms around her, mindful of the baby, realizing all at once how starved for a familiar face she was. Helen had been a good friend, under the circumstances, but Lori knew Annie better than anyone else outside of her immediate family. Annie had truly missed her.

"I thought you were bringing a boyfriend," Lori whispered in her ear.

"I never said boy," Annie whispered back.

"Kelly is in the second spare room. Where are we going to put her?"

"We can share. Lou said it was okay. I didn't know Kelly would be here."

"Of course it's okay."

"Ladies?" Louis called.

They broke apart. "This is Helen." Annie gestured down the stairs. "My roommate? Landlord?" She gazed down at Helen as she left the options dangling.

"Friend," Helen said with a disarming smile.

"A pleasure to have you," Lori said, coming the rest of the way down the stairs. "This is Kimberly."

"Kimberly!" Annie said. "Like we discussed."

"You have a beautiful home and family. Thank you so much for having me at the last minute."

"Any friend of Annie's is always welcome," she said. "Come on, let's get you settled."

Annie emerged from the bathroom and saw their bags sitting on the double bed on top of an expensive-looking quilt. Matching pillow shams rested against the headboard. There was no sign of Helen or anyone else, for that matter. Even the ancient cocker spaniel, Tubby, was nowhere to be found. He'd barked when they arrived and again when he waddled in from the backyard. He gave both Annie and Helen a suspicious sniff, dragging his wet muzzle along the tops of their shoes and then went to lie down on a round dog bed next to the den sofa.

Annie slid her fingers along their bed's wooden footboard, considering.

She could always sleep on the cream-colored leather sofa, she supposed. It was soft and luxurious but probably not ideal for sleeping on. She'd sweat all night, and it would squeak when she rolled over.

She looked at the narrow bed again. It wasn't the tiniest bed she'd ever shared with another person, and Helen was used to sharing her bed. She had a very Mother-Earth approach. She shared it with her children whenever they needed it, invited Annie to take a nap on it, or patted the mattress for Annie to climb up beside her so they could talk. Annie had technically been in a bed with Helen before, but she'd never slept with Helen. She'd never stretched out, elbow to elbow, under covers in the dark.

"Annie-bo-bannie?" Lori's voice floated up the stairs. "You want a drink?"

Helen was in the kitchen wearing an apron that matched Lori's, a sturdy fabric thing in a fetching pale green. Her hair was clipped back with a black velvet barrette. She had a wineglass in one hand and was looking over an open cookbook.

"We're making pies," Lori said. "Have you ever made pie?"

"I've eaten lots. Like, so many."

"That's a no." Helen smirked knowingly.

"Louis wants pumpkin and pecan," Lori said. "His parents are coming tomorrow too."

"Jesus, Lor. I didn't realize Thanksgiving would be such a big deal."

"Thanksgiving is a big deal." Helen licked her finger and turning the page to read the other side. "In my family, it was always a bigger deal than even Christmas, and we're Catholic."

"Then I'm doubly honored to have you," Lori said.

Helen smiled. "I think this crust recipe will work just fine. We'll just double it and put the dough in the fridge."

"Actually, you can go, Annie. Helen is all I really need," Lori teased.

Annie swatted at her. "Where are your children?" she asked.

"Louis put the baby down and then took Lindsay to the store with him." Lori pulled out a plain, black apron for Annie. "So it's just us girls."

Helen wasn't kidding when she said her friends' parents loved her. She handled Lori's questions gracefully. Sometimes the lawyer in Lori took over, and her questions felt like a trial—rapid-fire queries about Helen's family and past. When Helen said she had two children, Annie turned around to wash her hands in the sink, unable to look her in the eye.

"Your kids are still so little!" Lori said when Helen divulged their ages.

"They're with their father." Helen sounded defensive.

Annie picked up the bottle of wine and topped off Helen's glass, bumping her hip gently. Helen smiled in response.

"Say no more," Lori said. "My parents divorced when I was seven. It's not an easy situation."

"No," Helen agreed.

"Not everyone comes from a picture-perfect family like Annie," Lori said. "Have you had the pleasure of meeting the Weavers?"

"Lord no," Annie said. "Can you imagine them in Los Angeles?"

"I spoke to your mother on the phone once," Helen said to Annie. "Briefly. She was very polite."

"That's Midwestern for rude," Annie said.

"No." Helen shook her head. "Concerned, maybe."

"I'm going to be thirty years old, and they still treat me like a high schooler, no matter what I've accomplished."

"You'd think leaving the Company would buy you a little leeway." Lori tensed, glancing at Helen. "I mean—"

"It's all right," Annie said. "She knows about that."

In fact, Helen probably knew more about Annie's current life than Lori. She and Lori had been close, the best of friends, but time and distance had changed things. Likewise, Annie no longer knew everything about this confident, polished mother of two, the same woman she'd eaten greasy fast food and done tequila shooters with on the Tuesday night before a huge final. Anyway, being coerced into doing contract work for any law enforcement agency that requested her wasn't really something to put in a letter or chat about over the phone.

But she saw Helen every day, and she was so easy to talk to. She wanted to listen, and even though Annie wasn't usually much for sharing, something about Helen always made her want to spill.

She hadn't told Helen about Dasha, obviously, or Yeva, or why her time in Belarus and Europe and the CIA had ended abruptly. She'd given Helen the polished version that night through her tears. How she'd been recruited out of college. Trained and fast-tracked and thrown into the deep end. She still couldn't tell anyone what she'd done or why she'd done it because some things were classified, and other things were simply too horrible to say out loud to another person.

Things like seducing a married woman with a small child and getting them both murdered. Practically sending two of her coworkers to their deaths. Probably the husband's blood was on Annie's hands too.

"Honey?" Helen stood in front of her, gripping her bicep.

"Huh?"

"You okay?" Helen asked. "You were drifting."

"Oh." Annie laughed nervously. "Just tired, maybe."

Lori was looking at her strangely, but the sound of the garage opening distracted her. "Oh, that's Louis. We can have lunch!"

"Come on," Helen said. "Come help me with this pie crust. It's easier with extra hands."

Annie knew that was a lie, but she went along anyway.

After the girls went to bed, Louis got out Rummikub. He had campaigned for the Dune board game but was vetoed by everyone else in the room.

"We used to play Risk," Annie explained, "but I won too much, and they banned me."

"She was Machiavellian," Lori said, laughing. "She was ruthless!"

"She made Lori cry!" Louis snorted.

"That was once!" Annie said defensively. "One time and banned for life! Talk about unfair!"

"Well, this is more my speed anyway." Helen chuckled.

They set up their game trays as Louis mixed the tiles on the glass table, making a loud clatter that seemed to echo in the big, open house. It seemed like all the tables were glass panels on black metal frames, giving the illusion of transparency, of objects floating over the pretty walnut floors. It wasn't Annie's style, but it was impressive nonetheless, and certainly an improvement over the cinder-block-and-board shelving and used furniture of their college years.

"Helen likes to pretend that she's a hundred-year-old grandma, not a badass cop," Annie said.

"And professor," Helen added primly, winking at Lori.

"Oh yeah!" Annie said excitedly. "I signed up for her class next quarter."

"Kinky," Louis said, pulling tiles and setting them up in his tray.

Through the glass table, Annie saw Lori kick him. He jumped. "Ow! What?" He reached down to rub his shin. Lori pulled her foot back.

"How do you like UCLA?" Lori changed the subject.

"It's not Ole Miss," Annie said, "but it's all right."

"She got an A on her midterms in every class."

"That's supposed to be confidential," Annie pointed out.

"You left your grade report in the kitchen."

"Oh." Annie had read the grades to her dad over the phone. She must've left the report there, distracted by something or someone.

"I stuck it on the fridge," Helen said and turned to Lori. "Obviously, she hasn't noticed."

"If you kept the candy in the fridge…" Louis suggested.

Annie kicked him on his other shin.

"Ow! I swear to God."

"You were working a lot," Helen said. "I know it's been a crazy time."

"Wait, you're working too?" Lori asked.

"Oh—" Annie felt a rush of panic and searched for a lie that could convince Lori, someone who knew her well and was a lawyer. But Helen smoothly beat her to it, covering her own faux pas.

"Studying, I mean. Always at the library."

"Right," Annie said. "You know how it is."

"I do," Lori said. "I do."

Annie didn't mind lying, but she wasn't used to having someone on her side. To lie for her and with her.

Annie decided the best thing would be to change the subject. "I'm thirsty. Anyone want a drink?"

"What are we talking, water or…" Louis waggled his eyebrows.

Annie grinned. "Show me your booze, and I'll make something good," she promised.

Helen drunk was a sight to behold. Annie knew she could be a sloppy drunk herself, but she was the least intoxicated of the four by the time they all broke for bed. Lori was a tired drunk, the first to slink off toward a softer surface—the couch in the next room. Louis was loud, and Annie had to keep shushing him, reminding him about the little girls sleeping upstairs.

Annie wasn't exactly sober either. She felt warm and happy, and it was easy not to think about things she didn't want to think about. Her father's critical letters. The finals that loomed between Thanksgiving and Christmas. Mason Worth's lecherous handshakes. Agent Katz's hopeful, doughy smile. Minsk.

But Helen... Helen seemed to be glowing from within. It had to be the red wine that made her flush. Then they started adding hard liquor, and Helen had shrugged out of her sweater, revealing bare, pink arms. Every time she laughed, she added sunlight to a dark room. Annie couldn't stop staring at her, couldn't help reaching out to lay her hand on Helen's freckled, rosy arm. She realized that she was touching her over and over again, realized she needed to stop, but she couldn't. When Louis cracked a joke, they all burst into laughter, and Annie reached out to touch Helen's arm again.

Helen put her hand on top of Annie's and squeezed.

That was when Lori got up to go pee and never came back. They all had to get up early anyway, what with kids and guests and a huge meal to cook. Helen had already proven herself invaluable with the pies and had jumped into the head cook position. Lori thanked her for coming twice over, as if Helen were the guest and Annie the stranger. But no matter. It was the right body for the right job.

Louis asked if they needed anything else, told them to make themselves at home, and roused his drunk, tired wife from the sofa in the other room to walk her up the stairs.

"I can sleep down here," Annie offered.

"Nonsense," Helen said.

And that settled that.

Helen giggled as they crept through the upstairs hall.

Their room had a Jack-and-Jill bathroom that they shared with the other guest room, Kelly's room, but Kelly had gone out with friends after dinner and had yet to return.

"You go first," Helen urged.

Annie didn't want to fight, so she grabbed her toiletry bag and locked herself into the little bathroom, quickly changing into flannel pajama pants and a white T-shirt, then brushing her teeth. She knew she should wash her face but didn't have it in her. Buzzed Annie was even less responsible than sober Annie.

Helen was already in gray sweatpants and a black tank top when Annie came back into the room. One of the tank top straps was twisted in the back. Annie reached out, not waiting for consent, and adjusted the strip of fabric.

"Thanks," Helen said and took her turn in the bathroom. She wasn't long. Annie heard the toilet flush and the sink turn on and off a few times. While she waited, she busied herself with turning on the nightstand lamp and turning off the bright overhead light. Pulling the decorative pillows off the bed and tossing them to the floor. Turning the bed cover down.

"Left or right?" Helen said.

Annie spun around. She hadn't heard Helen come back in the room. Her cheeks were still flushed, but her face was damp and clean. She'd pulled her dark hair up with a scrunchie. Annie was suddenly self-conscious about her own smudged eyeliner and limp hair.

"What?" she asked.

"What side of the bed do you prefer?"

"I went from a cot to a twin," Annie said. "Side hasn't really been an option lately."

Helen laughed and pointed to the side Annie was standing by. "You." Then she pointed to the opposite side. "Me."

"Sold." Annie sat on the edge and looked around the little room. "I'm tired, but I don't know how sleepy I am."

"You'll be sleepy when you have to wake up at six a.m. to chop onions," Helen said with a grin. "You'll be sorry."

"You're the one who got yourself suckered into cooking practically the whole meal." Annie slid her legs under the blankets. But she didn't recline, just sat up against the headboard. Helen mirrored her pose. With her hair up and her face clean, she looked younger than her nearly forty years, but Annie could see little lines at the edge of her eyes and at the top of her lips. *Laugh lines*, her mom called them.

Annie couldn't take her eyes off them. In the low lamplight, they just made Helen more attractive.

It had been a mistake to bring her.

"I love cooking. I find it soothing and satisfying."

"Really?"

"Yeah," Helen said, her eyes half closing. "There's something about creating a complex meal out of simple parts. I can't paint, and I'm not much of a writer, but I feel like an artist when I make an elaborate meal. Especially if I get to watch people enjoy it."

"I've never thought of it like that," Annie said. "Well, I know Lori's going to be grateful."

"Thank you, for bringing me here. I like your friends, and I get to have a holiday when I expected to be alone."

"It's not a big deal—"

"Thank you for moving into my garage. Will you stay? I don't want you to move out."

Annie realized that Helen was still buzzed, that they both were, but she nodded. "Yeah. Of course. Anything. I'll do anything you want, Helen."

And then Helen leaned in and put her arms around Annie in an awkward hug. Annie tilted her face, closing the gap, pressing her warm, slightly numb lips against the stretch of pale skin between Helen's chin and ear, against those little lines that undid her. Helen's heart beat a rhythm against Annie's lips.

She'd ignored her feelings the first time she'd met Helen, who was struggling with a colicky baby, desperate to hold on to a job she couldn't afford to lose. She'd ignored them the first time she and Helen went shopping for furniture, when they'd eaten tacos in that hole-in-the-wall Mexican restaurant. She'd ignored them when Helen cried and when she laughed and anytime she sat across from her, their knees brushing, so that Annie could tell her what had gone wrong that day.

She'd ignored her feelings, and she saw Helen ignoring them too, talking to Sal, watching Annie come and go at all hours. She'd ignored the expression of serenity that washed over Helen's face whenever she looked at Annie holding the baby or talking to Ashley or helping Kevin with his subtraction homework.

But Annie couldn't ignore her feelings for Helen anymore.

She pulled back, embarrassed and ashamed, but Helen tightened her grip. "It's okay," she whispered, tucking her face into the muscle between Annie's neck and bony shoulder. She heard Helen suck in her breath, felt her fingers play with the ends of Annie's hair, tugging it gently. She lifted her head, nuzzling Annie's neck.

For a moment, Annie wondered if she was drunker than she originally thought. She felt a little giddy, reckless and impulsive. She put her hand on Helen's thigh. It was warm through her sweats. Digging her fingers in, she heard Helen gasp.

Annie didn't know who started the kiss.

Annie heard footsteps on the stairs. Kelly must have come home. Both doors to the bathroom were open, and the little lamp on the nightstand glowed cheerfully.

"Shh," Annie breathed, yanking her hand out of Helen's shirt and reaching across her to snap off the lamp. Kelly's light came on just as theirs shut off. "Shh," Annie breathed again. Helen nodded against the pillow. Annie pulled the covers up over them.

Kelly dropped something on the floor in her room. Her humming was interrupted by an "oh, shit," and they heard her step through the narrow bathroom door and pull it closed.

Annie breathed out, giggling nervously. They'd been lazy about the whole encounter, actually. Long, slow kisses. Fingers creeping under clothes.

She didn't really know what they were doing, and she didn't want to do anything Helen didn't like. She was nervous and turned on and anxious. She wanted to pick up where they left off, but Helen sighed. "It's very late."

"Yeah," Annie said, disappointed.

"We should sleep."

Just as Annie was about to roll over and fret the rest of the night away, Helen surprised her by reaching for her hand in the bed and pulling it back to her breast.

Annie turned back and kissed her again enthusiastically, relieved. Helen hooked her long leg over Annie's hip, pulled her mouth away, and said, "I need...I...Annie, I want..."

She couldn't manage more than that.

"Shh," Annie said one more time. "You'll have to be quiet."

Helen nodded against her in the dark. "I promise."

Annie had only slept with men since returning from Minsk. It wasn't a conscious decision. It was just easier. Certainly faster and less emotional, like scratching an itch. Like taking aspirin for a headache.

She already knew whatever this was with Helen wasn't that. She stroked Helen's breast, slid her hand down her soft belly. The sweats were loose, easy to infiltrate. Helen held her breath, finally exhaling in little bursts. Sucked in air again as Annie cupped her mound, then pushed inside her panties to test the waters.

Helen moved her hot mouth against Annie's skin, against her neck, against her shoulder where the T-shirt had been pulled aside, then her cheek, her mouth. As much as Annie wanted to drag this out, knowing Lori's little sister was next door made her nervous, so she pressed her fingers into the damp fabric between Helen's legs before moving it aside and coating them with lubrication while Helen gasped into Annie's mouth. Annie moved her fingers up until she had to swallow Helen's moan.

Helen grasped Annie's other hand and held onto it hard before dragging it down between Annie's legs.

"Come with me," Helen whispered.

She made it seem so easy. So natural to rhythmically move both hands, to focus on herself while she focused on Helen, to feel the heat on both sets of fingers—heat so intense, it should burn.

Annie tipped first, used to her own touch, but it was close. Helen gasped and hummed, satisfied.

Annie pulled her hand out of her pants and then tried to gracefully remove her hand from Helen's. She wiped both hands on the sheets, too afraid that Kelly might hear to even think about getting up and washing them.

Helen kissed her one more time and tucked herself against Annie's side.

She listened to Helen's heavy breathing taper out into sleep and then, with some difficulty, drifted off herself.

Annie woke up alone, sprawled across the bed. She usually liked sleeping alone, liked stretching out her limbs. But finding herself alone this morning was not a good sign.

She could tell from the amount of light streaming in through the window that she'd overslept. At least the shower was free, and she wasted no time. She stepped carefully into the old clawfoot tub, feeling unsteady, and drew the white curtain around. She stood under the hot spray for several minutes before realizing she didn't have any of her own toiletry items with her, so she used the Head and Shoulders 2in1 and hoped for the best. Then she lathered up a washcloth and ran it over her body, gently washing between her legs where it still felt a little swollen.

She slipped on the brown corduroy dress she'd brought to wear today. She'd packed it because she thought it made her look her age, but then she plaited her hair down both sides of her head to stave off dry, frizzy waves. The braids contradicted the effort to look more mature.

She went downstairs, barefoot and makeup-free, determined to face the consequences of what she and Helen had done.

CHAPTER 10

Lori was in the kitchen with both girls. Lindsay sat on a stool at the island, and Kimberly was strapped to Lori's chest in a baby sling, fast asleep. Annie felt shy at the domestic scene and hesitated in the doorway.

"Good morning, Mary Sunshine," Lori said when she caught sight of Annie lurking. "How do you feel?"

"Good. Sorry I slept so much. I guess I was tired."

"Well, we all feel like S-H-I-T. You want some coffee?"

"What did she spell?" Lindsay asked. "Something bad?"

"I have no idea," Annie shrugged. "I'm an awful speller."

"Oh," Lindsay said, then asked, "Can you make my hair be braided like yours?"

Lori set a mug of black coffee on the counter in front of Annie and nodded.

"I'd love to. I need two hair ties and a hairbrush."

"Okay!" Lindsay hopped off her stool and ran toward the stairs.

"Where's Louis?" Annie asked. Then trying to sound nonchalant, added, "And Helen?"

"Louis is picking up his parents from the airport. They should be back in half an hour or so. Your beautiful Miss Helen is out in the backyard, picking herbs from the garden for the stuffing."

"You have an herb garden?" Annie asked.

"It's nice to have fresh stuff."

"It's November. How is it even growing?"

"It's in the little greenhouse Louis made for me," she said. "Don't look at me like that, Annie. I went to law school so I wouldn't have to live in squalor well into my thirties."

"Tell Lindsay I've gone to the greenhouse and will return shortly," Annie said, adopting a snooty accent.

"You're just jealous," Lori called after her, and she was right. Lori had picked a lucrative law career, and Annie had chosen to work for the government. Now Lori had a greenhouse with fresh herbs, and Annie lived in a garage.

She made the mistake of going outside barefoot. The northern half of California was colder that what she was used to in LA. It wasn't freezing exactly, but the grass was dewy and the slate path cold as she headed toward the little structure near the back fence. She could just make out Helen's silhouette through the tempered glass.

She pulled the little door open, scraping the bottom along the concrete foundation. Helen looked up at the sound and waved her over.

"Good morning. Come smell this basil. It's growing like crazy."

Annie peered down at what looked to her like a variety of leafy weeds. She couldn't tell one plant from another. Helen broke off a leaf and held it under Annie's nose.

"Smells like pesto."

Helen laughed. "Imagine that."

"So," Annie said, tugging nervously at one of her braids, "did you sleep okay?"

"Yes, though not enough, I think. I got up at six to put the turkey in the oven, and then—well, you know how it goes in the kitchen."

She actually didn't. "You should've woken me up. I would have come down with you."

"We didn't both need to be overtired."

Annie clutched the braid in her hand and then, clearing her throat, let it go and dropped her arm. She wasn't going to survive this day if they didn't at least talk about what had happened.

"Right, but I just thought—"

"Annie!" Lindsay's voice rang out across the yard. "I have my brush!"

Annie looked at Helen and smiled. "I told her I'd braid her hair like mine."

"Smart girl." Helen reached out to touch one of the braids. "Looks good on you."

They walked back to the house together, then went their separate ways. Helen headed back into the kitchen to prepare the meal with Lori, and Annie went into the living room, where she could braid Lindsay's hair during *Sesame Street*. Lindsay hugged Annie when she was finished and then settled onto her lap to watch Big Bird.

It was easier to avoid everything until they sat down to dinner. She played Barbie dolls with Lindsay, who shadowed her all day. She talked football with Louis's father, Dean. She and Kelly ran to the store to pick up a last-minute bag of ice because the ice maker was acting up again—the one less-than-perfect thing in Lori's house she'd encountered so far.

Louis's mother, Betty, spent most of the day in the kitchen with Lori and Helen. Annie listened to them chatting and laughing, and it made her feel weird and out of place, as if she were a child, not an adult. As if she'd be relegated to the children's table with Lindsay at dinnertime.

Dinner was planned for three o'clock, and a few minutes before, she went upstairs to freshen up. She unraveled her braids and pinned her hair back. She instantly looked older; her hair wavy from the braids instead of curly. She was leaning over the sink, applying mascara, when she heard someone else come into the bedroom. She leaned back to see who it was.

Helen had gripped the bottom of her T-shirt to pull it over her head when Annie cleared her throat.

Helen jumped and dropped her hands. "Jesus! I didn't know you were there."

"I didn't mean to scare you," Annie said. "I was trying to avoid that."

"I came up to change. Try to look a little nicer."

"Me too. Or at least my hair."

Helen stood waiting.

"Sorry, I'll just… I'll let you have some privacy." Annie felt strange saying that. Helen seemed to have no reaction to the previous night's activities. Maybe she didn't remember? That seemed unlikely. Or maybe this was just how Helen dealt with emotional upheaval—she shut down.

Annie turned back to the mirror and picked up a tube of brownish-red lipstick, hoping for a more mature look. Helen, now wearing a dark green button-down blouse, stood in the doorway, watching as she dragged the tube across her bottom lip, tapped it along the top, then pressed her lips together.

"I hope you're not upset with me," Helen said, looking down to fiddle with one of her buttons.

"Upset? I'm not upset. I'm…" She was confused. She was wary. She was concerned. "Are you upset?"

"No!" Helen's response was emphatic, but then she shrugged. "Yes? It was a bad idea, but I'm not upset with you."

"Who are you upset with, then?"

"Myself," Helen said. "You brought me with you, introduced me to your friends, and I took advantage—"

"You did not take advantage of me." Annie cut her off. "Let's be really clear here. That isn't what happened."

Helen's eyes widened.

"I think we need to talk about it, but we really don't have time now." The time was early this morning. The time was in the greenhouse. There were pockets of time all day they could have managed it, but now it was too late, dinner was about to be served, and everyone was waiting for them to come downstairs.

"Sorry," Helen said. "You're right. God, you're right."

Annie nodded. "Okay, then." She took a deep breath and smiled nervously. "I know you worked hard today."

"The fun kind of work. Better than sitting around thinking about the kids all day."

Annie wanted to reach out and give her hand a comforting squeeze. Yesterday, she would've done it. Last night, she had. Instead she said, "There's a phone in the office. Why don't you go give them a call before dinner?"

"You don't think Lori would mind?" Helen asked.

"I don't. Not even a little."

She went back downstairs, where Lindsay was running around, swinging her Cabbage Patch doll wildly behind her. Louis and Lori were in the kitchen with Betty, having a strained conversation about why the rolls weren't ready when the rest of the food was. Lori had her hand on her hip, never a good sign. And somehow, Dean had ended up holding Kimberly, who was crying loudly.

"Here," Annie said, walking up to Dean. "You mind if I take her for a spin?"

"I suppose that would be all right," Dean said gratefully and handed Kimberly over with no hesitation.

As soon as she took the baby, Annie realized she had a soggy diaper. She headed toward the playroom at the back of the house, which was where Louis found them. Kimberly, who had momentarily settled down when Annie took her from Dean, was starting to fuss again. Annie was not an expert at changing diapers, and she was not going fast enough.

"Turns out I'm not good at everything," she said when she heard Louis come in. She had managed to pin the diaper without poking the baby, but her onesie was still unsnapped.

He chuckled and stepped in to finish up. "We're about to eat," he said. "Go on. We'll be right there."

Everyone except Helen and Louis had gathered in the formal dining room but still hovered around the table.

Kelly was sitting with Lindsay at the coffee table in the living room. "I volunteered," she said, winking and lifting her glass of wine in salute.

Lori and Louis sat at the ends of the table, his parents sat on one side, and Annie and Helen sat on the other. There were little place cards with names written in gold ink and little copper-foiled cornucopias that matched the large one in the middle. Cream-colored candles had been placed symmetrically around the ornamental container.

It was a little much for Annie's taste, but everyone else gushed. Helen came down the stairs just as Louis returned with Kimberly, and though Helen was all smiles, her eyes were rimmed with red. Louis put the baby in the high chair next to Lori. Once everyone had gathered, they sat.

"I thought we could say grace before we brought out the food," Lori said.

"That'll give the rolls enough time to finish browning," Betty said pointedly.

Lori rolled her eyes, but Louis stepped in. "I'll pray!"

Everyone reached out and grasped hands with the person next to them.

Helen gave Annie's hand a little squeeze.

"What is that?" Helen asked, turning the lamp on and squinting.

"My pager," Annie said, feeling a peculiar mix of guilt and anger. She glanced at the bathroom door, but it was closed. Kelly had moved to an air mattress in Lindsay's room to make space for Louis's parents, so they were more careful about closing the doors to the bathroom.

"What time is it?" Helen reached for her glasses, then answered her own question. "It's after midnight."

"Technically, no longer Thanksgiving," Annie muttered. "Assholes."

"So don't call."

"They have a real habit of ruining my life when I ignore them," Annie said. "I agreed to do this until I graduated, so I have to."

She got up, dug the pager out of her bag, and silenced it, then leaned against the dresser and rubbed her eyes. She wanted to ignore them; she really did. But she didn't want suspicious-looking cars parking outside Helen's house either, watching her or her children, and she didn't want ghosts from her past showing up to make veiled threats. She wasn't scared for her own well-being, but the idea of her parents getting hurt, or Helen and her family, was unbearable. It was the same sick feeling as when she saw Dasha clutching her dead child, and it threatened to overwhelm her now like a heavy stone of guilt and grief in her gut.

"I'll be right back."

But Helen got up and followed her into the office. There was no point in arguing with her, tired and bleary as they both were. Annie flipped on the switch, recoiling when the bright overhead light came on.

"What if they want you there right now?"

"They know where I am," Annie said, picking up the phone on the desk. She tucked it against her shoulder and dialed the number on the pager.

"Hello?"

The same familiar voice.

"Agent Juno, Akron," she said. "You all know good and well that I'm not in Los Angeles right now."

"I do," he said. "The FBI has requested your presence at their San Francisco office."

"Oh," Annie said. "Can they do that?"

"Can they do what?" Helen asked. Annie looked at her, a finger to her lips.

"It appears that they have," he said.

"What time?"

"First thing in the morning," the voice said. "Eight o'clock."

"So why on earth are they paging me now?"

"Oh. Well. That was my idea. I figured the more notice you had, the better. Was I incorrect?"

"No," Anne said. "Thank you. Tell them…tell them I accept. May I have the address, please?"

"You may," he said, sounding relieved.

When she hung up, she said "FBI" before she could think about it. "Uh, I'm not sure how best to play this."

"We'll get up early. We'll explain that I have to get home to my children," Helen said. "I'm happy to shoulder the blame here."

"You don't have to."

"I know you're in a difficult situation, even if you talk about it like it isn't." Helen smiled at her. "Let me help you."

"You'll have to come with me. It might take all day," Annie warned.

"One more day with you?" Helen asked, stepping closer. "I can handle that."

Annie reached out and hooked her pointer finger around Helen's pinky, then Helen leaned in and pressed her lips to Annie's.

A voice in the back of her head told Annie that Helen would pull away again in the morning, that Helen would have regrets, but Annie ignored the voice and melted into the kiss.

The alarm went off at six. Annie got into the shower while Helen packed her bag. Then they switched. Annie put on a pair of jeans and a pink and cream striped sweater, the only change of clothes she had brought. They'd planned to go home later that day anyway.

It was her mistake, one she wouldn't make again. There were no vacations from this job. She needed to always be prepared.

Helen came into the room wrapped in a towel, and Annie stared at her freckled shoulders, her dark hair dripping at the ends, her baby-pink toes and perfect calves and…

"Stop," Helen said, tucking her wet hair behind her ear. "You're looking at me like you're about to jump me."

"Sorry," Annie mumbled, stuffing her dirty clothes into her bag and then struggling to close the zipper.

When she looked up again, Helen was smiling.

Lori was already up, sitting at the island with Kimberly at her breast. She looked up from the newspaper when Annie and Helen came in. "I didn't expect to see anyone so early," Lori said. "Everyone else is still asleep."

"Actually," Annie said, "we have to go."

"What? We were going to do brunch!"

"I know." Annie was genuinely sorry. She was disappointed to have to cut the trip short. "It's a long drive, and Helen wants to get home to her kids. Now you can have real family time."

"You are family," Lori reassured her.

"You and me, maybe," she said. "Me and Betty?"

Lori snorted. "Consider yourself lucky."

Annie smiled. "Thank you for having me. Thank you for taking us in last minute."

"Anytime," Lori said. "Next time, we'll come to you."

Lori made them both travel mugs of coffee to go, telling them she'd get them back when she came to visit, then sent them on their way. She promised to pass along their goodbyes.

"What do you think they'll ask you to do?" Helen asked after they had pulled away. There was little traffic on the freeway. Not surprising, given the hour, given it was the day after Thanksgiving.

"Hard to say," Annie said. "Last time they had me translating tapes. The time before that, it was an interrogation that I helped exactly zero with. I honestly never feel like I help all that much. If they called me at the beginning of an investigation, if I could see everything happen in real time, then maybe I could be more useful. But I always come in at the end, after everything has already been screwed up, and they expect me to fix it."

Helen scoffed. "Of course."

"At best, I can tell them where they went wrong. Sometimes I get them confirmation of something they already expected. Or I might be the only one around who speaks Czech that day."

"You speak Czech?"

"Some," Annie said. "Anyway, if it looks like it's going take forever, you should head home, and I can catch a flight or rent a car."

"I'm not leaving you to the wolves!"

Annie chuckled, and Helen shot her a quizzical look.

To her own knowledge, Annie had killed five people, albeit indirectly. Dasha and little Yeva and the husband too, probably. He could still be alive somewhere, a prisoner of some civil war, but that was at least as bad as dying, if not worse. Wherever he was, two agents had died looking for him.

But five seemed low to Annie. She was smart enough to know that the information she extracted didn't improve foreign infrastructure or provide school lunches to hungry children or medical aid to countries whose citizens were dying of malaria. No, the information she was good at retrieving caused people to die. Sometimes foreign people, sometimes disloyal Americans. Annie was never responsible for worrying about the consequences, only the nuggets of truth that she panned out from the silt of lies.

Helen wouldn't be leaving her to the wolves. Annie was the wolf.

It was a drug bust, a crack cocaine ring. The FBI had partnered with the DEA for the operation, and they called Annie in to triage the interrogations. Each high-level player in the ring had to be ranked and processed and interviewed to get the most useful information out of them. While agents were still rounding everyone up, Annie was in with the thug who'd flipped, getting a sense of who might actually have the information they needed to make an airtight case.

She had to pitch a fit about allowing Helen to stay with her. "She's the LAPD officer in charge of making sure no one else gets slapped with an Internal Affairs audit," Annie had said as Helen quickly dug her badge out of her purse. "If you're working with the DEA and the locals, do you really think it's going to hurt anything to have someone watching our backs too? Keeping everything aboveboard? You want some cop to punch a drug dealer in the face and then everyone gets to walk free because you didn't let one out-of-jurisdiction officer cross your drawbridge?"

They had to wait nearly forty-five minutes while calls were made until they were finally given access to badges. While they waited, Helen leaned over to say, "I'm not exactly in charge—"

"Hush," Annie said. "Close enough."

"She's your responsibility, Weaver," the special agent warned with a scowl as they clipped on their badges. Annie was not threatened in the slightest.

In the elevator on the way up to the interrogation floor, Helen stared at her in awe. "You talk to these guys like…"

"Like I'm not a tiny girl?" Annie finished. "Yeah, I know. It goes a little better when I'm not wearing a pink sweater."

"Does it?" Helen asked. She looked unconvinced.

Annie shrugged. "Nobody ever likes me, and it's unrealistic to expect that they will. Once you let that go, everything else gets easier."

Helen looked at her with admiration and something else. Something that made Annie's spine tingle.

"I'm the first woman you've ever slept with, aren't I?" Annie asked. The words seemed to fly out on their own, and she knew the answer before she even finished the question.

Helen's face went from lust to shock and then shut down completely.

"That wasn't an accusation. You didn't do anything wrong," Annie said.

"I'm married. I have three kids—uh, two kids—and you live in my garage," Helen said. "What we did certainly wasn't right."

Annie never should have brought it up. She couldn't just let things lie.

An agent greeted them at the elevator doors. Annie made herself smile when they locked eyes. "Here we are," she said, sweet as honey. "Where do you want us?"

Annie drove the Jeep back to Los Angeles while Helen slept in the passenger's seat. She tuned the radio, hurrying the knob past the sad song about Eric Clapton's dead kid. On the next station, a woman sang about how she wished she were the other person's lover. She glanced over at Helen. Annie listened to a few bars of that and then moved the dial onward. The next station played Christmas music.

That was safe. It also reminded her that she needed to buy a ticket to Ohio. That she needed to not come home empty-handed. That she needed to think more than five minutes ahead, bouncing from class to class, assignment to assignment, while living in constant, low-grade fear of the sound of her pager.

She'd been wondering what the CIA would do when she went back home for a week, but now she knew. They'd loan her out there too, but her daddy wouldn't be so forgiving about her wanting to borrow the car at two in the morning without explanation. And what would she tell him? That somewhere along the way she'd made a mistake and people had died? Or was the mistake letting herself get recruited in the first place? Was it admitting that she had slept with a woman and then quitting because the possibility of a second catastrophic failure that ended in death was too much to bear? That Frank Clifton was using his power and influence to keep her working? That he was obsessed with her and she didn't know how to escape a situation where it was her word against his?

She looked over at Helen again and realized that had been a mistake too. It hadn't felt like it at the time, and to Annie, it still didn't; but she knew Helen thought it was.

Helen was slumped down with her head against the window. The seat was in the direct sun, the light slanting across her hips as it set. They'd be home soon, in time to get a few hours of sleep and then pick up the kids in the morning.

The carol on the radio ended, and a cheerful DJ started talking loudly, Helen shifted in her seat and opened her eyes. She looked at the clock and then over at Annie.

"I'm sorry that I complicated things for you," Annie said.

Helen blinked at her owlishly from behind her glasses, then sat up, pushing them up onto her head. She rubbed her face with both hands, then sighed and rolled her eyes. "You probably think I'm some sad, old woman having a midlife crisis," she said, laughing at herself. "You probably think I'm pathetic."

"I don't. Actually, I think you're kind of hot."

"Stop," Helen said, though she smiled. "I didn't know you…you know, liked women."

Annie shrugged. "I like men sometimes too."

"And your parents? What do they think about it?"

"Oh no," Annie said with a laugh. "No, no, no. I don't even tell them about the men, let alone the woman. Could you imagine? My dad would have an aneurysm."

"Ah. Just one woman, then."

"Well, two now, I guess. Counting you."

"Counting me? What happened? Never mind. That's really none of my business."

"It's all right."

"Just because *my* ex is an extroverted asshole."

"It just ended badly. That's all. And then I moved away." Annie signaled to move around a big truck and glanced behind her to make sure the lane was clear. They were on the outskirts of LA now.

"You're very smart," Helen said. "Watching you today was quite illuminating. You're really smart and pretty, and I think that… I can see how I let myself…because you're…"

"You don't have to explain anything."

"My issue right now is," Helen continued, "that you're going to actually be my student."

"Shoot. You're right."

"Yeah," Helen said. "We can't…"

"No, I get it. That would be inappropriate."

"Very."

"It's fine," Annie said. "Just a one-time thing, then."

Helen nodded. "Agreed."

Annie eased the car back into the right-hand lane, her hands gripping the wheel.

CHAPTER 11

Kevin did not want to go to the Paula Abdul concert.

Annie had purchased three tickets, figuring Helen would take Ashley and Kevin and she'd stay home with the baby, but now the baby was gone.

"You could take Aunt Sal," Annie suggested.

Ashley looked up at her mother questioningly, but Helen narrowed her eyes. "We can certainly ask her, but I'm finding that very difficult to picture," Helen said.

"What about a friend from…" Annie stopped, seeing Helen shake her head. "Ballet class? Or one of your cousins?"

"That won't work," Ashley said quietly.

"I'm not going!" Kevin called out from the other room, where he was parked in front of the Nintendo.

"Understood, buddy," Helen called back.

"Why can't you come?" Ashley asked Annie.

"I mean," Annie said helplessly, "your brother can't stay home alone."

"I'll ask Sal to watch Kevin," Helen said. "You bought the tickets, Annie. You should come."

"Don't you like Paula Abdul?" Ashley asked, eyes narrowing as if gearing up for a fight. They'd all heard the Paula-Abdul-is-the-greatest-dancer-ever spiel from Ashley more than once, and no one wanted to hear it again.

"Obviously I like Paula Abdul. She's the greatest dancer ever," Annie said.

Ashley looked pleased to hear her speech repeated back to her.

Truthfully, Annie had no strong feelings about Paula Abdul one way or the other, but she and Helen had diligently stayed away from one another ever since the trip to Lori's. It wasn't easy, but the routine of daily life helped. "I have to fly home tomorrow. That's all." Though it wasn't like she had never been tired on a flight before.

"Right," Helen said.

"But it'll be fine." Annie gave in when she saw Ashley push out her lower lip in a pout. "I can sleep on the plane."

"Okay," Helen said. "If you're sure."

"Are you sure you want me? No one else?"

"I'm sure," Ashley said.

"Maybe Sal can come a little early and cut your hair." Helen looked at her daughter with a critical eye. "I can barely see your face under those bangs. Your brother needs a haircut too."

"Sal does hair?" Annie asked.

"Yeah, she owns the hair salon down on Florence," Helen said. "She could do yours too, if you want."

Annie reached up and touched the ragged ends of her hair. "I mean, if she has time, that'd be nice."

Sal arrived with her daughters to keep Kevin occupied while she did haircuts. Annie went out to her room while Helen and Sal set up shop in the kitchen. Ashley came out with wet hair to get Annie for her turn.

"Have you ever been to a concert before?" Ashley asked as they walked back to the house. Annie shivered in the cool air. The sky was overcast with a gray pallor everywhere. She'd sat in front of a space heater, warming her toes while she waited her turn.

"I have," Annie said.

"This is my first one," Ashley admitted.

"Everyone has to start somewhere."

"What was one you went to?"

"Let's see. I think the last one I went to was New Kids On The Block," Annie said.

"Oh, I don't like them very much," Ashley said. "I like girl musicians."

"The nice thing about concerts is, even if they're not good, it's still fun to go with so many other people."

She opened the kitchen door for Ashley, then walked in behind her.

Sal was waiting for her. "Hi, doll! How you doing?"

"I'm just fine." Annie smiled. "How are you, ma'am?"

"Ma'am," Sal said. "Ha!"

"She's not from here," Helen said with a wink.

"Have a seat, kiddo."

Annie sat down, then unclasped the barrette holding the front of her hair back and curled it into her fist. "It's kind of wavy." There was a time when she'd spend the effort to blow it out or iron it flat, but now, between school and work, she didn't have the energy.

"It's beautiful! Don't worry. I've cut lots of curly hair." Sal buried her hands in Annie's locks, peering at her scalp. "Helen, look. Strawberry roots."

In fact, her real color had grown out several inches at this point.

"I told you it was real," Helen said.

"Why would you ever bleach this color? People pay top dollar for this."

"It was a foolish impulse." She'd done it so she could look like someone else. So she could blend into any crowd and be no one.

"The ends are rough," Sal said. "We should cut at least two inches."

"Two?" Annie stood up and turned to look at Sal. "I thought it was just going to be a trim!"

"Sit down," Helen said, laughing. "I'll make sure she doesn't shave you bald."

"Just a trim, though I need my other kit. Helen, stick her head under the sink, would you? I need her wet." She grabbed her keys and walked out the front door.

Annie looked at Helen, who looked at her over the top of her glasses and said, "You heard the lady. Let's get you wet."

"Helen!" Annie said.

Annie had been so good. Had been trying so hard. They both had, she thought. Annie didn't tease, she didn't make jokes. She didn't allude to what had happened, and she tried not to stare. She tried only to think of their encounter, their coupling in the dark, when she was alone so Helen couldn't read her face.

But she was thinking about it now. The heat spread through her like her heart was a pump meant exclusively for desire.

"You have something on under that sweater?" Helen asked. Her voice sounded strained.

"A camisole."

"Good. It's probably better if you take the sweater off."

Just as Annie reached for the bottom of her sweater, they heard a shriek and a thump upstairs.

"They're fine. They're just playing," Helen assured her. Annie pulled the sweater over her head and set it on the counter. Crossed her arms over her chest. Licked her bottom lip nervously.

"Now what?"

"Now lean over, just here." Helen put a dish towel over the edge of the sink and pulled the sprayer out. "I'll try not to make it too hot."

"I don't mind it hot," Annie said, leaning over.

"Yeah. I remember."

She turned on the water and stood behind Annie, gently pressing her hips as she leaned over her to get her hair up from her neck and under the water. Annie pushed back a little.

Helen shifted, leaned against her harder.

Then she turned the water off and stepped back. A towel was wrapped around her shoulders.

"Come on, kiddo." Sal had reappeared. "Have a seat."

"Why are we taking the freeway home when it's only one exit?"

"Because look: puts her right to sleep."

Annie glanced back. Ashley's chin was resting against her chest, her head lolling slightly to one side. She was out.

"I think she had fun."

"She had a blast!" Helen said. "I haven't seen her smile like that since well before Bruce left."

"What about her mom? Did you have fun?"

"I had a nice time," Helen said. "I've had enough Paula Abdul to last a lifetime. But I concede that she is a great dancer."

Annie laughed.

"What time does your flight leave?"

"Seven thirty, I think."

"You need a ride?"

"I was going to take a cab."

"I can take you."

"I don't want you to have to wake up the kids."

"Sal's spending the night," Helen said. "She's probably asleep in my bed right now. She won't mind staying through breakfast."

Annie had thought that maybe, after what happened earlier in the kitchen, she might find herself upstairs again. But with Sal there, that dream faded away.

It was for the best. She'd catch her plane, they'd have some time apart to cool down. When she came back, the quarter would start, and that would be that.

As they pulled into the driveway, Annie said, "Do you need help getting her into the house?"

"She's too big for either of us to carry," Helen said. "She'll wake up enough to get up the stairs and into bed."

"I'm going to go around the side, then. 'Night, Helen."

"Goodnight."

Annie's suitcase was half-packed, but she wasn't in the mood to finish right now. She set down her purse, slipped off her jacket, and kicked the space heater on with her foot. Stepping into the bathroom, she looked at her haircut in the mirror. Sal hadn't cut much off, but it did look better. Shinier and more voluminous. She'd put on more makeup than usual for the concert, and now she regretted it because she'd have to wash the eyeliner and the blush off before she could get into bed.

She was reaching for her washcloth when there was a knock on her door.

Her heart pounded in her chest. "Yeah?" she called out.

Helen let herself in, closed the door behind her, and leaned against it.

"Was there something else?" Annie asked, stepping out of the bathroom.

"We didn't talk about what time you need to leave for the airport," Helen said.

"Six o'clock should be fine, I think. She paused. "It isn't too late to change your mind, you know."

"Oh," Helen sighed "I hope that's true."

She stepped toward Annie, meeting her in the middle of the room, then put her hands on Annie's face and kissed her. Annie, terrified that Helen would freeze up and back out again in the next moment, didn't hesitate. She kissed her back—hard. Helen tasted like mint, like she'd brushed her teeth before coming out to find Annie.

Helen moaned and dropped one hand, fisting the material of Annie's T-shirt until it pulled taut at the collar. Annie reached for the bottom of Helen's blouse, tugged it gently out from her jeans, and rested her hand on Helen's stomach. It was smooth and soft. Helen gasped in surprise at the touch and moaned softly when fingers grazed the underwire of her bra. When Annie unbuttoned Helen's jeans, Helen tore her mouth away, breathing harder, and Annie moved to kiss her cheek, her jaw, her neck, pressing the tip of her tongue against her skin, tasting the salty and the sweet.

Annie slipped her hand down the back of Helen's jeans and, wiggling her fingers under the elastic of panties, grabbed a handful of warm flesh. The night at Lori's had been a surprise, but now that it was happening again, she was going to do things differently. She was going to take her time, make sure she got Helen as naked as the day she was born, leave the light on, and look as much as she touched. Catalog what she had missed the first time around.

Helen kissed her again, pressing hard against Annie until she had to move or fall on the floor. With Helen pressing on her, she backed up to the mattress and sat. Helen stood over her, lips glued to Annie's, and buried her hands in Annie's hair while Annie worked Helen's jeans over her hips. The briefs underneath—lavender with scalloped white elastic—went down partway with the jeans, stopping at the widest part of Helen's hips and giving Annie a tantalizing view of what was yet to be revealed. Helen was breathing hard now, her glasses sliding down to the edge of her nose.

Annie pushed Helen's jeans down her thighs.

"Wait," Helen said between gasps. "I still have my shoes on." Putting her hands on Annie's shoulders, she steadied herself while she toed off one shoe and then the other. When the movement caused her jeans to fall the rest of the way, she stepped out of them, kicking her discarded clothing to one side.

The only sounds were the hum of the space heater and their heavy breathing.

While Annie undid the bottom buttons on Helen's blouse, Helen undid the top until they met in the middle. The shirt hung open, revealing a beige bra and an impossibly pale stomach dusted with freckles. Annie leaned in to kiss just above her belly button, and when she leaned back again, goosebumps had blossomed across the skin. Under Helen's belly button was an almost imperceptible white scar from a C-section.

"I shouldn't have teased you earlier in the kitchen," Helen said, her voice deep from arousal. "That was mean."

"Doesn't seem mean now." Annie hooked her thumbs into Helen's panties and tugging them down.

Helen gasped. "I'm…I'm not…" Helen swallowed. "I'm sorry, Annie. I'm so sorry. I'm sorry about all of this. I tried to stop, but I couldn't."

Helen's hands were shaking as they moved up to cradle the back of Annie's head.

Annie stroked her hand over the curve of Helen's hip. "I'm not sorry."

Helen threw her head back and groaned. Annie pressed her thumb against Helen's slippery clitoris, exploring with her fingers until Helen lifted one leg and put her foot up on the mattress. Annie glided a finger in and out a few times, then a few moments later, eased in a second finger.

Helen clenched her eyes shut. Her face was flushed, her chest red and splotchy. Annie wanted to lay her down, to reach around her and unhook her bra and release those beautiful breasts, but it seemed cruel to stop, so she pressed her fingers deeper, curving them, searching. When she found what she was looking for, Helen gasped out, "Oh, my God."

"Mmm," Annie hummed. "That's a good sign."

Helen emitted a short laugh, but it turned into a groan, and she dug her nails into Annie's shoulder, thrusting harder against her hand. Annie moved her thumb against Helen's clitoris, resting her head against Helen's torso. All she could smell was sex, all she could feel was Helen, and all she could hear were the wet strokes of her fingers moving inside Helen.

A grunt escaped her that Helen might have meant as a warning just before there was a flutter around Annie's fingers and Helen came with a cry, her body pitching forward to curl over Annie. The weight of her pushed Annie back onto the narrow mattress with her head nearly hanging off the other side as Helen shuddered on top of her. Annie eased her hands away, wrapping them around Helen, stroking her back with one sticky hand where her shirt was damp with sweat.

It was a risk, letting Helen go first. Last time she'd gotten off by her own hand, Helen's pleasure had been enough to send her flying, but if it happened again, it would create a pattern of Helen taking what she wanted and leaving Annie to mop up.

Helen rolled off Annie, onto her back, and pushed the hair off her sweaty forehead, her eyes still closed. She licked her lips, then opened her eyes slowly, like a lizard on a rock.

"Still sorry?" Annie asked softly.

Helen looked at her and chuckled. "Not very, anyway."

"Good," Annie said. She felt a little strange with Helen basking in afterglow and herself still fully clothed. She still had her shoes on too.

"I thought maybe I was going crazy," Helen whispered. "Have you ever gotten so turned on that you couldn't function?" She didn't wait for an answer. "I saw you today in the kitchen, and I just… And then we spent the whole day together, and it was too much for me. I couldn't… I only had to make it one more day before you left for Christmas, and I couldn't do it."

She pushed herself up on an elbow. Her blouse slipped off her shoulder, framing the curve of one breast with the sheer fabric.

Annie shifted, pressing her thighs close together, feeling pleasure from the pressure. She had to move. She reached down and pulled her shirt over her head, shaking out her hair and sucking her bottom lip between her teeth.

Helen got the same look on her face that she'd had at the kitchen sink, the same look as when she'd let herself in and leaned back against the door to ask her made-up question about the airport. It was the face she made when she was thinking about kissing Annie.

It was Annie's favorite expression.

As long as they were pressed together as close as possible, chest to chest, thigh to thigh, they could fit on Annie's twin bed. She'd thrown a sheer pink scarf over the top of the lamp, and now everything was bathed in a rosy light.

Annie had dozed off briefly, and Helen had her head propped up on her hand, watching her sleep.

"Hey, kid," she said. "You think you got one more in you?"

"One more what?"

Helen winked, pushed up off her side, and scooted down to the middle of the bed.

"You don't have to do that," Annie said, though she was already parting her knees to make space.

"I've been practicing."

Annie propped herself up on her elbows and asked incredulously, "On who?"

"In my mind," Helen clarified. "I've been thinking about how I would do it. What I like and how I'd share that with someone else."

She positioned her face and propped one of Annie's legs over her shoulder. "Is it strange I think you're beautiful down here?"

Annie felt her face grow warm. She thought it was strange that anyone thought any part of her beautiful.

"Don't take it personally if I can't," Annie warned. "It's not you. The second time doesn't always go as easy."

"Don't fail me before I've even started," Helen said. "I'm the professor. I do the grading here." She leaned in, kissing up one thigh and down the other, then zeroed in between Annie's legs and licked, tentatively at first, then more boldly. She slid a hand up to part Annie's lips to better penetrate her with her tongue, then circled her clit with her mouth, sucking lightly.

Annie squirmed.

"You like that," Helen said. "You got wetter."

"Are you going to go down on me or are you going to narrate?"

"I can do both."

The first orgasm had taken Annie by surprise, though she'd been so turned on, it shouldn't have. She had been sitting with her legs crisscrossed, Helen's fingers inside of her and Helen's mouth on hers. She'd used her own hand as a guide—a little to the left, a little faster. When she finally relinquished control, she came gently, like the tide lapping at the shore. Soft waves, quiet gasps.

But now she was at the mercy of Helen's mouth. Annie clutched at the sheets, trying not to grab Helen's head and thrust against it. Whatever Helen had meant by practicing—endlessly fantasizing or *whatever*—it was working. Helen wasn't teasing or trying to drag it out. Her tongue worked fast and hard, and Annie moaned loudly; she couldn't help it.

She threw one arm over her head, looking for something to grasp, finding the bedpost and wrapping her fingers around it. With her other hand, she reached for Helen's head, curling her fingers into that thick hair, tugging it until Helen moved her mouth to comply.

Just a little bit more…just a little…

Annie cried out as the force of her orgasm thrust her hips upward.

When she finally opened her eyes, Helen was sitting up on her legs, watching.

"All right?" she asked.

"A-plus."

Helen had left Annie to sleep a few hours. When Annie finally forced herself to get up, it was still dark out. She was sticky between her legs and felt clammy from sweating. She smelled like sex.

As the shower heated up, she looked in the mirror. Her hair was a tangled mess, and there was a red line on her clavicle, a dark splotch on her neck, a red patch between her breasts. A map of where Helen had been.

She showered, washed her hair, and shaved under her arms while her conditioner set. She took a few extra minutes to blow-dry her hair, brushing it out to straighten it as she went. She pulled on a pair of black slacks and a dark pink sweater, then slipped on her ballet flats. She transferred what she had already packed into a suitcase into a smaller duffel bag that would be better for traveling. She had plenty of stuff at home, so she didn't need to pack a lot of clothes or toiletries, just some underwear, an extra pair of shoes, one nice outfit, and her makeup. She had to take some books; she had too much studying to do for the next quarter's classes to leave it all behind. Helen hadn't lied: her midterm grades were hanging on the refrigerator next to Ashley's spelling test and a dinosaur drawing Kevin had made.

That was her: just one of the kids.

Coffee was ready when she got to the house. She poured herself a cup, then double-checked that she had her driver's license—she'd finally gotten a California one—and her plane tickets. She had a layover in Salt Lake City. She was just pulling her keys out of her purse when she heard footsteps on the stairs.

"Good morning." Helen leaned against the kitchen doorframe.

"Yeah." Annie felt stupid that she couldn't come up with something more clever. "Um, I'm going to leave you my car key in case you need to move my car for some reason."

"I promise not to let Kevin take it for a joyride."

"Much appreciated," Annie said. "You know, you don't have to do this."

"I'm taking you. And then Sal and the kids and I are going to get a Christmas tree."

"I'm sorry I won't get to see it."

"We'll leave it up until you come home," Helen promised. "Which is?"

"December 29. Not till late, though."

"Call from the airport if you need a ride," Helen said. "Is that your only bag?"

"I'm just going home. I don't need much." She slung the duffle over her shoulder and picked up her old purse. The strap was really fraying now. Her mom would sigh when she saw it, embarrassed for her.

"You ready, then?" Helen asked. She was dressed in jeans and an old gray sweatshirt. Her hair was damp and her face scrubbed. She looked beautiful and relaxed. "I'm sorry you didn't get much sleep."

"I'm not."

Helen smile widened. "Let's go."

It was only about a thirty-minute drive to the airport in light traffic, but it was too early, and they were both too tired to really talk about what had happened between them, which was just as well.

"What airline?"

"Delta."

The airport was busy with Christmas travelers. Helen pulled up to the curb just as another car left. "I could park. Wait with you at the gate for a little while?"

"That's okay. You have a tree to get," Annie said. "Um, thanks. For the ride and for…the other stuff."

Helen snorted. "Yeah, I liked the other stuff too."

Annie rolled her eyes, trying not to let her own embarrassment immobilize her. A car behind them honked, and she opened her door.

"It's good that we got it out of our systems," Helen said.

That felt like a kick to the ribs, and Annie tried not to flinch.

"Merry Christmas, Helen."

"Travel safe, honey," she said, reaching out and squeezing her forearm.

Annie closed the car door, being careful not to slam it. She forced herself not to look back.

She spent the first flight trying not to think about the night before but failed miserably. She could still feel Helen's mouth on her, drumming up echoes of that spectacular orgasm. She shifted in her seat. And then she felt stupid because Helen was merely getting something out of her system and Annie, conveniently living in her garage, was just the girl she was doing it with. The midlife crisis. The rebound. The student.

She got off the plane in Salt Lake City, famished and feeling the first throbs of a headache. She bought a muffin and chocolate milk at a newsstand, then found the monitors showing arrivals and departures. She pulled out the yellow envelope that had been delivered to her mailbox at school. She looked up at the flights leaving: Albuquerque, Atlanta, Boston, Charlotte, Cincinnati, Cleveland.

Two monitors over gave her what she was looking for: San Francisco, Toronto, Washington. She checked her ticket and then looked back up at the screen to make sure the flight numbers matched. She arrived at her gate with just enough time to eat her muffin, drink her milk, and then pee before boarding.

She slept a little on the plane, though it wasn't restful. The plane was packed and noisy.

When she finally landed at Dulles, she was exhausted. She waved down a taxi and gave the driver the name of the airport hotel provided in the envelope. She asked the driver for a card to get a ride in the morning.

She had arranged for a late check-in, and the desk clerk was waiting for her. He gave her a room key on a bright orange keychain. "There's no room service, but the restaurant over there is open for another hour and a half," he said.

She ordered a hamburger, fries, and a slice of chocolate cake and took the food to her room. She ate sitting on the bed, then called her mom.

"I'm good," she said. "Just packing up. Can't wait to see you. I'm sorry I get in so late tomorrow."

"It's all right. We're just happy you're coming home! Your father will pick you up, no matter the hour."

The envelope contained the plane ticket, including the one that took her back west to Ohio, the hotel information, an address, and a time. Nothing else. But she knew the address well enough. She used to work there, after all.

She didn't think she'd sleep, but she drifted off easily, tired from traveling and the lack of sleep the night before. When she first got into bed, she thought about calling Helen but decided against it. She knew better, dumb as she was. At least she was smart enough to know she was dumb.

CHAPTER 12

She checked out of her room and called the taxi the next morning, but they sent a different driver than the one from the previous night. And even though she told them over the phone where she wanted to go, the driver still grumbled about having to drive anywhere so early, as though he were doing her a favor. It would be a twenty-minute drive, half an hour if they hit traffic, so she ignored the complaining, digging deep for her manners.

She held her duffle bag on her lap, clenching the purse strap in her hand.

The taxi driver smoked, leaving the window cracked, so it was freezing in the back seat, and she snugged deeper into her jacket. Washington DC in December seemed much colder than she remembered it. How quickly she'd acclimated to the mild California climate despite having spent several years in DC and then in Eastern Europe, where the cold burrowed so deep that Annie had slept in a ski cap and gloves.

The radio was tuned to the news. The broadcaster was talking about the upcoming inauguration, making fun of the Clintons—his accent, his wife's stiff demeanor, their preteen daughter's looks. Annie felt bad for the girl, having to live in the national spotlight at the most awkward time of her life.

Annie cleared her throat and told the driver where to turn.

"Ah," the man said in a heavy Middle Eastern accent. "I did not know they let little girls be spies!" He laughed at his own joke.

"Here is close enough," Annie said and reached into her purse to pull out the exact fare. She handed him the money through the center window. "Next time if you want a tip, maybe don't call women little girls."

She closed the door on his swearing and walked toward the security gate that was barely noticeable behind a copse of trees.

It took time to get through security. The guard searched her duffle thoroughly, pawing through her bras, her stick of deodorant, and even flipping through the pages of her books before issuing her a visitor's badge and directing her to the main building where they were waiting for her.

It was a cold walk, the wind cutting right through her, and she regretted not renting a car for the day. She hurried to get to the main building, then waited for someone to show up and take her to the meeting room. She was hurried down the hall and then waited for nearly forty-five minutes for someone to actually appear. After all of the hurry up and wait, Frank Clifton's secretary finally arrived to take her to his office three floors up. She barely looked at Annie, even though she had known her since she was twenty-three.

"Thanks, Shirley," he told the woman with a fake warm smile. "We'll be busy for at least the next hour."

"I'll hold your calls, Director Clifton," she said and closed the office door.

Frank's smile for her was much more menacing as she stood awkwardly holding all of her things. "Well, now," he said. "Nice to see you still come when called."

It was work to stay neutral. Talking back was her natural response, but she didn't give him the pleasure. Didn't even let her distaste for him cross her face. She refused to show him the anger she felt at her situation, the guilt over what had led her here, or the shame of being treated as an outsider in a place she had once belonged.

"Sit, sit," he urged.

She set her duffle down and sat across from his desk, leaning back just a little. Comfortable but not relaxed. She was hungry and tired and had planned her day poorly. She could see the big picture—see all the pieces at once and how they fit—and she could live in the moment. But the short-term planning always tripped her up—what clothes to pack for a week, how to make things last until they could be replenished, making sure she ate before a meeting. She'd been so focused on her nerves that she didn't think about how she would feel when she got here.

"I could use some coffee." Annie surrendered to her need for fuel.

"Let's take a walk," Frank said.

The building had a huge cafeteria with burgers and fries, sandwiches, pizza, Chinese food, Mexican, pho. But it was too early for lunch, and so they went to the coffee cart. She allowed Frank to pay only because purchasing anything required a company badge to complete the transaction. She threw a blueberry muffin on the counter as he pulled out his wallet. He laughed. "Of course."

They went out to a courtyard and sat on a bench in the cold. She ate her muffin and sipped her hot coffee. The brew was achingly familiar, like how church coffee always tastes the same—watered down, made in bulk by little old ladies.

She thought about her old desk and her stateside colleagues. Most of them would be here still. She'd already seen more than one familiar face that wouldn't meet her eye. They knew she'd washed out of the Company and quit. The way no one would look at her told her that Clifton's little project was still under the radar. Surely, they couldn't keep this up forever. She was costing his department a lot of money.

"I have to say, you've held up your end of our bargain quite well," he said. "I expected less, and for that I apologize. Your flaws have never been in your work, Miss Weaver."

"You and my grandma should have backhanded compliment competitions." She balled up the paper from the muffin.

"Belinda Marie Weaver, 71 Beaverwood Lane, Yellow Springs, Ohio," Frank recited cheerfully. "Currently retired. Mother to Benjamin, Kenneth, and Leighanne. Has a dog named Magnolia."

Annie stared at him, horrified.

"I believe they call her Maggie," he added.

"Yeah."

"You see, there isn't anything I don't know about you, and my memory is just as remarkable as yours. I know your file. I keep you right in here," he said, tapping his temple. "I know you as well as you know yourself, and that's why I know that eventually you're going to come back to me."

"You haven't given me a lot of wiggle room," she pointed out. "You sabotaged my housing. You implied that you'd derail any alternate career prospects. You threatened to turn me in for treason."

"Nonsense," he said. "You have an entire country of wiggle room. I don't tell you how to help or how to run the cases they call you in for. All we ask is that you show up."

She drank her coffee; it was cool now.

"You've built a good reputation out there, you know," he said. "So good, in fact, that the funds we set aside to pay you with have already been depleted."

There it was. The money.

"Is that why you called me out here? To fire me while I freeze my ass off?"

"I've never understood why someone would name a pet something and then call them something entirely different. Why not just name her Maggie from the start?"

Annie stared at him.

"Let's go back inside," he said.

They walked back to his office in silence. There was no way he was going to cut her loose. No, he wanted to alter their arrangement somehow. She just hoped she could live with the change.

Shirley didn't look up as they walked past her desk into Frank's office and resumed their seats, Frank behind his desk and Annie on the other side. Frank reached into a drawer, pulled something out, and tossed it onto the desk.

A pager.

"We'd like your old one, please," he said.

"What's the difference?" she asked, rummaging in her bag.

"This one is better."

She set the old one on the edge of his desk so he'd have to lean over to reach it. She put the new one in her purse without looking at it.

"So, how am I getting paid when this thing goes off?"

"There's been some concern about what you're doing on the CIA's dime, so I've arranged a different source of funding. It's fine when you translate tapes or help find missing little girls. It's the interrogations that are causing concern."

"You've never been interested in legalities before," she said. She highly doubted he was discussing her jobs with his superiors.

"You'll be paid a salary, and your tuition will be paid for the foreseeable future."

"You want to pay for my school?" she asked, incredulous. There had to be a catch.

"I honestly didn't think you'd last the quarter, let alone do so well. So we've decided that a master's in criminology would be a good thing for the FBI's new liaison to have."

"FBI?" she squawked. Her cool exterior was crumbling under the weight of what he was telling her.

"Only technically," he said. "We give them money from whatever funding source we choose, and they pay you through their books."

"Launder me through them, you mean."

"It's a situation where everyone's happy."

"Everyone except me!"

"You'll be doing the same thing but with a free ride through school and a steady income," he said. "Of course, you'll have to work at least twenty-five hours a week, so maybe don't take more than two classes, hmm?"

"No, absolutely not," she said. "It'll take me forever to graduate."

"Miss Weaver, I have made a very generous offer." His tone turned chilly. "It's obvious you are filling a need, and this is the least you can do for your country."

She looked down into her lap. "My country." She liked it a lot better before she saw the inner workings up close.

"Let me remind you what a fragile position you're in. You have nothing to bargain with. You have no leverage. You cannot get by without me. You will not find a better job, not at another government agency, not at a Neiman Marcus, not even flipping burgers at McDonald's. No bank will give you a loan, no school will accept your transfer."

He never raised his voice, but the impact of his words set her back. He might as well have picked up the coffee mug on his desk and smashed it down again.

"And need I remind you that you have people you care about? Your family. Your friend in San Rafael and her young children." He leaned in. "What happened to you in Belarus, well, one could write that off as undercover work. You aren't the first agent to seduce someone's wife. But two is a pattern, Miss Weaver. What you do affects not only you but all the women you let between your legs. Do you want to ruin Helen's life as well as your own? Kevin and Ashley's?" His lip curled in disgust. "Do you want the world to know what you are?"

"What's that?"

"A dyke and a quitter," he said softly. "A tragic combination for someone with so much promise."

"Enough." She gripped the arms of the chair until her knuckles were white. "You've made your point."

"My point, Annie, is that you crossed a line in Minsk, and I'm the only one who can help you now. This could have been so much easier." He got up and walked around his desk, stopping to rest a hand heavily on her shoulder. "Together we can make this right."

She shrugged his hand off and stood up to face him. "I did what I thought would give me the best chance to get useful information. It didn't work. The cleanest fix was to leave the Company."

He sighed. "And so we find ourself at this impasse. I will make it plain for you: if you'd like your private life to remain private, I suggest you take this deal."

She couldn't imagine bringing Helen home to meet her parents. Her grandparents. The LAPD already treated her like garbage, calling her a bitch behind her back. The last thing she needed was rumors that she was a lesbian.

Annie nodded. "Fine."

"Good. We'll put this ugly talk behind us, then. You, young lady, have a plane to catch! And when you return to Los Angeles, we'll make the adjustments to your schedule."

"After my finals, I hope," she said.

"I told you I wouldn't interfere with your classes, and I am a man of my word," he said. "I like what you're learning out there, Annie. It's useful. It's practical."

"How so?"

"There's more to interrogations than gathering information and analyzing it to get to the truth. You're getting to see it in action. What you find saves lives. And we'll be saving lives together for many years to come."

She picked up her duffel and her purse. "I need a ride back to the airport," she said.

"Very well. Shirley will have security at the gates call you a cab." As she opened his office door, he added, "See you around, FBI Agent Weaver."

Shirley looked at her and reached for the phone.

She called Helen from the airport. She hadn't intended to, but she had so much time to kill before her flight after she'd gotten something to eat. She'd bought a magazine and flipped through every page. Bought a fresh book of crossword puzzles and filled out three before she wandered to a pay phone and dropped in a quarter.

It rang three times before Helen answered with an out-of-breath "hello." Christmas music played in the background.

"Hi," she said. "It's Annie."

"Oh!" she said. "You got home safely!"

"Yeah, I did."

After a boarding announcement, Helen asked, "Where are you?"

"I'm at the airport again. My brother's flight is late coming in."

"I'm glad you phoned. The school called. They said they'll have a room ready for you by the first of the year. They left a number. You got a pen?"

A reward for doing Frank's bidding, no doubt.

"Oh," she said. "Hang on." She pulled her pen out from the book of crosswords and flipped the book over. "Go on." She jotted it down on the glossy back cover, the ink already smudging.

"They said they wanted you to return their call. I didn't feel like it was my place to tell them you didn't want it."

"Right."

"You don't, right?" Helen asked softly. "I know things were up in the air when we talked about it, but you really do fit in here, and the kids like you. So if you want to stay, please stay, Annie."

"You don't think it's a bad idea?"

"It's certainly your choice," Helen said. "But we want you to stay."

"I'll call them back after Christmas. No one will be in the office now anyway."

"Okay. Hey, while I've got you, why don't you give me the number of your parents' house? In case we need to get ahold of you."

"Sure. But I wouldn't call today. We're all here waiting on Danny."

"Of course. I should let you get back to your family. Why don't you call me when you get back home? The kids'll be in bed by then."

"Yeah," Annie said. "I can do that."

"Talk to you later."

"Bye." Annie hung up the phone and picked it up again. Dropped in another quarter and punched in the number. "Mom? Yeah, it's me. My flight is just about to board. It should be on time. Dad will be there to meet me?"

"Of course," her mom said. "Fly safe."

Her flight wouldn't leave for another two hours, but she settled in at the gate with a textbook, her puzzles, and Helen's voice looping in her head, asking her to stay.

Her parents' house still felt like home. Her family had moved a lot while she was growing up, due to her father's military career, finally staying in one place when she was fourteen. It had been a luxury to go to the same high school for four years.

Danny had already arrived at the house when her father parked in the driveway after picking her up. Only family was staying at the house this year: her parents, Danny and his wife Megan, and their daughter, Jenny. Her niece was four, just like Lori's daughter Lindsay. They were going to stay until Christmas Eve, then head to Megan's family for Christmas Day. Patty was disappointed, but the one year the two families had tried to combine Christmas while Annie was overseas, it was reportedly a disaster, and no one really liked Danny's in-laws enough to try again.

The extended family would arrive early on Christmas Day. Grandparents and aunts and uncles and their children would be crammed into the house. Christmas had always been a big affair. Not Annie's favorite holiday—that title went to Halloween while she was young enough to go trick-or-treating, then switched to any major holiday that paid her to stay home before her work took her overseas again.

There was candy all over her parents' house, and she grabbed a handful of chocolates from a bowl by the door as she walked in.

"That all you brought?" her mom asked. Patty was wearing her red flannel nightgown with a white collar.

"All my warm clothes are here," she said.

"Well, don't fill up on sweets," she said, eying the red- and green-foiled candies in Annie's hand. "I saved you some supper."

"I won't," she promised, though she ate four as soon as she got upstairs. The rest she squirreled away in her nightstand. She'd unpack later.

She looked around the small bedroom. Nothing had changed. Danny's room, when he moved out, had become her father's study, but hers had the same twin bed, same ruffled curtains, same books on the shelves. Her old Nancy Drew books, *Eloise,* and *Harry the Dirty Dog.*

Her father and everyone else had gone to bed, but her mom sat with her while she ate.

"How come you've never changed my room?" Annie asked between bites.

"You want to redecorate?" Patty asked. "I don't think we have time this trip, but if you came home for the summer…"

"No," she said. "That's not… I mean, why haven't you made it a guest room or a sewing room or a home gym or something? Danny had barely left before Dad was measuring for a desk."

"Boys leave, and you know you'll never get them back." Patty waved a hand in the air. "We knew that when he married Meg so young. But you're my girl, Anabelle. Girls should always know they have a home to come back to."

"Well, that's sweet, but I don't think it's necessary," Annie said. "You could put a bigger bed in there, have more guests."

"What if you want to come back again someday and you don't feel like you have a room of your own?"

"I don't need the same things I had at sixteen to recognize this as my home, Mom," she said with a laugh.

"I like to think I'll get you back one day, honey." She reached over and patting Annie's hand. "You're a hard one to let go. Anyway, you came back once before!"

First Frank Clifton, then Helen telling her to stay. Now her own mother. Annie felt like she was being pulled in too many directions, and she wondered what it would feel like if she could do exactly as she pleased. Where would she go? Who would she choose if there were no strings attached? California was supposed to be that place for her, but it seemed like she could never get far enough away.

She cleaned her plate, put it in the dishwasher, kissed her mother, and went to bed.

On Christmas Eve, her dad let her take his car to the mall. She'd been far too busy to buy gifts before she left.

Although the mall was a madhouse, the worst place to be on Christmas Eve, she managed to buy her father a sweater, her mother a silk scarf, something for Danny, and some toys for the kids. She was climbing the stairs to the third floor of the parking garage with her shopping bags when an unfamiliar sound began emanating from her purse.

She dug out the new pager and chastised it. "You have to be *kidding* me," she said. "Here?"

She put her purchases in the trunk and disappointed a harried woman waiting with two kids in the car for the parking spot. Annie mouthed an apology, but the woman gunned her engine and peeled out.

She found a pay phone just inside the side entry, pulled a quarter out of her pocket, and called the number.

"Agent Juno, Akron," she said.

"Merry Christmas to you too," said the familiar voice.

"Do you know where I am right now? I can tell you it's nowhere near Los Angeles."

"I do know where you are," he said. "I don't actually have a job for you."

"Oh," she said. "So you're calling just to see if I'd answer?"

"I couldn't possibly say," he replied cheerfully. "But you have answered, despite your location, and I'll pass that along to my superiors. Happy holidays, Anabelle Weaver."

"And to you, sir."

She hung up and headed home.

After so many months abroad, finding ways to disappear without a trace—covering her tracks, burning scraps of paper and maps and instructions, finding notes taped under park benches, fishing brown paper bags out of public garbage cans, and shaking out her hair as she pulled off a wig—the pager felt strange. It was a permanent fixture, and carrying it around felt counterintuitive, even after so many months. She knew she'd passed their test and that they probably wouldn't call her again until she was back in Los Angeles, but she still felt like she had to check it every hour.

Every time she told herself she was feeling paranoid, she remembered the two cars that had followed her across the country. No doubt Frank Clifton wanted to know how long before it took her to realize she was being followed and how she would react. Now that she had the pager, he didn't need to tail her; she suspected it had a tracking device.

On Christmas morning, Annie woke up with cramps and blood. She found an old box of menstrual pads in her parents' bathroom and took it to her room. After she cleaned herself up, she crawled back into bed. She had barely settled back in before there was a sharp knock on the door.

"Anabelle," her mother said. "It's Christmas, and your grandmas are here."

The living room was packed with relatives by the time she showered and made it downstairs. She tolerated the hugs as much she could, then picked up her cousin Stephanie to use as a shield against any more contact. She was nearly too old to be lifted, but she wrapped her long legs around Annie just the same, clinging to her for protection against the crush of people so early in the morning. Stephanie hung on to her until she saw her own mother again, then struggled to get down.

Patty and Billie, her maternal grandmother, were preparing breakfast. Feeling guilty that she hadn't gotten up earlier to peel potatoes and crack eggs, she fell in line, picking up a knife and helping Billie slice a pile of oranges into wedges. Billie kissed her cheek and said, "You look flushed, Anabelle."

"I'm just warm."

"You look puffy too."

"Thanks," she said dryly.

Her mother shot her a warning look.

"You been eating too much sugar?" Billie asked.

"No, Grandma," Annie said. "It's just my personal time of the month. That's all."

Her mother chimed in. "And she eats too much sugar."

"You two stop picking on her!"

The voice came from her other grandmother, Belinda, who was in her father's reading nook just off the kitchen, partially obscured by a tabletop Christmas tree. Belinda was never much for crowds.

"How's Maggie?" Annie asked. She had always been closer to her paternal grandmother.

"She's staying with the neighbors, who feed her table scraps, so she's probably happy that I'm away," Belinda said.

Annie pulled another orange toward her.

"Take the little stickers off first," her mother said.

"I know, Mom," she replied, struggling to control her agitation. Maybe small talk with her cousins and bear hugs from her uncles would have been better than this after all.

By the time she made it through the pile of oranges, the ragged skin on her nail beds, the dry areas around her knuckles, and the papercut she had on the inside of her finger stung from the acid. She stuck the finger with the papercut into her mouth to soothe it.

"Carry that out to the table, Anabelle," Billie said, waving a spatula at the bowl of orange wedges. "It's almost time to eat."

"Yes, ma'am."

The afternoon after Christmas, her mom called up the stairs.

"There's a gentleman on the phone for you!"

The gentleman turned out to be a former friend from her high school days, Casey Pickett. His mother was church friends with her mom. He'd gone to a different high school, but growing up, they'd seen each other at church once a week. When they got a little older, they went out a few times to football games and dances. She went with him to his junior prom; he went with her to her senior prom. They'd never officially been boyfriend and girlfriend, but she liked Casey; he always made her laugh.

They'd spent a lot of time parking in his daddy's pickup truck, getting as close to the cliff as they could without taking the plunge, but she'd been a good girl at that age. Sort of.

She picked up the phone. "Hello?"

"Annie Weaver." Casey's deep voice was still familiar. "Will you go to the dance with me?"

She laughed. "No, sir," she said. "I'm too old for that."

"Oh," he said, feigning disappointment. "How about dinner and a movie?"

"Well, that sounds fine."

He picked her up at six thirty, which felt a little early for dinner—she was still on California time—but he took her to a decent restaurant.

"Mel Gibson frozen in time, Steve Martin as a con man, or a paralyzed soap opera star in the bayou?" he asked as they stood outside the cinema box office, studying the movie times.

"Frozen Mel Gibson, obviously."

Casey held her hand during the movie, and she let him, pushing Helen out of her thoughts. After the movie, they drove to where they used to park. Casey leaned in to kiss her, and she let him, trying not to think about Helen's lips and tongue.

They didn't go past a little light necking—it was, after all, her time of the month—but she wondered if she would have let him go all the way. Helen had used Annie to get something out of her system. Annie could use people too. Could be spiteful. Could be casual.

Casey dropped her off at home, kissed her cheek at the door, and said, "It was good to see you, Annie."

"Likewise," she said and watched him walk back to his car.

Her parents were still up. She told her mom she'd had a nice time, then kissed her daddy's cheek. Climbed the stairs, washed up, and crawled into bed, trying so hard not to think about Helen that she'd circled right back to thinking about nothing else.

Here she was, in her old bedroom in her parents' house, and she was lonely and homesick. She went on a date with a lovely young man who still doted on her, wanting nothing more than to make her happy, and all she could do was compare him to her landlord.

She turned and pressed her face into her pillow.

CHAPTER 13

Patty sat in Annie's desk chair and watched her pack.

"You sure I can borrow this little suitcase?" Annie asked from inside the closet.

"You can have it, honey," her mom said. "We got a new set just last year, remember?"

"Okay. Thank you again, then." She started pulling work clothes off the hangers, items that she'd left behind when moving. Blouses, skirts, slacks. She packed them loosely enough to make her mother wince. Annie ignored it. If her mom wanted to take over packing, she would gladly step back and eat the rest of the chocolate in her nightstand.

"Can I ask you a question?"

Now it was Annie's turn to wince. Up until now, there'd been so many people around that she'd been able to dodge her mother's direct queries, but it seemed her time was up.

"Of course."

"Are you happy out there?"

That was not the question Annie was expecting, and she froze, her hands hovering over the suitcase.

"As happy as I could be, I suspect," she said. "I miss you and Daddy, though."

"You just seem"—Patty shook her head a little—"spread thin, I suppose."

Annie shrugged one shoulder. Tucked her hair behind her ear.

"Why do you need all those work clothes, anyway?" her mother continued. "Are you working again?"

"Part-time," Annie said.

"Doing what?"

"You know, helping out here and there."

"Helping out who, honey?"

"The police," Annie said. "The FBI and sometimes the sheriff."

"Really?" Patty seemed genuinely surprised. Not the faux kind of surprise where she put her hand to her chest even though she clearly knew all along.

"Yeah." It felt strangely good to be telling the truth. An unfamiliar feeling, a rare, small pleasure. "Turns out there aren't so many people who can do what I do, so they use me when they can."

"Isn't that clever," Patty said, "setting all that up."

"It took me no effort at all." Annie zipped the suitcase closed.

Her parents had given her a beautiful black leather tote for Christmas, so she felt like a new woman as she walked through LAX with a proper suitcase and a purse that wasn't fraying right off her shoulder. She called Helen from Salt Lake City to remind her that she was perfectly capable of taking a taxi home, that it was a short distance, that it wouldn't even cost her that much, but Helen just said, "We'll be there."

She next called the university housing office. No one answered. They probably didn't staff the place between Christmas and New Year's, and it was just as well that she didn't have to talk to a real person. She left a message that she was declining their offer of a room and felt only a little silly after she'd pitched a fit when she arrived at the UCLA campus. But it didn't matter, and she refused to dwell on it.

She fidgeted through the last leg of her flight, which seemed interminable, and by the time she landed in California, it was dark and felt late though it was only dinnertime.

The flight had arrived on time, so hopefully Helen would be waiting. She was grateful for the ride but exhausted. She wanted to get back to her own bed, her denim jacket, her good candy stash, the rest of her makeup. Her privacy and solitude.

She expected to find Helen parked at the curb in her red Jeep, but when she made it to baggage claim, she found Kevin holding a cardboard sign with her name scrawled in red and green marker. Then she saw Ashley. Helen was just behind them, holding a baby in her arms. Right away, she could tell it was Zach. Even from a distance, she could see that something wasn't quite right. When she got closer, she saw the cast on his leg and a bump on his head.

"Hey, guys!" She hugged Kevin and waved at Ashley. Helen looked tired but happy. "So, what did I miss?"

"We got Zach back," Ashley said. "He's hurt, though."

"Hey, buddy," Annie said.

Zach, suddenly shy, curled his face into Helen's neck.

"Long story," she said. "Welcome home."

"I can't believe you brought the whole gang," Annie said.

"They insisted," she said. "Is that all you have?"

"Yeah."

"Okay. Come on, everyone. Come on, come on," Helen said. "To the car."

Annie leaned into Kevin. "I just love the sign."

He sighed happily. "I knew you would."

It was good to have Zach in the house again. He was a solid buffer. Helen kept him with her, so he was always between them; though he was also a time suck. Helen admitted that she'd enjoyed having extra time and less responsibility after he was taken away. No day care, no car seat, no diapers.

"This is better, though," she said. Zach was asleep on the couch between them. The kids were in bed and Annie was exhausted, but she felt like she should stay up with Helen for a while longer. She'd picked her up from the airport, after all, and then bought her dinner.

"What happened?" Annie asked.

"I'm not sure, exactly," she said, "but I saw the police report. Apparently, his mother was driving a borrowed car while high and crashed it into the cement base of a lamppost in a parking lot."

"Well, didn't the car seat protect him?"

"He was in her lap," Helen said. "His leg got caught in the steering wheel. That's how it broke. Hit his head on the steering wheel too. He had a concussion." She shook her head.

Annie reached out and lightly brushed Zach's hair aside so she could see the bump. "What did the doctors say?"

"That he's a very lucky little boy. We got him back two days ago. They called in the middle of the night. I thought about you—how you must feel getting up at crazy hours of the night to go do something heroic."

"Hardly heroic, what I do."

"A debate for another time, maybe," Helen said. "Anyway, the cast stays on for at least another few weeks, but…babies heal fast. And he seems to remember me."

"Of course he remembers you!"

"It'll be much, much harder for her to get him back this time, so while I can't say this is permanent, it's at least for a while."

"Good," Annie said. "Which reminds me: I turned down the dorm room, so it looks like you're stuck with me too. That's okay, right?"

"It certainly is. I'm…relieved."

"It's not going to change anything, right? It's not too late. I can drop the class. I actually have to drop a couple of classes anyway."

"You do? Why? How many are you signed up for?"

"Four," Annie said. "But… Well, they're changing the source of my funding, and I have to work at least twenty-five hours a week, so I think carrying more than two classes is going to be difficult."

"And you're getting something in return, I hope."

"Oh yeah. More money and a free ride."

"They're going to pay for your degree? That's wonderful!"

It was designed to look wonderful. It was designed to be a very lovely trap, a way for them to seem gracious and accommodating. More money, free school—a dream come true. But she didn't have a say in the matter, not really, and it was the lack of freedom that chafed.

"It's going to take me longer to graduate," Annie said. "I don't really know what to expect but…whatever. It doesn't matter. I can drop your class, Helen."

"No, don't. It's probably going to be my last quarter there anyway. I make more on the force, I get good benefits, and I can go full-time if I want to… I'm holding on to the teaching job for the wrong reasons."

"I'm sorry," Annie said, and she meant it.

"It'll be nice to have at least one good student in the class."

"Okay, then."

"We can be professional." Helen waved her hand in the air, though it sounded more like a question than a confident statement. "It'll be fine."

Annie nodded. "Yeah, totally."

Zach sighed, and both women looked at him. His cheeks were bright and rosy. He kicked out his good leg.

"He's cutting a new tooth," Helen said. "He was gone a month, and I feel like I missed so much." She placed her hand lightly on his stomach, and he soon stilled.

Helen knocked on Annie's door just before eight in the morning on the day before New Year's Eve. Annie thought it might be one of the kids. They were both early risers and didn't have good boundaries about the garage as a separate personal space. To them, it was still their backyard.

She opened the door, tired and cold and half asleep. "What?"

Helen held out a cup of milky coffee.

"What's that for?"

"Kind of a good news, bad news situation," she said.

"You need me to babysit?"

"No, nothing like that," Helen said. "The good news is I got you a Christmas present. The bad news is I forgot about it until now."

"And you had to wake me up to give it to me?" Annie asked, sipping the coffee. It was sweetened just right and not too hot.

"Well, he's here to install it right now, so…" Helen screwed up her face. "Sorry?"

"What the hell kind of Christmas present needs to be installed at eight a.m. on a Wednesday?" Annie asked.

Helen laughed. "He's from the phone company. They're installing a line out here so you don't have to cross the yard in the middle of the night if your little beepy thing goes off."

Annie reached for her robe. "Okay, that's a pretty good gift."

"I know," Helen said. "You can go lie down in my bed."

"I will." Annie was too tired to consider whether or not getting into Helen's bed was a good idea. She slipped up the stairs, avoiding the man from the phone company and the children watching cartoons in the living room. She made her way into Helen's bedroom and closed the door. She took another mouthful of the sweet, warm coffee, then set it aside to grow cold and crawled into Helen's unmade bed. She pulled the covers up over her, breathing in Helen's scent—one deep breath, two—and then she closed her eyes and fell asleep.

She woke up when Helen came in carrying the baby and Annie's beeping pager.

She bolted upright. She'd forgotten the pager!

"It's all right." Helen tossed it onto the bed. "I've had it the whole time. It only just went off."

"Oh my God, you're so good to me." Annie rubbed the sleep out of her eyes.

"There's a phone on the nightstand," Helen said. She put the baby down on the bed and turned to get a diaper.

Annie reached for the phone and then, seeing Zach start to roll, put her foot on his shoulder, holding him in place until Helen returned her attention to him.

The usual person picked up on the first ring.

"Hello, mysterious voice," she said after she'd given her identification code words.

He chuckled. "Well, hello to you too."

"What do you have for me?"

"You are to report to the Los Angeles office of the FBI Monday morning at nine a.m.," he said.

"All right."

"I also need to inform you that you'll be receiving your orders through the FBI from now on. You need to continue to keep your pager on you at all times in case you need to be reached," he said.

"So they can track me, you mean?" she muttered.

"I know nothing about that," he said. "Annie, this will be our last call, I suspect, for quite a while."

Her stomach flipped. She liked this voice at the other end of the line. He knew as well as she did that she was being used. "Oh," she said sadly.

She saw movement from the corner of her eye. Helen had looked up from changing Zach's dirty diaper. "See you around, I guess."

"See you on the other side, my dear," he said and hung up.

"What's the matter?" Helen asked as she picked Zach up and moved him to his crib.

"Nothing." Annie shook her head. "Just…I'm not real great with change."

"Who is?"

"Well, you," Annie pointed out. "Your life is six kinds of crazy right now, and you handle everything with humor and grace."

Helen rolled her eyes. "I cry every time I'm alone. It's just that I'm hardly ever alone unless I'm in the shower."

"Nothing wrong with crying."

"Do you have to leave?" Helen asked.

Annie shook her head. "Not till Monday morning."

Helen smiled. "Good."

"I can get out of your way, though." Annie threw the covers off and swung her legs to the floor. She felt suddenly self-conscious.

"I'm going to put the baby down for his morning nap," Helen said. "But don't go too far. There's breakfast if you want it."

Breakfast was leftover French toast, which Annie preferred cold to hot anyway. The syrup always ran off hot food, but when it was cold, it stuck, and Annie liked her food as sweet as possible. Helen sat with her at the kitchen table, watching her in silence, then asked, "What are you doing for New Year's Eve?"

Annie wiped her mouth with a paper towel and shrugged. "Haven't thought about it. I've been mostly trying to survive Christmas."

"Sal's having a party."

"Sal has a lot of parties, seems like." Annie stuck her fork into the last bite. It was so drenched in syrup that it dripped onto the plate, barely missing the table.

"Yeah," Helen said. "That's Sal for you."

"Are you going? What about Bruce?"

"He'll be in Vegas," Helen said with a snort. "I can't remember the last time Bruce Everton was in California for New Year's."

"Oh."

"Will you come?"

"I guess. If I'm not working."

"You don't have to go in until Monday, I thought," Helen pointed out.

"Right. I mean, I'm happy to go. I love Sal. It's just…do you think it's a good idea?"

"I think it'll be fun," Helen said firmly.

Annie knew she should say no. She knew she wouldn't.

Ashley sat on the toilet lid with her knees pulled up while Annie put on her makeup. She was small for eleven. The hours of dancing kept her slim, and her genetics made her petite. She watched Annie in comfortable silence, and Annie didn't bother to fill the quiet with small talk.

"I've never seen you put on so much eyeshadow before," Ashley said finally.

"It's a party," Annie said. "It's what people do."

"It's dark, though."

Annie leaned back and inspected herself in the mirror, studying the black eye shadow she'd been brushing onto her lids. It made her look a little dangerous. She liked it. "You think it looks bad?" Annie asked.

Ashley shook her head. "Different."

"I can live with different."

"What are you going to wear?"

"I haven't decided," Annie admitted. "I have a dress, but I think I'll be cold without stockings, and I don't really want to wear them."

"Or?"

"Or pants and a blouse," Annie said with a shrug.

"I've been to Aunt Sal's parties before," Ashley said with an air of authority. "I don't think you'll be too cold. It's always hot at her parties."

"That's a good tip. Thanks." Annie flashed her a grin.

"Oh, I know," Ashley said brightly. "The makeup—it makes you look like you have a secret. Especially when you smile."

Annie applied mascara to one eye and looked at her reflection. The longer lashes looked better. "I guess when you see people, you have to decide whether or not they're hiding something. Whether what they have might be worth keeping secret." Annie applied mascara to the other eye.

"What about me?" Ashley asked. "What do I look like?"

"You? Honey, you look like you're stuffed with secrets. All filled up to the brim."

Ashley tucked her chin against her knees, considering, then said, "Can I have some blush?"

Annie dusted some high onto Ashley's cheeks and then sent her out to show her mother.

Justin, one of Helen's nephews, arrived to watch Zach just before they left for Sal's. He was Helen's brother's son, and he arrived with a black backpack stuffed nearly to bursting. He wore glasses that made him look bookish and a faded flannel shirt over a T-shirt, and he had barely enough facial hair to look like he needed a shave.

Helen handed him the baby. "We'll be home by one at the latest," she promised.

"Dad is at home, if you never come back," Justin said. "He said we could leave Zach on the steps of the church."

"Ha, ha, ha," Helen said. "Help yourself to anything in the fridge. Zach ate, but he'll need a bottle before he goes to bed."

"I know." From the way Justin handled the kid, he probably did know. He had to be the oldest of a whole bunch of siblings, probably volunteering for this babysitting gig to find some peace and quiet.

"I left his car seat in the den, but if something happens that's bad enough to take him to the ER, just call an ambulance."

"Mommy, come on," Kevin complained. "Let's go."

"You guys go get in the car," Helen said. Annie followed the kids out to the Jeep and got in the front seat. Ashley and Kevin saw her as an adult with a job, but because Helen was older, she often felt stuck in between. The only time she didn't feel that way was when she was alone with Helen. She forgot that Helen was older. She forgot that they shouldn't.

"I'm going to stay up until midnight," Kevin announced as they waited.

"No, you aren't," Ashley retorted.

"Am too."

"You're going to fall asleep just like last year."

"Staying up until midnight isn't so great," Annie said. "It's over in a flash, and all you get for your trouble is being tired the next day."

"Then why do grown-ups make such a big deal out of it?" Kevin asked.

"Because grown-ups like to drink," Ashley said.

"You mean Daddy," Kevin said.

"Don't worry about your daddy," Annie suggested. "Your mother said he won't be there."

The conversation was interrupted when Helen opened the door and slipped into the driver's seat. She fastened her seatbelt and started the car.

"Mom, can I stay up until midnight?" Kevin asked.

"You can certainly try," Helen said.

Annie reached out and turned on the heat, fiddling with the vents so that warm air would blow on her legs.

"Don't worry." Helen glanced over. "Sal's place will be warm with so many people."

"Yeah." Annie turned around and gave Ashley a wink.

"How come Zach can't come?" Kevin asked.

Helen pulled out onto the road. "Because it's past his bedtime and because Justin is saving up for college, so I hire him whenever I can."

"How come you don't hire me for stuff?" Kevin asked.

"Because you don't know how to do anything that's worth money," Ashley said.

"Hey!"

"What if we sat in silence, hmm?"

The kids clammed up. They knew their mother well enough to know that her suggestion was an order, and no one wanted to arrive at a party already in trouble.

The kids went right upstairs to play with their cousins. Annie was introduced to the few people who had arrived early—some of Sal's work colleagues, family members she'd met at Ashley's birthday party. People complimented her hair, her dress, her makeup, but she still felt like a fish out of water. She rarely bothered to make friends. She was bad at anything that wasn't work or school.

"Here, kiddo," Sal said when Annie wandered into the kitchen. "Helen says you're a deft hand at a bar. Can you help me set up?"

"I can even bartend."

Sal's face lit up. "Seriously?"

"Sure," Annie said. "It would give me something to do." Something besides wandering from room to room, sitting awkwardly next to someone she barely knew or standing stiffly listening to other people talk. Something besides watching Helen and then deciding she was watching her too much but not being able to stop. Walking away, then finding her again. Everything a cycle, like when the washer load was unbalanced and the machine rocked against the wall. Annie—an uneven load.

She played bartender like it was a role, a persona she could slip on for the evening. She could be flirty enough to make everyone feel special. Laugh at their jokes, roll her eyes with the women behind the men's backs. She could make most drinks without looking them up. One old portly fellow she didn't recognize asked for a Manhattan and was about to tell her how to make it when she smiled sweetly and said, "Why, that's my daddy's favorite drink."

"My father," Sal said, walking up after he left the room, "in from Texas."

"Very pleasant fellow." Annie topped off Sal's flute of champagne. "Liar."

Annie shrugged. "Your brother looks like him."

"Cut from the same cloth." Sal shook her head. "I love Bruce, but he's a real piece of shit."

"I don't see how anyone could leave a woman like Helen," Annie said, looking at her as she talked to one of Sal's coworkers across the room.

"You don't say," Sal said with a small smile. But then someone came up to the bar and asked for another beer, and when she looked for Sal again, she was gone.

Bartending was a good diversion, but the problem was that every time she made a shaker of something, and it was a little too much for the glass, she drank the remainder. By the time it was eleven o'clock, she was drunker than she'd been in a long time.

Sal must have noticed because she shooed her away from the bar. "Go get some air, honey. I've got this."

But what Annie really needed was to pee. The door to the bathroom downstairs was closed, so hanging onto the banister, she carefully climbed to the second floor to find another bathroom. Her face felt numb, and her hands were clammy.

She walked past the bedroom where Ashley and her cousin Gina were playing a video game, staring at the television screen. Kevin was asleep on the bed.

She found an empty bathroom and locked herself in, emptying her bladder with a relieved sigh. As she washed her hands, she studied her reflection in the mirror, looking critically at her skin, her eyes, her hair.

"You're an idiot," she said to her reflection.

She dried her hands and turned around, stumbling a bit, then opened the door.

Helen was in the hallway, leaning against the wall. Waiting.

Abruptly, surprising herself, Annie reached out and yanked her inside, locking the door.

"What are you doing?" Helen asked, surprised.

"Technically," Annie said, "the quarter hasn't started yet, right?"

Helen went very still for a moment, then breathed, "Annie."

"Helen," Annie whispered, pulling her closer until their lips almost touched.

"Oh, what the hell." Helen kissed her.

CHAPTER 14

Annie was in the laundry room just off the kitchen, pawing through a tangled load of clean darks in her white plastic basket. She had pulled on a pair of denim shorts over tights and put on a bra, and now she was looking for a black T-shirt. To hell with looking professional for school, she'd decided. She wore slacks and blouses every other day, but today she was going to her Thursday class in comfortable clothes. Besides, these ones were clean.

She turned around when Helen came in, a look on her face like someone had turned up the gas, like she was about to catch fire.

They couldn't seem to stop having sex. Following Sal's party and the days after that, they'd rationalized that the quarter hadn't officially started, but now it was Thursday, and Helen's class literally started at four o'clock.

Now Annie was sitting on the kitchen counter and Helen was trying to yank her shorts off in full view of a photo on the refrigerator of the kids at the La Brea tar pits.

"Wait, wait," Annie said, tearing her mouth away. Helen had abandoned the shorts and was now working on unclasping Annie's bra. Helen pulled back to look at Annie just as the clasp popped open. Annie quickly held the bra in place.

"What's the matter?" Helen asked, gasping for breath.

Annie thought about saying they should stop, opened her mouth with every intention of saying those words. Instead she said, "Can we go upstairs?"

Annie had slept in Helen's bed, cried in it, shared it with Helen and Zach, but this was the first time they were going to have sex in it.

They had the house to themselves, but Helen still closed the door out of habit. The midmorning light brightened everything in the room.

Helen shimmied out of her clothes and lay back on the bed, spreading her legs in invitation, while Annie pulled off her shorts and tights. She lay on top of Helen and, pressing her thigh between Helen's legs, parted them. Annie got her off right away, so fast and hard that Helen could only thrash her head around on the pillow. And then Annie made her come again more slowly, drawing it out and teasing her, leaving her on the edge until Helen begged for release, and only then did Annie use her mouth and tongue.

Afterward, Helen pulled her into the shower, turned Annie around to face the wall, and slipped her hand between Annie's legs under the spray of hot water. Annie whimpered into the tile.

As they lay on the bed wrapped in towels, Helen said carefully, "We're going to do better."

"I'm going to drop the class," Annie said firmly. "I'm not even going to go today."

"Yes, you are. Child welfare is something you already deal with in your career, so why not become familiar with California laws?"

"I'm not saying your class isn't important," Annie said. "Just that we seem to be bad at not having sex."

"You were standing in my kitchen in your bra!"

"It was the laundry room."

Helen snorted and covered her mouth with her hand.

"Well, if you think I should go to your class, then we should actually go," Annie said.

"May as well go together." Helen met Annie's eyes.

But Annie reached out and brushed her fingers along Helen's freckled arm. Helen looked up and smiled, her eyes crinkling up at the corners, making Annie's heart flutter.

Annie's desk at the FBI building was in an open bullpen populated by midlevel agents—people in their late twenties and thirties who had put a good chunk of time into the organization but who were years away from moving into any sort of management. They all hated

Annie. Resented her presence and resented the fact that she wasn't even a real agent.

She absolutely wasn't. She wasn't super familiar with the FBI's training methods or their caseloads. She'd never trained at Quantico, and she didn't know the culture. She knew how to be a government employee, but even that was different, depending on where one landed. The CIA was different from the NSA, which was different from the FBI, and probably the FBI offices in DC were different from the ones out here on the West Coast. She might have been able to fake it in DC, but this?

So she stayed quiet and played dumb. She asked where the break room was with big eyes and fluttering lashes. She smiled at the dumb jokes and ignored the sexist ones. She did the menial labor the assistant director tossed her way because he was stuck with her and he couldn't just leave her with nothing to do. She translated audiotapes. She watched videotaped interviews. She read backlogged and cold cases. If she had nothing else to do, she did her homework. She worked Monday through Wednesday, so they also resented her for not putting in forty-hour weeks.

On her second day, she was in the far stall of the bathroom when she heard one of the female agents say, "I heard she defected from Russia."

Annie raised her legs and held them straight out in front of her.

"Come on," said a different voice. "She doesn't even have an accent!"

"You don't call that an accent?" The first woman snorted.

"Not a Russian one," the second voice said.

"Well, she wouldn't. They train their spies deep. She's probably been selling our secrets for years right on our own soil, and now they have her sitting two desks away from me. It's disgusting."

"I heard she was up in San Francisco when they caught her sleeping with an assistant director, so they shipped her down here to get rid of her."

"Oh yeah? Who told you that?"

"I heard it from Agent Katz. He said she was up there on that drug bust."

Annie shook her head in disbelief. How did they even know about that? And furthermore, Agent Katz hadn't been there.

"Oh, well, if that alcoholic told you, it must be true."

They both laughed.

Annie put her feet down and flushed the toilet. Suddenly, the two women got very quiet. She walked out of the stall and glared at them both, then turned to the sink and washed her hands, watching them in the mirror. The shorter woman, stout and blonde, looked horrified, but the tall dark-haired woman stared back at Annie.

"Those Clintons have been in the White House not two seconds and they're already hiring commie ex-spies. Can you believe it?" Annie asked.

"Let's go," said the taller lady. Annie dried her hands as they walked out.

Whatever. She'd never been particularly popular in the workplace. No one ever liked the smartest person in the room.

Helen's class was interesting. Annie found her teaching style engaging—when she could make herself focus on the lecture and not on the way Helen sat on the corner of her desk with her shapely legs crossed. The first week, they'd gone straight from bed to the classroom, and it was jarring. Annie sat in the back, unable to look directly at her.

The second week, they arrived separately. Helen wore her LAPD uniform, her hair pulled back, her shiny badge on display. Everyone *oohed* and *ahhed*. There was something commanding about her, and it was interesting to Annie that everyone else had the same reaction, especially since police officers still weren't particularly popular in Los Angeles. Even without her uniform, though, Helen was beautiful and commanding.

Annie hung around after class instead of fleeing as if the place was on fire, like she had the week before. She watched Helen toss things into her tote bag. "I have to figure out how to be in two places at once," Helen said when she looked up and saw Annie.

"What happened?"

"Work ran late, obviously." Helen indicated her uniform. "I still have to go pick up Zach, and I was supposed to get Ash from ballet class ten minutes ago."

"I can go get Ashley," Annie offered, then glanced behind her. Two guys were packing up their books, and one woman stared unabashedly.

"Could you?" Helen asked. "She's going to be so pissed. She hates when I'm late."

"I'll go right now."

"Okay," Helen said. "I'll get Zach and then pick up something for dinner…"

"Just get the baby and go home, Helen. You leave dinner to me."

Helen looked like she wanted to reach out and touch Annie, but she didn't. "Thank you."

They walked out together, ushering the other woman out with them so Helen could lock the classroom door.

At the parking lot, they went to their separate cars. Annie hustled to get going. Ashley was usually pissed anyway, so she could only imagine the cloud of joy she was going to find at being picked up late.

The ballet studio was not too far from the house. Annie had been there once before to watch the fall recital. She didn't really understand tiny girls in tutus, bouncing around on stage to extravagant music, but the parents all seemed to eat it up. Ashley was at the stage where she was about to outgrow this studio and would soon have to decide if ballet was just a hobby or if she was going to make it her life.

She was waiting when Annie pulled up. An older girl was sitting on the concrete steps with her. Annie put the car in park and pulled up on the emergency brake, then opened the car door and called out, "Ashley!" Ashley looked up with a squint and seemed to deflate a little.

"That's my ride," Annie heard her say.

"That's not your mom," the other girl said.

"It's the lady that lives in my garage," Ashley said, shouldering her backpack. "Bye, Cecile."

Ashley got in the car, dropped her backpack down by her feet, and slammed the door shut. She still wore her leotard and tights under her jacket, though she'd taken off her ballet slippers and put on sneakers. Her cheeks were red. She wiped her nose with the back of her hand.

"Where's Mom?"

"She was running late, so I offered to come get you. Hope that's okay," Annie said.

"Not like I have a choice."

"I guess I could make you walk," Annie offered. Ashley rolled her eyes. "Well, I also told her we'd get dinner, so what do you think? Pizza?"

"Whatever."

"We could do Chinese or hot dogs or pasta."

"Pizza is fine."

"Pizza it is," Annie declared and pulled out of the parking lot.

At the Pizza Hut, in an effort to shake Ashley from her mood, Annie offered her a quarter to play one of the arcade games while they waited, but she declined.

Annie persisted. "Come on. Something good must've happened to you today."

"Well," she said, "my ballet teacher told me she wants to start me *en pointe*."

"That's awesome! That must mean she thinks you're really good."

"Most girls don't start until they're twelve, and I'm only eleven. Mom isn't going to say yes."

"You don't know that. You haven't even told her yet," Annie said.

"She thinks ballet is too hard on my feet already. She thinks it stunts my growth."

"Your mother is smart. I'm sure she doesn't think your growth is stunted by exercise," Annie said. She couldn't comment on the feet thing.

"Once I'm *en pointe*, I qualify for full-time ballet school with tutoring. I wouldn't have to go to regular school," There was a note of desperation in her voice.

"That sounds…" *Expensive.* Helen was already working two jobs and had taken on a tenant to make ends meet. "What's so bad about regular school anyway?"

Ashley scowled, but then her bottom lip started to wobble.

"Oh, honey. Oh no," Annie said.

Ashley lunged at her and buried her face in Annie's chest. Annie put an arm around her, patting her awkwardly while she wept.

On Monday, the assistant director, William Baker, intercepted her as she approached her desk. "Weaver, you're with me today."

The buzzing in the room stopped, and everyone turned to watch as she followed him. Baker was Bill to his equals and Buck to his buddies in the office. And yet, Baker didn't even seem to know any of the women's names. He called them "honey" and asked them to bring him coffee anytime his secretary wasn't available. They got it for him too.

Annie had met him briefly on her first day.

"Oh yeah," he'd said. "Our new spy."

She opened her mouth to tell him that wasn't why she was here, but he waved her off before she got a word out. "I know you're as stuck with me as I am with you, sweetheart," he said. "I suggest you just lie low until you get something to do. No one likes change, and they're certainly not going to like you."

Which had been true. Baker might be a bureaucrat and a misogynist, but he wasn't a moron. No one got to his position by being stupid.

She followed him down to the parking garage and into his car. She didn't ask questions, though she did check her pager as he pulled out onto the street. She hadn't received a page since her last call just after New Year's.

Baker drove in silence until they were on the freeway, then said, "They tell me you did espionage in Eastern Europe."

"'They?'"

He laughed and rolled down the window a crack. "You mind if I smoke?"

"No, sir."

He reached over and pushed in the cigarette lighter, then fished a cigarette out of his shirt pocket.

The lighter popped from the dash. "You mind?" he said.

She pulled it out and held it to the cigarette dangling from his mouth. He took a deep drag. The smell reminded her of the cigarettes her daddy had smoked before he quit. She told herself not to equate this man with her father.

"You ever kill anyone over there?" he asked. "Communists?"

"You ever kill anyone?" she shot back before she could catch herself.

He took another long drag from his cigarette, then said, "You gotta crack a few eggs to make an omelet."

"I did my job."

"Very well, I hear, and now you're here with me," he said. "Because, what? You're going to school to be a cop?"

"I'm going to school to have options."

"Oh, that's a load of total bullshit," he said. "With a brain like yours in that hot little body? Any police force or private sector business would hire you. Shit, I'd hire you."

"I think there was a compliment buried in there somewhere," she said. "Somewhere deep."

"I mean, more power to you, getting the government to fund this little detour—"

"You think this was my idea?"

"—but I really think you're doing yourself a disservice," he said, ignoring the interruption. "Wasting away in LA."

"Well, thank you, sir. Your opinion is noted."

He slowed down to turn in to a neighborhood with big houses and well-manicured lawns, then flicked his cigarette butt out the window. He drove down half a block. "This house is 4572."

She looked at the house and waited for him to say more, but he simply drove deeper into the neighborhood. He slowed again. "This one is 2381." And again. "And that one is 6714."

They circled out of the neighborhood and back onto the main road that would take them back to the freeway and downtown. "Tonight," he said, "you're going to meet someone at the south entrance of Griffith Park to collect what you need. By the end of the week, you'll have implanted listening devices in all three of the houses we visited today, as well as two others."

"Not a lot of prep time."

"You'll get some background along with your bugs."

"You know, my specialty is really interrogation," she pointed out. "Working for the CIA doesn't automatically make me James Bond."

"You're saying you can't do it?"

"No," she said. "I'm saying there's no way I'm the most qualified person in Los Angeles, though."

"Well, sweetheart," he said, "you're the most qualified one that works for me."

She sighed. "What time tonight?"

She arrived an hour early, parked a few blocks away, and headed to the meeting place. Found an obscured place to wait, pulled out her binoculars, and made herself comfortable. In her work and her travels, she found that things always went better when she had sufficient information. Espionage wasn't about elaborate outfits or code words or guns with lasers; it was about patience. It was about listening and waiting and watching.

So she listened and waited and watched, munching through a bag of peanut M&Ms until, finally, a car pulled up and parked. The engine cut off, the lights went out, and then a man got out and looked around.

That was likely her guy.

She approached cautiously, moving through the dark easily enough that she startled him and he swore. In Russian. And it wasn't anything like her Russian. As fluent and proficient as she was, she would never sound like a native speaker.

Why was this man, obviously a native speaker, helping the United States government? A defector, maybe. That had happened a lot during the Reagan administration and just after as Soviet spies realized that life was better in America. They defected for money, promising Soviet secrets to maintain their Western lifestyles.

She reached out for the envelope he held and said, *"Eto vse?"*

"Da," he said.

She turned around to head back to where she'd left her car.

"Wait." His accent curled around the word.

She turned to look at him.

"You are just a girl," he said, scanning her up and down. "How can you be the spy I am to meet?"

She turned away from him. "That question is annoying every single time," she muttered.

If anyone in the office noticed that she left for long stretches in the middle of the day, they didn't say anything. If their resentment came with a heavy dose of not giving a shit, that suited her just fine. She'd already mentioned to Baker's secretary that she'd be in and out during the day completing his assignment, and the secretary promised to pass it along.

Breaking into people's houses midday would be easier for her. She didn't look suspicious. She was just a girl, after all.

The information in the packet she'd received contained only the addresses, the names of the people who lived there, whether they had families or not, and their estimated times of arrival and departure. Nothing about why they were being bugged. She could do her own research on the names; she had full access to government databases. But she figured the less she knew about them as people, as humans, the better.

The first house was on a cul-de-sac, which was unfortunate. Cul-de-sacs tended to breed nosy neighbors. She pulled up to the house. A gray SUV was parked in the driveway.

Perfect.

Annie shrugged out of her jacket and pulled on a white lab coat. She put on a pair of weak reading glasses in large frames that she'd bought at a drugstore along with a wooden clipboard. She'd found and printed out official-looking forms at the UCLA library. Her hair was gathered into a tight knot and secured at the base of her neck. She exchanged her flats for smart black pumps. Then she applied some neutral lipstick, completing her professional look. The listening device that she was to install was in the wide pocket of her lab coat, along with the tools she needed to install it.

She walked up the front walk and rang the bell.

A woman opened the door. "Can I help you?" she asked. The woman's Slavic accent was barely noticeable, and it gave her an uneasy feeling.

"Mrs. Posp…Pospisil?" Annie said, purposefully butchering the pronunciation.

"Yes?"

"Oh good. I'm from SoCal Gas, and I'm going door-to-door in your neighborhood to investigate reports of a leak."

"Leak?" she said, frowning.

"Oh yes. We're trying to determine which house it might be coming from. Tell me, have you been getting headaches?"

"Oh," the woman said. "No… I mean, I'm not sure."

"You mind if I come in and take some readings?" Annie smiled and held up her clipboard. "It'll take me five minutes to rule out your house as hazardous."

"Yes," the woman said. "Yes, please."

Annie smiled and stepped inside.

The gas company ruse worked on three of the houses that day, and she returned to the office to stow the other two bugs in her desk. They'd be safer inside a secure building as opposed to her car or her garage room. She left the lab coat and glasses in the car, but even so, when she walked in, it felt like everyone in the room stopped and stared.

Someone had left a handwritten note on her desk that said *Go see Buck*.

The secretary stood up when Annie walked into the outer office. "He's waiting for you," she said and knocked on his door, pushing it open without waiting for a response.

Annie stepped in. "You wanted to see me?"

"Close the door," he said.

She complied, nervous but determined not to care about whatever he had to say. They were forcing her to work here, forcing her to do the work of a CIA agent, even though she'd been clear about not wanting to do that anymore.

She took a seat in front of his desk.

"It was implied," he said, "that you would bug these houses at night."

"Are you having me followed?" She was surprised, but more than that, she was disappointed in herself. If she had learned anything over the years, it was that Big Brother was always watching.

"Yes," he said without apology. He must have been in charge a long time and was used to answering to no one.

She'd been so preoccupied with her work that she hadn't even noticed the tail. But that was no excuse for letting herself slip.

Buck was watching her, waiting for her to continue.

"People are in their houses at night," Annie finally said.

"There were people in their houses today too! You spoke to them."

"The information packets were all on the husbands," she countered evenly. "I talked to the wives."

He stared at her levelly. "You have a habit of that, it seems."

She stared back, unwilling to confirm or deny the accusation.

Finally, he said, "It's dangerous for them to see you."

"It's all dangerous, Mr. Baker. That's why you're having me do it."

He shook his head and reached down to open a desk drawer. "Well." He pulled out a handgun. He set it on the desk with a thud.

"I think murder is a little bit of an overreaction." She kept her eyes on the gun.

"I can't issue you a firearm. It would be too complicated," he said. "But I don't think you should go out there unarmed."

She stood and reached out for the gun.

He intercepted her hand before she could pick it up. "You do know how to use this, correct?" She merely gave him a look. "Okay. Try not to use it."

"Thank you, I suppose," she said and picked it up, checking that the safety was on before tucking it in the back of her skirt under her jacket. She could hear the screams of every firearm instructor she'd ever had.

"What about your last two houses?" he asked.

"I'll get them by the end of the week."

"See that you do."

When Annie got home, she did something she hadn't done in a long time. She parked in the alley and came in through the gate. It had been a while since she'd carried a gun, and she didn't want to walk through a house full of children with it.

It was dinnertime, and across the yard, the kitchen glowed brightly, but she stayed in the garage and ate snacks for dinner. She worked on her homework, doing the reading for Helen's class first and then writing a reaction paper in longhand for her other class. By the time she finished, it was after ten and she was ready for bed.

She stood up, stretched, and walked around the room, trying to decide if she wanted to shower before she went to sleep or if she wanted to do it in the morning. She glanced out the window at the house. Helen was standing at the sliding glass door, looking out at her. She lifted her hand and waved.

Annie waved back, looking at her longingly and feeling a familiar wave of desire.

She turned away from the window. Went straight to the bathroom and turned the shower on so hot that it quickly filled the tiny room with steam. By the time Annie got in the room to strip down, the mirror over the sink was fogged up, so she didn't have to see the expression on her face.

CHAPTER 15

She studied for a test in Helen's class while sitting in her car outside of the fourth house she needed to bug, waiting for the people inside to leave. It was one thing to win the trust of a woman alone in a house, but she didn't fancy meeting any of the husbands face-to-face. Just when she thought she was going to be late for class, the white SUV pulled out of the driveway and moved down the street. After it turned the corner, she got out of her car.

She'd bought a lockpick set at the hardware store closest to campus. The guy ringing her up looked at her strangely and asked to see her ID, even though it wasn't illegal to purchase. She produced her student ID with a glare that dared him to say something, then snatched the receipt out of his hand.

She hurried around to the side of the house and approached the garage's side door. Picking a lock was like riding a bike—she was a little wobbly before muscle memory kicked in. She closed her eyes, listening for the series of faint clicks that would grant her access. She crept in silently, praying there was no dog or elderly mother-in-law or any other surprise. But the house was still and quiet and settled. She headed for the stairs and, at the top, turned left into the home office. She scanned the room.

Bugging the lamp on the desk would be easier than opening up the phone and tying the bug in with the wiring, though the phone, of course, would be better for whoever was listening. But when she thought of Buck condescendingly reminding her to bug the houses at night, she picked the lamp.

Annie got to Helen's class without a minute to spare. Parking had been a hassle, and it had been a stressful week. She was already tired, but she still had one more house to do and wanted to get it done tonight so as not to ruin her Friday. She'd take the test and then go back out. It should be easy.

She tried not to think about the last bug—or the gun—waiting for her in the trunk of her car as she rushed into the classroom.

The only seat left was at the front, just to the right of Helen's desk. Helen watched Annie collapse into the chair and said, "I was starting to wonder."

"Yeah, yeah," she said. "I'm here."

Annie glanced at the woman on her left. It was the same one who had stared at them the other week, and she was staring at them now.

"Hey, do you two know each other?" she asked.

"Yeah," Annie said tersely. "I'm taking this class. How we know each other is happening right now."

The woman rolled her eyes and looked away.

"Okay," Helen said, standing up, a stack of tests in her hand. "Put everything away. It's time."

Annie wasn't worried about taking this test. Helen's syllabus was very structured, and the reading wasn't difficult as long as you kept up.

Helen handed her a few tests and touched her lightly on the shoulder before moving on to the next row. Annie took one and passed the rest behind her.

The test was twenty-five multiple-choice questions and an essay. She blew through the multiple-choice, then read the essay question. She glanced up to see Helen looking at her with a Mona Lisa smile.

Annie looked down and fidgeted, trying to ignore the heat between her legs.

She just had to put pen to paper, that was all. She knew exactly the reading Helen was looking for with this question, had the answer already half written in her head. She started writing, doing her best to push away thoughts of what they could do on Helen's desk if they were alone.

She crossed out what she had written and rewrote it, willing herself to focus.

Helen cleared her throat, and Annie looked up at her. She was writing something, her hair falling down in front of her face. She reached up and tucked the hair behind her ear.

Annie pictured putting Helen's earlobe between her teeth.

She uncrossed and recrossed her legs. Redoubled her efforts to focus.

"Fifteen minutes remaining," Helen announced to the class. Someone behind her sighed raggedly. The girl next to her started writing faster, her pen scratching loudly against the paper.

Annie wrote four more sentences and, rereading them, nodded. A conclusion and she could go.

Maybe they were going about this all wrong. Not having sex was supposed to keep things more professional between them, except for the fact that they weren't great at it. Sure, they hadn't done it since the class started, but that didn't stop Annie from thinking about it all the time, especially when she was in class. They weren't even doing a good job of pretending they didn't know each other, judging by the reactions of the young woman next to her. Annie didn't know why they were bothering to feign indifference. She'd found Helen from a list provided by the university. It was basically like the school was sanctioning their friendship. That was one argument, anyway.

She scribbled out a few more sentences and set her pen down. Some of the students had already dropped their tests on Helen's desk and left. Annie gathered her things and stood. Helen winked at her when she set her test face down on the desk.

"See you later, Professor," she said softly.

"See you later, Miss Weaver," Helen replied.

Cheeky.

She should leave. She should get in her car and go find that last house. She didn't want to show up at work on Monday and have to tell Buck Baker that she hadn't completed her assignment. She didn't want this gig, but if she was going to do it, she'd be the best.

But instead of walking out of the building, she found herself climbing the stairs, passing the empty receptionist desk, and waiting outside of Helen's office.

Helen appeared fifteen minutes later, her tote bag with the exams on her shoulder, her keys in her hand. She slowed when she saw Annie.

"I thought you'd gone!"

"Not yet."

"I'm glad." Helen slid the key into the lock and opening the office door. "I feel like I haven't seen much of you lately."

"Yeah, I've been working a lot."

"Nothing too bad, I hope." Helen flipped on the lights and tossed her tote bag on the desk.

"Just going here and there," Annie said vaguely, walking in after her and closing the door behind her. "Sorry I haven't been around."

"Hey, Sal has the kids tonight. You want to go get something to eat?"

"What about Zach?"

"Sal took him too. Gina is twelve now and wants to start babysitting, so we thought between her and Ashley, it'd be a pretty safe practice session," Helen said. "It turns out I'm free."

"I have to do some work. But I wanted to see you. I needed to see you."

Helen looked at her sympathetically. "It's late, Annie. What do they have you doing?"

Annie forced a smile. "Don't worry about me."

"I wish it were that easy." She lowered her eyes, looking at Annie's mouth.

"I know we're not supposed to…but maybe…" Annie swallowed, took a step toward Helen. "Maybe just to take the edge off."

Helen reached for her, met her kiss eagerly.

She'd known Helen for less than a year, but being with her already felt like home. The way she smelled, the way she tasted. Even as they became more comfortable and familiar, Annie's desire for her didn't diminish. Instead, she wanted more, wanted what she couldn't have. Dates and domesticity. A partnership of some sort. But Helen had a family and a life, and Annie just had secrets.

She pushed her thoughts aside and lost herself in Helen's kiss, their tongues twisting together. Annie moved forward, pressing against

Helen until she leaned against the edge of her desk. Helen pulled Annie closer until she was nestled between her knees.

Helen pulled her mouth away, then nuzzled her face into Annie's neck. "I'm not sure how, but you make me want to do bad things."

Annie pulled back. "I know," she said. "I'm sorry."

Helen looked at Annie, confused. Then she leaned in again to kiss Annie, softly, sweetly.

The tender moment was interrupted by a knock on the door.

Annie sprang back, wiping Helen's kiss from her mouth, nearly tripping over the garbage bin before almost falling onto the loveseat by the wall. She righted herself and crossed her legs, trying to look casual.

"Relax," Helen said quietly.

Helen opened the door. It was the young woman from their class.

"Mallory, what are you still doing here? It's awfully late," Helen said in the same tone she used to tell Kevin to go back to bed.

"Thank God you're still here. I can't find my keys!" she said, her voice panicky. "I was hoping you'd unlock the classroom for me so I can see if they fell out of my"—she glanced at Annie on the loveseat, who gave a little wave—"purse."

"Of course," Helen said. She turned to Annie. "We'll be right back."

While she waited, Annie pulled a file out of her backpack and skimmed the single page of information she had on the last house. A single man, lived alone, worked from home. Not exactly a lot to go on. If she had more time, she'd stake out the house for a few weeks, get to know his habits. When he went to the grocery store. When he went to work and came home. But as it was, she had to figure out how to do this last job before the end of tomorrow. If she couldn't get into the house when he wasn't home, she would wait until he was asleep.

She wanted Helen to come back, take her up on her offer for dinner, spend the night in bed. But she was past kidding herself; they were so laughably bad at professionalism that there was no point in keeping up the charade.

She should have just dropped the class.

She was shoving her intel back into her backpack when Helen returned and closed the door behind her.

"Did you find the keys?"

"Yep." Helen dropped her own keys onto her desk.

"You think she left them on purpose?" Annie asked, frowning.

"I really don't care." Helen grabbed the hem of her blouse, she yanked it up over her head, exposing her white bra and her ivory skin.

"Here?" Annie said.

"Right here." Helen nodded. "Right now."

"Lock the door."

It was easy to lose track of time with Helen. They might kiss for what seemed like a minute, and the next thing she knew, fifteen had passed. They could spend hours in bed without realizing it. Annie was determined this time to get them both what they wanted before they saw the sun rise from the tiny window of Helen's office.

Helen shoved paper clips and pens and papers off the ink blotter to the edge of the desk. Something fell off as she was undoing Annie's blouse, but they didn't turn their heads. Annie boosted Helen up onto the desk, and Helen pulled Annie between her legs, thrusting her hips upward. Together, they undid Helen's pants, and Helen lifted her hips enough for Annie to shimmy them down her legs. Heat emanated from Helen, and Annie plunged one hand into Helen's underwear.

That elicited a groan.

"You're awfully wet," Annie murmured. "What were you thinking about during that exam?"

"Shut up," Helen whispered, whimpering when Annie's fingers grazed her clit. Annie pressed her mouth to Helen's, swallowing the sounds she made. The building seemed empty, but there could always be someone, somewhere.

Annie slid Helen's panties off and threw them on top of the pants that had landed inside-out on the plastic mat that covered the thin carpet. She pulled up the visitor's chair to where she could lower her head between Helen's legs. Helen leaned back, propping herself up on her elbows to watch.

But it was over quickly. Helen came easily. Annie didn't think it was any deft skill of her own, rather something that the woman reacted to in her. Helen's eyes darkened; her lips parted as she gasped for breath. Annie knew how close Helen was when she fell all the way back, her head hanging off the edge of the desk.

"God," she moaned. "Just…just like… God, Annie, God!"

And then she tipped, her thighs tightening around Annie's head, her hands in Annie's hair.

She panted as Annie sat back, wiped her mouth with the back of her hand. When she finally caught her breath, Helen sat up and looked at her with a mixture of pleasure and distress.

"Good?" Annie asked, suddenly unsure.

Helen bit her lip and nodded.

For a moment, Annie thought that Helen was about to cry—her eyes were glassy—but before she could ask about it, Helen hopped off the desk, wobbling a little, and pulled Annie out of the chair, guiding her to the desk. She turned her around and pushed her forward. Annie leaned on her elbows to brace herself while Helen stroked her back and her bottom and then reached around to undo her pants. She helped push them down along with her underwear. They joined Helen's clothes on the floor.

Helen slipped her fingers between Annie's legs. "Wet," she murmured. "Wet, wet, wet."

Annie squeezed her eyes shut. It was a little strange, having her back to Helen and being leaned over like this, but not seeing Helen didn't stem her arousal. And from this angle, Helen's fingers reached deep. Annie shuddered, clenched.

Helen kissed her shoulder, the side of her neck. "Good girl," she whispered into Annie's ear. "My good girl."

Annie moaned and dropped her forehead on the desk.

Helen made her come so easily.

It felt so good, so blissful.

They walked out of the building together, brushing against one another. Annie said something that made Helen laugh, and Annie reached out to take her hand. Helen squeezed it briefly before their fingers slipped apart.

"Where are you parked?"

"Student lot," Annie said. "It's okay, I can walk."

"I can drive you. I have to go right by it."

Annie nodded. "All right. Thanks." The lure of a few more minutes with Helen was too much to resist.

They climbed into the car. Helen reached past the gearshift and rested her hand on Annie's knee. "I know…" She cleared her throat and started again. "I know we're being kind of reckless."

"Yeah," Annie agreed. "Feels worth it to me."

"Me too," Helen said. "I've just…never… And it's not just the sex."

"I mean it's good, right?"

"It's great, are you kidding me? I've never had sex like this before, and I just want you to know that even if we weren't… I still think you're worth fighting for, okay?"

"Okay."

Helen smiled and leaned in, pressed her mouth softly to Annie's. Pulled back and watched Annie get out.

She waited until Annie got into her car and started it before she drove off. In turn, Annie waited until she pulled out of the lot before she turned her car off again, then got back out and popped the trunk. She took off her denim jacket and pulled on her black sweatshirt. Then she gathered up her hair—it was getting long again—and secured it in a ponytail. She grabbed her leather bag containing her gun, the lockpick set, and the bug and set it next to her on the front seat.

When she started her car and backed out, she noticed a nearby car flip its lights on.

The car followed her all the way to the freeway. Paranoia prickled her skin, and she abruptly cut across several lanes to exit. The other car kept going. She sighed and took surface streets to her destination.

She parked several houses down from her target and walked on the opposite side of the street before crossing over. She'd studied the house from outside as best she could and decided that entering through a back door would be easiest. It was a solid door that led into what she guessed was a laundry room. She didn't know a lot about the floor plan, though. The info she'd been given for this address was sparse compared to the others. She knew there was a second floor, but she wouldn't need to bother with that. She'd stash the bug somewhere in the kitchen or the living room. A lamp, the phone, under a table.

She shouldered her tote bag, then hopped the fence. She crouched down at the door with a pocket-sized flashlight in her mouth. She pulled out her tools, intent on picking the lock, then twisted the doorknob to give it check. If it was deadbolted as well, she'd have to find another way in.

But the knob twisted easily, and the door clicked open.

Well. She hesitated and wondered if this was dumb luck or an omen? She stepped in cautiously. The house was nearly pitch-black, save for the light from a digital clock, and she swept the room quickly with her flashlight beam. The windows were covered with dark, heavy curtains. The furnishings in the kitchen were sparse, with nothing but a folding card table and a single chair. The table wouldn't hold her weight, so she decided against using the light fixture on the ceiling. She moved through the open doorway, through the dining room, and into the living room. Shining the flashlight around the room, she spotted a lamp with a shade on an upside-down milk crate.

Whoever this guy was, he either hadn't been here long enough to buy furniture, was extremely poor, or wasn't planning on staying long. It was a nice neighborhood of somewhat pricey houses, so she suspected it was the latter.

She set her leather bag down and turned off the flashlight. She unscrewed the lampshade and set it aside. She didn't see a great place to hide it. Had she more time and light, she might have taken the lamp apart to hide the bug inside. She'd just stick it next to the bulb and hope this wasn't the kind of guy to look inside his lamps.

She didn't feel guilty about doing a slapdash job. The FBI had told her what to do, and she was doing it. They'd given her little to go on.

She stuck the flashlight back between her teeth and depressed the button on the end with her tongue. The flashlight came on. She thought of Helen and what she had done with her tongue earlier and smirked.

She replaced the lampshade. Now all she had to do was walk back out the door. She didn't even have to lock it. Soon she'd be back home.

Maybe she'd sneak into Helen's house too, climb the stairs, slide into her bed. Wake her up so they could take their time.

She clicked the flashlight off and picked up her bag.

From deep within it, the pager started to beep.

She groped around, trying to find it to silence it, but it was too late. A light came on upstairs and she heard footsteps. She decided to cut her losses and just try to get out. She ran for the kitchen, but the doorway was right by the staircase, and whoever was coming down reached out over the banister and grabbed her ponytail. She grunted and fell to the floor, pain spreading like fire at the back of her head.

She scrambled to find her footing again, but the man jumped the banister and landed in front of her. She rolled and reached for her purse, but the man kicked her, catching her under the chin. The pain exploded through her like a knife. Spots appeared in her vision, and she struggled to catch her breath. She could taste blood.

The overhead light came on.

"Ja ciabie viedaju," he said, and she looked up. It took a second for her vision to clear, but when it finally did, she realized she knew him too. Father, husband, midlevel politician from Minsk.

"Wait," she pleaded.

"Špijon!" he bellowed. Reaching into the waistband of his sweatpants, he pulled out a gun. *"Zabojca, špijon!"*

She reached out to grab something, anything to defend herself with. Just as she touched her bag, he leveled the gun at her and hissed in English, "Spy!"

And fired.

The bullet hit her in the shoulder, and the force of it flung her backward. Someone screamed, and she realized it was her. She didn't want to go down like this. She gritted her teeth through the pain, her mouth still full of blood, and scrambled for her bag with her other hand. Felt the gun inside and wrapped her fingers around it just as he cocked his gun for another shot.

With her arm still in the leather bag, she swung it around, pointed her gun at him, and pulled the trigger. Bits of hot, black leather exploded into her face.

Her aim was true. She didn't miss.

She was aware that someone was picking her up. Someone strong and large who smelled faintly of stale booze. The next time she woke up was in the midst of commotion, bright lights, and unbelievable pain.

"We're going to operate," someone said. "We've got to get the bullet out. Can you hear me?"

With difficulty, she opened her eyes, tried to match people to voices.

"No," said a familiar voice. "I think we ought to keep her sedated until she arrives in Ohio."

Frank. She struggled to open her eyes but then slipped back under. Just as well.

"Anabelle!"

She was so tired.

"Honey, it's time to rise and shine!"

No mistaking that voice.

She forced herself to open her eyes through the layers of fog, but it was bright, so bright that she squeezed them closed again. Her head hurt, and she thought she might be sick to her stomach.

"That's my girl," her mother said. "Come on, try again."

She pushed herself into a semi-sitting position. Her mom was sitting in a chair next to her bed. She was surrounded by beeping monitors. A mounted TV was showing a game show. A little light came in through a narrow window.

"You're in the hospital," her mom said. "You were mugged, honey." The cheer in her voice sounded strained.

She tried to look down at her shoulder, but the motion proved costly. A new, sharper pain made her hiss and then left behind a thudding ache.

"Mugged," she repeated. She remembered the dark house, the pager, Dasha's husband being her mark. Her shoulder hurt because he'd shot her, and then she'd killed him. So why was her mother here?

She moved her neck a little, experimentally, then tried to move other parts of her body that weren't bandaged. Everything hurt with a dull ache, and she wondered what painkiller they had given her to make the pain bearable.

"Where's Helen?" she croaked.

"Who?" Patty asked.

"My friend Helen," she said. "My…my landlord."

"Honey." Her mom reached for the plastic remote next to her on the bed and pushed a red button. "We're in Toledo."

"What?" She tried to sit up more and, groaning, gave up.

"Calm down, Annie. Calm down. Don't you remember? Your Mr. Clifton had you brought here so I could look after you while you recovered," her mother said. "Where is that nurse?"

"Frank Clifton?" Annie asked, tears filling her eyes.

"Yes. He explained to us what happened. How he came out to LA to talk about giving you back your job, the mugging, how he saved your life. I'm glad you decided to go back to work, Annie, but I don't understand why you never tell us anything! Your daddy was so mad… Oh, here she is."

A woman in pink scrubs entered the room and smiled at her. "Well, well, well. Lookie who decided to rejoin the world of the livin'!"

The nurse checked her vitals, asked her a few questions, and then told her that the doctor would be by in a while.

"You hungry?" she asked Annie.

"I don't… I'm not sure." She still felt nauseous.

"I'll have someone bring you some food," the nurse said. "Just in case."

After she left, Annie said, "Mom, I have to go back to LA. I can't just quit school."

"I think you're confused. You don't have to worry about anything right now except getting better. Mr. Clifton said that once you recover, your job will be there for you."

"But—"

"Enough, Anabelle. You'll tire yourself out."

She was tired but figured if her mother wouldn't answer her questions, someone else might. She just had to behave for a while. When her food came, she ate as much as she could stomach. She talked to the doctor about her shoulder, listened to his instructions. Her mom stayed until visiting hours were over, then promised she'd be there again in the morning, bright and early, with her daddy in tow.

After her mother left, she had plenty of time to think about what had transpired. What Frank Clifton had clearly orchestrated from the very beginning. The shift to the FBI. The task that Buck Baker had given her. The man who would surely recognize her. The pager that hadn't gone off in weeks. Clifton knew she'd be in that house, had known exactly when to page her, had made sure Agent Katz was available to carry her to safety if she survived the exchange of gunfire.

Perhaps Frank had grown wary of their arrangement. Perhaps he wanted to force Annie out of Los Angeles. Blowing her cover would do that. He either had a lot of faith that she would survive the situation or didn't care whether she lived or died. Either way, Annie wasn't sure she wanted to know the answer.

And now she was back in Ohio, thousands of miles away from where she wanted to be. Clifton's plan had worked.

Later that night, when everyone expected her to be sleeping, she adjusted the bed until she was sitting up. She reached across the bed with her good arm and, gritting her teeth, picked up the phone. Sweated through dialing Helen's number only to have a prerecorded voice tell her that long-distance calls were not permitted.

She threw the receiver to the ground. It clanked against the side of her bed, tangled up in the metal rails, and hung swaying until it started to beep, beep, beep.

Frank came to see her wearing khakis and a short-sleeved polo shirt. She'd never seen him out of a suit before.

"You won't be going back to school, Annie," he said by way of greeting. "You've lost your funding for that, I'm afraid. We've packed up your things and explained to your, ah…what do you call her? Your landlord?" He chuckled. "They told Mrs. Everton that you wouldn't be returning and paid your rent for several months to compensate her."

"But why?" Annie said quietly. "I don't understand why."

"You failed at your task! You killed a man! I think we can safely say you're scrubbed from Los Angeles for a while," he said. "But no matter. After you heal up, you'll come back to me, like we discussed."

She stared numbly at the thin blanket covering her knees. They were weaning her off the painkillers before she went home, which only exacerbated her misery. She almost wished that Dasha's not-so-dead husband had killed her after all.

"It'd be better if you didn't try to contact her," Frank said. "Better for Mrs. Everton and her children. Make a clean break."

She didn't see a way out. Not anymore. She would never do anything to put Helen or her family in danger. She couldn't live with herself if Helen lost her job because of her. Frank wouldn't hesitate to do that.

She nodded at him. She was so tired. "All right," she said. "You win."

Because there was fighting for what she wanted and there was banging her head against a wall, and she knew what her life had become. She resigned herself to a predictable existence. Better the devil she knew, even if that devil was Frank Clifton with her whole career mapped out in his head.

CHAPTER 16

Los Angeles, 2005

She officially started working as the chief of the LAPD's financial division on Monday, but she rolled out Sunday afternoon on a pharmaceutical bust that had already been in the works. A break in the case was a break in the case, and she wanted to be there as it unfolded. Still, she felt left behind and out of sorts as she slipped on her police windbreaker and sent one of her lieutenants to get her a badge and a firearm. It probably wasn't the way things were done, but the need to jump in trumped procedural decorum. She'd apologize when it was over.

This was how she lived her life now that she was in her late thirties. She'd spent too much time trying to please other people at her own expense, and for what? To be chronically single and eternally lonely?

When she officially began work on Monday, she was running on only a couple hours of sleep. The rest of her division was just as worn out.

And they didn't like her.

She didn't expect to be greeted with open arms by a bunch of men who'd spent their years on the force climbing the ranks, only to be passed over by a woman just approaching middle age. That would never be a peaceful transition. But she naively thought maybe one or two of them would be more open to new blood.

She wasn't going to put much effort into winning them over either. She could turn herself inside out trying to get them to like her and never succeed. No, the only path to success was to do the work and do it well. That was the only thing she was good at anyway.

Besides, it wasn't like she joined the LAPD because she was passionate about putting an end to commercial crimes. Financial fraud was the least interesting thing to investigate. But she'd have to liaison with other law enforcement agencies, which was why Mason Worth thought of her. He remembered her from the '90s when she'd worked for everyone and no one. He also remembered her from the late '80s when, after she worked for the CIA, she refused his offer to join Metro PD.

Would she refuse him again?

It had been less of an interview and more of an invitation presented on a silver platter of benefits and rank. A very beautiful trap it was too, one that would leave her indebted to him for a while. That was a situation she did not want to find herself in again. Though she reminded herself that there was no longer any way Frank Clifton could get away with what he had back then.

She'd given him five more years of her life and labor before his bad behavior caught up with him. Ironically, it was the money trail that got him. Someone found out that he was using his budget to fund his little side projects. Like being Annie's ball and chain on the West Coast, farming her out to whomever needed her, despite the fact that the CIA was never supposed to interrogate its own citizens. That rule was disregarded all the time, but still. It turned out that Annie wasn't Clifton's only side project. He'd spent decades treating his staff like his personal pawns, spending funds for his own purposes and even renaming line items in his budget to cover his tracks.

But as departments converted to computerized databases, Clifton's suspicious spending became too obvious to ignore, and he was forced into retirement to save face. Both his own and the CIA's.

After he left, Annie spent some time looking through the documentation he left behind. She discovered that Frank had known all along that Dasha's husband was still alive, even as Annie was quitting her job, wracked with guilt over the deaths she'd caused. Frank ordered him flown out of Belarus to Virginia and, months later, had him relocated again to Los Angeles. The two agents who'd been killed were not killed while investigating where Dasha had gone but had died during the extraction.

The note in her file read *reintegrate or terminate*. Annie knew Frank well enough to know that it meant that he thought either seeing Dasha's husband was going to spook her enough to make her return to DC or it was going to get her killed. Annie found several other similar instances of Frank using intelligence assets as pawns to manipulate agents working under him.

She'd written up the report and shown it to her new superior.

He'd looked it over and scoffed. "What do you want? The man already left in disgrace. What use is it dragging his name through the mud now?"

Annie left the CIA not long after that. While she wasn't surprised that Frank's treatment of people was overlooked, she was disgusted that his financial crimes had gone unprosecuted. The irony of her shift to investigating financial crimes was not lost on her. It was funny how things worked out sometimes.

Annie knew that she could handle someone like Mason Worth better now that she was in her thirties than she could have ever handled Clifton in her twenties, when she was still green. Clifton had manipulated her to the point that she'd felt like a caged animal, and then hopeless, until she'd felt nothing at all. He threatened her family, he threatened her future job prospects with his knowledge of her sexuality, and he made sure to isolate her from the rest of the team so she didn't have any allies.

Worse than that, he did what he'd promised never to do: he sent her overseas again.

She'd been terrified to go, terrified that the power she wielded as an agent of the United States government could get someone killed with a mere slip of the tongue.

Annie was the kind of person for whom everything came pretty easily: she didn't have to work at being smart, she didn't have to study particularly hard in school, she was fairly attractive without a lot of effort, and success came quickly and easily to her. All of which made her wildly unprepared for the amount of blood that she found on her hands.

Later, after some therapy and time away from the CIA, she came to understand that she'd been traumatized. The trauma of what happened in Belarus had sent her running for reasons she couldn't explain, least of all to herself. And then Frank Clifton had traumatized her further by shoehorning himself back into her life, with his threats and his conditions and his hand on her thigh.

He died of colon cancer, she learned later, about three years into his forced retirement. She went out and bought a bottle of champagne, drank it alone, raising her flute every time she thought of him shitting himself to death.

So, no, she didn't fear Mason Worth. He might be a big fish, but after being out in the world, the LAPD seemed like a small pond.

"Does Helen Everton still work here?" Annie had asked at the end of her interview with Worth.

"Uh, yeah. Internal Affairs. She's a commander now."

That was all Annie really needed to know. She accepted the job.

The LAPD paid for moving expenses and put her up in a hotel near the airport that had been designed to hold conferences. The lobby teemed with flight attendants and pilots and people in suits wearing lanyards and holding paper folders. She was supposed to be finding a place to live while adjusting to her new role. Her stuff was scheduled to arrive in two weeks, so if she didn't have a place by then, she'd need a storage unit to hold her dining set, her couch, and her bed. Everything else, she had gotten rid of.

She worked Monday and Tuesday, and on Tuesday evening, as she lay in her hotel bed with her half-eaten room service, she decided to go to see Helen the next day.

She'd really thought that maybe Helen would seek her out; there was no way she didn't know Annie had joined the force. A few women had stopped her in the hallway to introduce themselves, clearly excited to have a high-ranking female officer in their midst, but most people averted their eyes when they saw her. She heard them whispering to their buddies after she passed. Busting the pharmaceutical thing had helped break the ice, but most of that legwork had happened before she'd arrived, so everyone knew that it wasn't really her win.

A hundred times over the last decade, she'd thought about picking up the phone to call Helen. But by the time Clifton was gone, six years had already passed since Annie had left LA, and it had felt too late to open that can of worms again. And Helen had let her go too. She'd never gotten a letter or an email or a phone call. Helen was a cop; she knew how to find people if she wanted.

Annie tried telling herself that she hadn't returned to Los Angeles specifically for Helen, that if Helen didn't want anything to do with her, it wasn't the end of the world. Annie liked California independent of the Evertons and the kindness they'd shown her.

But the pain in her heart was like a bruise that wouldn't heal, the protective layer as thin as wet tissue paper that would dissolve at the slightest tug.

A heavyset man with a gray buzz cut told her that she needed to wait for Commander Everton to return, but Annie breezed past him and opened the door. "I'm just going to wait right here," Annie told him, making sure the gold badge on her hip wasn't obscured by her jacket. It was an unsubtle way to pull rank, but the man understood it and held up his hands. "Suit yourself, Chief."

Twelve years was a long time to be away from someone. Annie remembered Helen as a warm and loving mother of three, a relatively new officer. Someone in a transitional period between married and not, straight and not. Twelve years later and Annie still remembered how Helen's mouth had felt on her in that small garage bedroom. Some things were simply unforgettable.

However, Helen Everton now had gold letters on her office door and an impressive rank. Commander Everton had no reason to acknowledge their old friendship or acknowledge Annie in any other way. But still, Annie was drawn to Helen's memory strongly enough to risk disappointment and embarrassment.

She stepped into the office, leaving the door slightly ajar, and looked around, thinking back on Helen's closet-sized office on campus. This space was easily twice the size, if not more, and contained an impressive wooden desk, a decent-sized window, and a row of filing cabinets. Everything was meticulously organized, from the pens in the holder to the typed labels on the file drawers. No dust or clutter accumulated on visible surfaces.

A single personal item appeared on the console next to the desk: a framed photo of three people—two adults and a teenager. Ashley, Kevin, and she assumed the teenager was Zach.

"Chief Weaver, I never permit people into my office when I'm not in it."

The cool and clipped voice interrupted her admiration of the photo in her hands, and she flinched. She carefully put it back exactly where she found it, then turned around.

It was Helen. Older, certainly, but more refined, in a tailored pencil skirt, silk blouse, and fitted blazer. Her chestnut hair had been dyed into a shiny and dark chocolate-brown, sleek and styled.

She looked a little nervous too, though it was hard to see under the professional veneer. Annie considered her options and decided that a casual familiarity was best. She picked up the photo again and asked, "Are these the kids? Is this Zach?"

"Please don't touch my things," Helen said stiffly.

Or not. Annie returned the photo to its place once more and stepped away from the desk. Helen was holding a salad in a clear plastic box and a bottle of water.

"I can see I've interrupted your lunch. I meant to come earlier, but we had a break in a case over the weekend and..." She shook her head as she trailed off. She was losing her train of thought, losing control of this interaction. This was all wrong.

"Yes, one of your lieutenants signed out your firearm. Another thing I generally do not permit." Helen stepped past Annie to set her lunch down on her desk, then turned to face her.

Annie fought the urge to edge closer to the door. "I came to apologize about that," she said. "And to...to say hello to you."

"Hello. Welcome to the LAPD." But her words were cold and overenunciated.

Annie's face was getting hot. She was just going to say what she came to say and leave.

"Helen—I mean, Commander Everton, I owe you an apology. You have every right to be mad at me, and I'd be mad at me too, but I want you to know that I never would have left if I'd had any control over the situation. Everything I did was because I thought it was best for you and your family. I know it was a long time ago, but I wanted to say that first thing. And say that I'm sorry."

Helen stared at her a moment, then said, "Sure. All right."

"I…uh…wasn't very good at long-term planning back then. I was just sort of running on adrenaline all the time. But once I started working for police departments, I made a plan to get back to Los Angeles. I know it's been twelve years, but this was the last place I was really happy, you know? And most of that had to do with you and your family. I know I messed up any real chance I had of us being friendly when I disappeared, but I'm back here now, and whether we're colleagues or acquaintances or enemies or whatever, I'm just really glad and relieved to have you in my life again. Even if it's just a tiny bit."

Annie forced a smile. "That's it. That's all I've got to say. Wait. Also, you look very pretty. Okay, I have to go. We have a case." Annie edged out of the office and out the door. "Bye now, Commander. Bye-bye."

She bolted out of the office, past the man who'd tried to stop her. He had a knowing look.

Standing in the elevator, she tried to catch her breath. This was not the time or place to burst into tears. She couldn't let her team see weakness this early on.

By the time she got back to her office, she had recovered. Los Angeles was still a great place to live, and she was fine.

Another week passed, and she was no closer to finding a permanent address. Her real estate agent, Beverley DeAngelo, kept sending her listings, but every time she let her know of her interest in one, it had already been snatched up.

It's a tough market, Beverley wrote for the fifteenth time in her latest email. *You have to move quickly!*

The next day was Saturday, and Annie promised Beverley that she would spend the whole day going to open houses and checking out off-market listings. She needed to do it if she was ever going to get out of the hotel, but she dreaded it. Plus, her mother kept calling, asking her whether or not she was settled. Patty was horrified that Annie had moved without having a place to live set up, but her start date had not given her much opportunity. She promised her mother she'd figure it out. She always did.

But for now, she would change into something more comfortable and sit at the hotel bar with a cocktail. And when she was buzzed enough to endure another night in a hotel bed, she would order room service and eat dinner in the shallow bathtub.

The bar was never busy, even on a Friday night. Usually there were people occupying two or three high-top tables and maybe a few people at the bar. Annie had become friendly with Arturo, the bartender, who would start making her martini as soon as he saw her.

It wasn't unusual for the bar to be mostly empty. It was unusual, though, to see Helen Everton sitting on a barstool.

She panicked and froze, considering whether to turn around and bolt after the reception she had gotten from Helen a week ago. But then her fear ebbed away, and common sense took over. It was unlikely that Helen was here by happenstance. She'd come for Annie.

Helen looked up and turned her head, spotting Annie at the entrance.

Annie made her way to the counter. By the time she got there, Arturo had made her drink and brought it to her.

"Thanks," Annie told him, then turned to Helen. "Hello."

"Chief Weaver," Helen replied, her expression neutral and her tone even.

Annie had always found Helen difficult to read. She wondered if she resented the fact that Annie now outranked her. "Are you here to see me?"

"Honestly, I hadn't decided." Helen sipped at her glass of red wine. She had a manila folder open in front of her, and when she saw Annie looking at the form on top, Helen closed it.

"Mind if I join you?" Annie asked. "Since you're here."

Helen paused to consider, then nodded. "All right."

Annie pulled out the barstool next to Helen's and sat down. Her heart was pounding. "Can I refresh your drink?" she offered.

"No, I'm fine," Helen said. "Never more than one glass for me these days."

Annie nodded and sipped her martini. Helen looked up at the television above the bar that was showing highlights of various games.

"I'm glad you're here," Annie said, "but I'm surprised to see you."

"Honestly? My sister-in-law told me I should come talk to you." Helen's eyes never left the screen.

"How is Sal?"

Helen turned her attention to Annie, her eyebrows raised. Then she seemed to soften a little. "Right. Of course. She's well."

"That's nice to hear."

"How are things going for you? I mean with your division?" Helen asked.

"Oh, they hate me," Annie admitted. "Truly, utterly despise me."

Helen pulled her wineglass a little closer. "You made an unorthodox entrance into our force."

"More or less unorthodox than the last time I was here doing work for the LAPD?"

"They don't know about that."

Annie sipped her martini. "Give them time." The alcohol on an empty stomach was having an effect. "I haven't had dinner. Do you want to go get something to eat?"

"Well…"

Annie pushed a little. "I was going to have a drink, then walk down to the Mexican restaurant a few blocks away." It was utter bullshit, of course, but she had tucked her ID and credit card into her back pocket along with her room key to leave her options open.

"Ah."

"I know I sort of ambushed you before. I get that. But you're here, which means…maybe I could tell you a bit more about what happened?" Annie was desperate to explain herself. Helen and her children deserved more than Annie disappearing into the night. Of all the terrible things she'd done in her life, abandoning Helen with no explanation was among the worst. She'd worked hard to get back to LA so she could make things right, and she was terrified she was going to blow it. Or that she already had.

"What happened?" Helen repeated softly. "What happened is you left, Annie."

"I did," Annie said, "and I'm not going to make excuses. But I think you deserve some answers all the same."

Helen ran her hand along the front of her closed folder. "I could eat. Let me just pay my bill."

"Arturo can just put it on my room tab," Annie said. She finished her drink and slid off the stool, then caught Arturo's attention and pointed to their glasses.

They walked down the street, the sound of Helen's work heels filling the silence between them. Annie had a million questions: about Helen's kids, about the house, about what happened after she left. But she held back from asking them, wary of scaring Helen off.

The Mexican restaurant was busy but large enough that they were seated right away. The server dropped a basket of warm tortilla chips and a bowl of house salsa onto the table. Another server brought cool glasses of water.

Annie cleared her throat. There was no time like the present. "When I was in my early twenties, I went to Eastern Europe on assignment, and the work I did there ended up getting the family of a government worker murdered. A woman and a little girl. The husband went missing and was presumed dead. I returned to the States, quit my job, then decided to go back to school."

"Annie, you don't have to tell me everything in the first five minutes."

"I just want to get it out," Annie said.

"All right. So that had just happened when you met me? Those people had died?"

Annie told her about Clifton and his machinations. "I think he thought I'd get tired of it and go back."

"Didn't you?" Helen asked softly.

"No," she said, "because I met someone and fell in love."

The server approached to introduce herself and drop off menus. Annie glanced over the menu, but the words didn't make sense.

"I know what I want," Helen said and ordered.

Flustered, Annie pointed to a number and handed the menu back. She would eat whatever came. It didn't matter.

After the server left with their orders, Helen prompted, "Go on."

Annie told her about the assignment with the houses, how she broke into the last one at night and encountered the missing man from Minsk. How Clifton had set off her pager intentionally, but how no one knew that the man had a gun. Annie thought that her rescuer had been one of Clifton's goons but found out later that Buck had had her followed just in case. Agent Katz, the assigned agent, rushed her to a hospital when he heard shots fired.

In the end, Clifton got what he wanted. Annie recovered at home with her parents and then moved back to Washington. Clifton had made good on his threat and had nearly gotten her killed. She had no reason to doubt that he would do it again.

"It took me a while to realize that it wasn't normal—his obsession with me or the things that he used his power to do."

Helen leaned forward and rested her elbows on the table. "Okay. Then what happened?"

"He got caught and was forced to retire."

"I meant with you." Helen had replaced her wire-framed glasses with dark, plastic ones that accentuated her brown eyeliner and the lashes heavy and black with mascara. "You could have called me and explained all of this back then."

Annie shrugged, though she was embarrassed because she'd never been sure whether or not she'd made the right choice by not reaching out. "By the time I felt like it would have been safe to call you or write to you, it had been years and—I don't know. I figured you were probably better off without me. And I figured since you never got in touch with me, it was best to let sleeping dogs lie."

"But you're here now."

"I like LA," Annie said.

"I did try to find you," Helen admitted, leaning back in her chair. "I suspected you went back, but I didn't know why. I thought maybe you were unhappy with us. That you decided to drop out of school and were embarrassed to tell me."

Annie shook her head.

"I contacted the CIA, trying to find out… I just wanted to know if that's where you went back to."

"What happened?"

"Someone from the CIA called the chief of police and told him that I was poking around. The chief called me into his office and said if I wanted to keep my job, I should mind my own business, that I wasn't a detective."

"Jesus."

"Annie, I had three young children. I couldn't afford to lose my job."

"I know." Annie stared at the basket of tortilla chips. "I loved living in your garage, for the record. I loved your family. I loved—"

The server returned and set their plates in front of them.

Annie stared at the food, a lump in her throat. This was harder than she'd thought it would be. Opening up to Helen was fostering hope in Annie, and hope without fulfillment was going to be torture. It was going to fester inside her.

Helen picked up her fork but held it suspended above her plate. "When you left, it wasn't easy. You broke my heart. It's comforting to hear, I suppose, that I didn't do something to drive you away, but just because I got hurt all those years ago doesn't mean I want you to fail in your new position."

"Thank you." Annie took a bite of her burrito. "I'd like to hear about your kids. If you don't mind."

"Well, now," Helen said, cutting into her enchilada. "Ashley is a dance teacher. She lives in Austin. Kevin is in school for computer science. He goes to UC Santa Barbara. And Zach is in high school."

"You got to keep him." Annie smiled. "That's wonderful."

"We had a party when I adopted him officially. He's a great kid. Smart, sensitive. I'm really proud of him."

"You should be."

"And your family? All good?" Helen asked.

"Sure. Well, Ken and Patty are Ken and Patty. They're always trying to get me to move closer to them, but it never feels quite right. I mean, I don't have a place to live yet, everyone at work hates me, and I don't know anyone in this city besides you and Mason Worth, but I already feel like it's home. Or it's going to be. Do you think that's strange?"

"No, not so very strange," Helen said. "It's a city of transplants. People come here for all sorts of reasons."

Annie took a bite of her food and chewed thoughtfully, considering whether or not to ask her next question. She had been surprised when Helen showed up at the bar, when she agreed to come to dinner, when she listened to Annie's explanation, and now she was about to blow it all on a question she had to ask. She looked at Helen's hands, her bare ring finger, and said, "You never remarried?"

Helen sipped her water and looked down at her plate, not answering for so long that had Annie any cash, she might have dropped it on the table and walked out.

"After Bruce, I was soured on marriage. And I never…wanted anyone else after you left."

"Helen…"

"I tried. Went on some dates, even slept with a few people, but it was just easier on my own with the kids. After all, people leave."

Annie looked down.

"You know," Helen said, putting her fork down and leaning in. A paper lantern hanging above the table reflected on her hair. "You're the age now that I was when we met."

Annie had thought about that too. Helen had seemed so grown-up back then. She owned a house and was married long enough to have children. But Annie didn't feel all that different than she had at twenty-seven. She was more prepared to face whatever challenges might appear, surely, but she didn't feel older. She just *was* older. Helen must have felt so scared when Annie had swooped into her life like a breath of fresh air, then disappeared just as quickly, taking the air right out with her.

There was nothing Annie could add to what she had already told Helen, so she simply nodded and said, "I know."

They walked back to the hotel together. When they reached the lot where Helen was parked, they stopped.

"Well," Annie said, "what do you think?"

"About what?"

"About us being friends. You think we could give it another try?" She held her breath. Hope was burning a hole in her sternum, shining so brightly that surely people on the top floor of the hotel could see it streaking up into the sky.

Helen nodded. "Let's see how it goes."

"Okay." Annie exhaled. "Good."

"See you later, Chief Weaver," Helen said and turned toward the parking lot.

It felt wrong to watch Helen walking away. Annie desperately wanted to keep talking, to hold onto the progress they'd made today. And because some things never change, she knew she wanted too much. Wanted more of Helen than she deserved.

"Helen?"

Helen turned back to her, waiting to hear what Annie had to say. She shifted her purse on her shoulder.

"Friends is good," Annie said. "Friends is great, even. I like friends. But if you want to come upstairs"—she nodded toward the lobby doors—"that's an option too." Her heart was pounding so hard she was dizzy. Depending on what Helen decided, she would either fall to the sidewalk or float into the sky.

Helen studied Annie for several long seconds, then stepped toward her.

OTHER BOOKS FROM YLVA PUBLISHING

www.ylva-publishing.com

HONEY IN THE MARROW
Emily Waters

ISBN: 978-3-96324-724-8
Length: 237 pages (78,000 words)

New widow Stella is facing middle age alone in LA. Without being a prosecutor and wife, who is she anymore?

When an ex-colleague, a beautiful but cold LAPD captain, helps her back on her feet, Stella can't keep pretending she's not attracted to her. And there's no way she feels the same way. Is there?

ART OF THE CHASE
Jennifer Giacalone

ISBN: 978-3-96324-835-1
Length: 207 pages (74,000 words)

Warring detective exes hunt a taunting art thief in a lesbian romantic suspense fusing the line between love and hate.

Fleur jumps at the chance to snare the elusive art thief who ruined her life six years ago…even if she has to work with her fiery ex-wife.

Will the case push them back into each other's arms, or shatter what's left of Fleur's heart?

LOOKING FOR TROUBLE
Jess Lea

ISBN: 978-3-96324-522-0
Length: 312 pages (109,000 words)

Nancy hates her housemates from hell, useless job, and always dating women who aren't that into her. She'd love to be a political writer and meet Ms. Right.

Instead, she meets George, a butch, cranky bus driver who's dodging a vengeful ex.

When the warring pair gets caught up in a crazy Melbourne election, they must trust each other and act fast to stay alive.

A quirky lesbian romantic mystery.

REQUIEM FOR IMMORTALS
Lee Winter

ISBN: 978-3-95533-710-0
Length: 263 pages (86,000 words)

Requiem is a brilliant cellist with a secret. The dispassionate assassin has made an art form out of killing Australia's underworld figures without a thought. One day she's hired to kill a sweet and unassuming innocent. Requiem can't work out why anyone would want her dead—and why she should even care.

ABOUT EMILY WATERS

Emily Waters is a Children's Librarian who loves reading picture books and middle grade fiction and doing storytime for little ones. A citizen of the internet, Emily is a fan of all things fandom and pop culture. Her other interests include reading, binge watching old television shows, drinking coffee, and saying "Gasp! A dog!" anytime she sees a dog.

Emily currently resides in Northern California with her family.

CONNECT WITH EMILY
Website:www.emilyraywaters.com
Facebook: www.facebook.com/emilyraywaters
Twitter: twitter.com/emilyraywaters
E-Mail: emilyraywaters@gmail.com

Two Is a Pattern
© 2024 by Emily Waters

ISBN: 978-3-96324-880-1

Available in e-book and paperback formats.

Published by Ylva Publishing, legal entity of Ylva Verlag, e.Kfr.

Ylva Verlag, e.Kfr.
Owner: Astrid Ohletz
Am Kirschgarten 2
65830 Kriftel
Germany

www.ylva-publishing.com

First edition: 2024

No part of this book may be reproduced, scanned, or distributed in any printed or electronic form without permission. Please do not participate in or encourage piracy of copyrighted materials in violation of the author's rights. Thank you for respecting the hard work of this author.

This is a work of fiction. Names, characters, places, and incidents either are a product of the author's imagination or are used fictitiously, and any resemblance to locales, events, business establishments, or actual persons—living or dead—is entirely coincidental.

Credits
Edited by Genni Gunn, Michelle Aguilar, and Julie Klein
Cover Design and Print Layout by Streetlight Graphics

Printed in Great Britain
by Amazon